A CUT ABOVE

It's 1962 and Freda Scott and her five schoolmates are eager to embark on their life journeys. Madly in love with the dashing but unattainable Ewan, Freda instead throws herself into a hairdressing career, and soon she and her best friend Robin have established their own flourishing business. The future looks rosy, until Freda's life is turned upside down by a brutal attack. As Freda struggles to come to terms with what has happened to her, she relies on her old friends more than ever. However, a chance meeting with her old love Ewan, brings a potentially life-changing dilemma. Does Freda dare to finally put herself first?

A CUT ABOVE

by

Millie Gray

Magna Large Print Books
Long Preston, North Yorkshire,
BD23 4ND, England.

British Library Cataloguing in Publication Data.

A catalogue record of this book is
available from the British Library

ISBN   978-0-7505-4648-5

First published in Great Britain 2017 by
Black & White Publishing Ltd.

Published in Large Print 2018 by arrangement with
Black & White Publishing Ltd.

Magna Large Print is an imprint of Library Magna Books Ltd.

Printed and bound in Great Britain by
T.J. (International) Ltd., Cornwall, PL28 8RW

For my daughter Rosemary

ACKNOWLEDGEMENTS

Special thanks go to May Steele, for willingly sharing her memories of her hairdressing apprenticeship and career with me; Diane Cooper, for assisting me with a first edit and tweaking a certain bit of the story; my sister, Mary Gillon, who has an encyclopaedic knowledge of our formative Leith days, and last, but certainly not least, all the very professional and supportive staff at my publishers, Black & White.

ONE

JULY 1962

By continually rubbing her hands together, fifteen-year-old Freda hoped she would be able to keep her rushing, bubbling excitement under control. She just couldn't believe that, at long last, she was sitting in Michael's, her favourite ice cream parlour on Easter Road, with two of her long-time school friends, Molly Duncan and Hannah Lindsey. All three were impatiently awaiting the fourth member of their unique circle, Angela McDonald.

Surely, Freda thought as she began biting on her lip, she cannot have forgotten that this was the day the four of us are to have a sitting with Meg Sutherland. Meg Sutherland the renowned clairvoyant fortune-teller, who they not only had to beg for a sitting with, but also had to book at least a year – yes, a full calendar year – in advance.

'Freda,' exclaimed Molly in a rather posh voice. This affectation did not surprise Freda because Molly had been speaking with a posturing accent ever since being offered a trainee seamstress position at the exclusive famous ladies' outfitters Greensmith Downes, on Princes Street. Sighing, Molly continued, 'What are we going to do? If you wish to know what I think, then it is that we should be making our way down to Iona Street to meet up with Meg Sutherland. After all, I am fifteen years old now and will be starting work...' She paused as she began to giggle, 'Oh Freda, did I tell you that Greensmith Downes have...'

'Yes you did,' Freda grunted with disdain, whilst resisting the urge to add 'at least eight times in the last two days'.

Ignoring Freda's lack of enthusiasm, Molly blithely continued, 'In that case you will understand that I must know immediately what else my wonderful future holds for me.'

Before Freda could respond, Hannah chipped in with, 'And that goes for me too ... even if it isn't as bright as Molly's.'

'Okay, I accept that both of you are looking forward to the sitting but we have to give Angela another five minutes. And before you say anything else, you know that because we are all still at school–'

'Until next Friday,' Molly reminded.

'Point taken, but as we are not wage-earning yet, Mrs Sutherland agreed to give us twenty minutes each for ten shillings, so that means we all have to pay a half-crown share.'

'So?'

'Don't be so huffy, Hannah. It's just that I only have my own half a crown, so I can't pitch in with as much as another penny if Angela doesn't turn up.'

Before either Molly or Hannah could reply, their attention flew to the café entrance, where they were confronted with Robin. Dapper Robin, who really believed he was the fifth member of the gang, jumped towards the girls, exclaiming, 'Olé!'

'Olé to you too,' snivelled Molly.

'Problem?'

Freda scowled before nodding. 'Angela's not turned up...'

Giving a short demonstration of a bullfighter swinging an imaginary cape, Robin swaggered and danced. 'But surely,' he chortled, 'you guessed when you heard that our late developer, brainy Ewan, had been invited down to Leith Academy Senior Secondary School to discuss transferring to a course more suited to his mammy's vaulting ambitions that our lovesick Angela—'

'And what does his mammy want?'

Robin shrugged. 'Och Molly, you ken fine she wants him to be a lawyer.'

'Right enough, the snobby bitch does. And I see what you mean that our too-smart-by-half pal Angela will be down there too. Aye, she will not be asking but begging them to allow her to change her mind and stay on at school there until she's eighteen.'

All the banter between Molly and Robin diverted Freda's attention from her money worries. Back she was to remembering what seemed to be such a long time ago, when they were all just eleven years old.

It was the year that they had to sit the Eleven-plus Qualifying Examinations. The papers had just been collected in when confident Angela, the brightest of the 'fabulous four', as the girls wished to be known, announced that even though the papers were still to be marked, she knew she had passed well above average.

On the day they were to be told their results

and which school they would each be transferring to – this would be either a Senior Secondary School, which was the equivalent of the English Grammar School, or to a Junior Secondary School – the children were all lined up in the playground after the mid-morning break. It was then that the headmaster, Mr Sanders, appeared on the school steps, accompanied by the class teacher, Miss McLeod. Mr Sanders pulled on the lapels of his academic gown before he graciously invited Angela and four others to follow him back into the school.

However, before he was out of earshot, Miss McLeod said, 'Headmaster, what shall I have the other children do in the meantime?'

Halting to look back disdainfully over the playground, Mr Sanders curtly announced: 'Just have them pick up all the litter until I am ready to speak to them.'

Before Angela left to follow Mr Sanders back into the school, she turned to Robin and his friend Ewan Gibson, who were both to remain behind. The boys hunched their shoulders and shook their heads before Ewan snapped, 'Well, folks, we now ken that us dunderheids are all for Norton Park Junior Secondary School. And oor dear heidmaister has just telt us that aw we will ever be good enough for in life is picking up rubbish.'

'Aye, I agree that's what he thinks,' huffed Robin, 'but know something, we can all make our minds up here and now that the stupid baldheaded old pig will eat his words when we prove him more than wrong.'

Not surprisingly, it turned out that Angela was

offered a place at Leith Academy Senior Secondary School. It was also true that she was thrilled at her success. However, as she had developed a crush on Ewan, she thought that it was in her best interests to transfer to the same school that he would be attending. This meant that Angela, who was being reared solely by her father since her mother had died, had to persuade her dad that she just really wished to go to Norton Park Junior Secondary School. It came as a surprise to him when Angela went on to explain that she wished to be a secretary when she left school, so the superior commercial course being offered at Norton Park would suit her needs better than the academic course at Leith Academy. Of course, Mr McDonald meekly agreed – but then he would, because Angela, like her mother before her, ruled the roost. Poor Mr McDonald was quite incapable of standing his ground where the women in his life were concerned.

By the time the group reached fourteen, they had all worked very hard at school and were succeeding in the paths they wished to follow. Naturally, Angela excelled in everything she studied, but she remained convinced she had done the right thing in following the commercial course at Norton Park. This was all true until Ewan, as he matured, started showing signs of being as intelligent – or more so – than Angela. Indeed, to everybody's amazement, he advanced so quickly that by the last month of term, only four short weeks before he was due to leave school and possibly take up a trade, the headmaster had summoned him to his office.

Mr MacLean's commanding voice, asking Ewan to come into his private province and stand to attention in front of his imposing desk, held no terror for Ewan. He knew that he had done no wrong and he was more than able to defend himself. However, Mr MacLean explained that he had had a chat with three of Ewan's teachers: Mr Anderson, Mr Mack and Dr Muir, who was affectionately known by the pupils as 'Docky'. All three were of the opinion that Ewan should be afforded the opportunity to transfer to Leith Academy Senior School and continue his education there. The matter had also been discussed with the rector of Leith Academy, Mr Drummond – or, as all the pupils called him, Bulldog – and he had agreed to interview Ewan.

As soon as the news about Ewan's possible transfer to Leith Academy reached Angela's ears, she was devastated. Immediately she started to hound her father, begging him to contact Bulldog and have him grant her an interview also. This meeting would of course result in Angela saying that she now realised she had made a terrible mistake in opting for anything other than the superior and privileged education she had once been offered at Leith Academy Senior School – an education that she now realised would assist her in her desire to go to Moray House Teacher Training College.

Freda's trip down memory lane was abruptly brought to an end when Robin called out her name.

'Here, Freda, now you know that Angela is away to beg Bulldog at Leith Academy to allow her in, how about letting me take her place at the spooky meeting?'

'Have you got half a crown?'

'I've got ten bob.'

'How have you got ten bob when you don't get paid your paper delivery boy's wages until tomorrow?'

Before he could reply, Molly started for the door and called out for the others to follow her.

Iona Street was a modern, spacious, well-designed tenement street. Meg Sutherland's ground-floor flat was situated at the Easter Road end of the thoroughfare. Freda shrugged and shivered as she noted that Meg's house was very different to what she had been led to believe mystics lived in. In the stories she had heard, mystics sought to dwell in basements – dank, dark, eerie places – because that was where the spirits of the world beyond felt most comfortable. It was true that she was pleased that Meg lived in a bright, airy house but, unlike the others, she was not so concerned with what life held for her in the future. No, she had her very own personal reason for visiting a spiritualist and she hoped that Meg Sutherland would be able to help her, despite not living in a gloomy basement. If Meg Sutherland was as good as her reputation, she would be able to work out exactly why Freda had come.

Before Freda could contemplate further, Molly pulled the doorbell. The door was immediately opened by a sprightly, twinkling-eyed, middle-aged woman who exuded charm and self-assurance.

Freda's jaw dropped. Last week one of her other schoolmates, Ida Spence, had told her about her own visit to a gypsy fortune-teller called Madame Isabella, who lived down darkest Salamander Street. According to Ida, the woman was like the dark, damp, dingy hovel she lived in with her mangy, scrawny, venom-spitting cat. This weird and ghoulish woman was a legend. She was so good at her job that only last week she had refused to tell a lassie her fortune, returning not only her four-bob fee but also her shilling deposit. It turned out the lassie didn't have a future and therefore Madame Isabella couldn't tell her anything. Naturally the lassie was upset, but not for long, because while meandering her way home along Albert Street she was knocked down and killed by the number 13 Edinburgh Corporation bus.

Freda felt suddenly hesitant about her appointment with Meg Sutherland. If all that Ida had told her was true about Madame Isabella, who Ida also claimed was a genuine Romany Gypsy, could someone as seemingly ordinary and engaging as Meg Sutherland – even if she was of Highland lineage and the seventh daughter of a seventh daughter, meaning she should have the second sight – ever be as good as spooky Madame Isabella?

The three girls had just got themselves seated on the three chairs in the hallway, leaving Robin to support himself against the wall, when Meg said, 'Now, who is coming in first?'

Freda nodded to Molly, who jumped into Meg's living room before Hannah could protest. As soon as the door closed Freda whispered to

Hannah, 'Look, you are next, then Robin. I am last because I have the money to pay her and I will only hand it over if everybody thinks she has been worth it.'

'Worth it!' exclaimed Hannah. 'But she normally charges five bob each and she is doing us a cheapo.'

'Yes I know we are getting it half price and she assured me that we wouldn't be getting short-changed, but you never know.'

The trio then sat in silence. All were lost in their own contemplations. Hannah's thoughts were on what she was going to do with her life. She conceded that it was probably a mistake to be taking the clerkess/typist job with Edinburgh Corporation, even if she did – as her mother hoped – end up getting courted and married to a white-collar man. She would much prefer to become a shop assistant.

Robin's mind, on the other hand, was on how his mother would cope with telling his father about his choice of job. He also worried about how Joey, who his mum and dad now communicated through, would cope with their inane bickering about it.

As to Freda, well, her thoughts were suddenly put on hold as the door to Meg Sutherland's office opened and a flushed and excited Molly bounced out.

Freda and Robin wanted so much to ask Molly how she had got on, but they had agreed that nothing was to be said until they were all back outside in Iona Street. However, in order for Freda to know whether Meg was worth the money it had been suggested that after each sitting, if the recipient was happy with Meg's service they would nod their head and give a 'thumbs up' signal. If they were not impressed, they would just shake their head. When Molly emerged, she nodded so vigorously that Freda and Robin were left in no doubt that Meg had more than met Molly's expectations.

Meg did not keep to the twenty-minute time slot and although Hannah and Robin gave the thumbs up, it was a nerve-wracking hour before Freda was invited into the inner sanctum.

She had just closed the door behind her when Meg, who was sitting at a small table, smiled at her and signalled to her that she should take the seat opposite her. As soon as she was seated Freda noted that her seat faced into the room and that Meg's chair was positioned so that she faced the bright, sunlit window.

'Now,' Meg began in a low, soft voice, nodding her head, 'you are welcome.'

Freda was startled as she became aware that Meg was not speaking to her, but to someone standing behind her. Instinctively she moved to see who the other person was, but she felt Meg's hand grasp hers and she turned back to face her.

'No,' Meg whispered. 'You won't be able to see him, not unless he wishes you to. You see – Freda, isn't it?' Freda could only nod her head as Meg continued, 'Freda, when you came into my home today, the man who walks every step of your life with you followed you in.'

Freda was now panting. Fear was choking her. It was true that unlike the others she had not really come to Meg to find out what lay in store for her in the future. No, she had come in the hope that her deceased father would send her a message. Freda had been just five years old when her darling daddy died from complications of influenza. Sitting before Meg, she found herself vividly recalling her very early years. Every night her special daddy would sit her on his knee and tell her tales that transported her into the land of make-believe. He always had her believe she was a beautiful princess and when danger threatened, a handsome prince – the image of himself – would gallop to her rescue. All this took place before he would tuck her safely up into bed and kiss her – his special princess – good night.

Placing her elbows on the table, Freda supported her drooping head with her hands and mumbled, 'Are you saying my dad is here?'

Meg nodded. 'Yes. Now come on, he doesn't wish to see your tears today. He has seen them so often of late.'

This was true, and it was because of her mother's second husband. A few years after her father passing – too soon, in Freda's opinion – her mother, Ellen, had married Drew Black, an uncouth brute of a man who Freda feared. A couple of years later, Ellen gave birth to Susan, who was now a tender and lovely five-year-old. Susan was the reason that when life became so unbearable for her older brother Stuart and herself at home, she had decided to stay instead of joining Stuart in going off to live with Jack and Rosie Scott, their loyal and supportive paternal grandparents.

For the rest of her life Freda would remember Meg breaking into her thoughts and saying that her dad wished her to know that she should never doubt that when things went awry, he would always be there with her to assist her in getting her life back on track.

Before the sitting finished Meg also said, 'Freda, like I pointed out to your pals, I am not a fortune-teller. I am a medium, a spiritualist. No one can predict all the paths your life will take. This is because all of us come to crossroads in our lives, and as to which road we will follow ... well, that's a choice everyone is free to make. Also, even if you sometimes choose the wrong road you will somehow get back on track. What I am saying is that you have a life before you and that, no matter what, it will always be worth living. A life where there will be more happy times and good achievements than there will be trouble and failure. Just believe that whatever happens and however desperate you feel, you will rise up again and tap dance on the road.' Meg stopped to look over Freda's head before she slowly continued, 'Imagine where you wish to be and, as you are a bit of a dreamer, the road you choose will always be the "Yellow Brick Road".' Meg leaned over and patted Freda's hand before adding, dreamlike, 'Finally, I have to add that one day you will think that you are about to lose everything, but someone in the spirit world – I think your father – will come back and save that dreadful day for you.'

Freda was now in a world of her own with her treasure trove of memories. She was remembering how her dad, just two months before he died, took her to see a re-release of *The Wizard of Oz*, her favourite film as a child. Her head was full of sweet memories of how when the wicked witch was screeching and careering about on her broomstick terrifying Dorothy, Freda was cuddling into her dad. She could still smell the reassurance of his manly odour and feel the wonderful sense of security that came with him being there to assuage her fears and encircle her in his strong arms. Those arms that seemed then – and even now, in the stillness of the night – to hold her safe and protect her from the dark.

Meg put an end to Freda's daydreaming, asking if there was anything else she would like to know. Wistfully, Freda shook her head; she accepted that there was nothing else of any importance that she wished to ask Meg. No, she had been told all she wished to hear so there was nothing left to do except fish in her pocket for the four half-crowns and hand them over to Meg.

In response, Meg's eyes twinkled and she winked at Freda. 'So I take it I honestly met your expectations and therefore earned my fee?' she tittered.

Freda squirmed. How did Meg know about the agreement? Lifting her left hand, she placed it over her right shoulder, where she now knew, thanks to Meg, that her dad would be standing.

Both Meg and Freda then knew that the audience was over and as a more-than-satisfied Freda prepared to leave she smiled at Meg, before saluting her with a courteous nod.

Outside, Molly and Hannah were so full of what Meg had predicted for them that Freda and

Robin were afforded the space to quietly contemplate.

Naturally Freda's thoughts were on her desire to truly believe, which she now did, that every day and night her dad walked with her. That he understood how she missed him so. That he knew how she thought her mum had betrayed him by marrying again – and to someone, in Freda's estimation, who was so... She hunched her shoulders and shivered, as was always her reaction when she thought about Drew Black. She knew he had a reputation as a violent man down at Leith docks and although he hadn't yet raised his hand to her or her mother, she was deathly afraid. Also, the way he sometimes stared at her when her mother was out at the bingo made her shudder. Dropping her shoulders, she breathed in deeply as a warm, loving glow embraced her.

'Freda, do you think you could just come back to earth for a minute?'

She jolted. 'Sorry, Robin. You want to tell me something?'

'Aye, for two days now I've been trying to tell everybody that is interested about how I have my dream job all lined up. Start on Monday next, I do.'

'Oh, oh, oh,' gasped Freda as she threw her arms around him and kissed him on both cheeks.

Molly and Hannah exchanged shocked glances at the embrace. Both, without saying a word, acknowledged that although Robin was a nice guy, he didn't exactly ooze virility like John Wayne – or even Clark Gable. Oh no, he was quite naturally, well, one of the girls!

'What is it and where is it?' were Freda's next remarks.

'Hairdresser's apprentice in Stuart's, would you believe.'

'Stuart's!' she squealed. 'Are you saying that you're going to do an apprenticeship in Stuart's, the ever-so-posh hairdressers up town?' she added, playfully patting his cheeks.

However, Robin's remarks had a different effect on Hannah and Molly, who both had to put their hands over their mouths to stifle their giggles.

Pointedly ignoring Hannah and Molly's reaction, Freda continued, 'Oh my darling boy, I didn't know that you wanted to train as a ladies' hairdresser.'

'Oh, but I do. And Freda, not only will I be good at it, I will be the very best.'

Drawing up abruptly, Freda bit on her lip before simpering, 'But what will your dad say? After all he is a coalman, and did he not say that he would get you a start at his yard and that would soon put some muscle on you?'

Robin nodded and shrugged. 'Don't worry, Mammy and my wee pal Joey are going to tell him of my success tonight.'

When Moira Dalgleish moved into her lower-flatted villa home in the tucked-away colony of Woodbine Terrace she felt elated. After all, it meant that Stevie was finally earning enough to give her and their future children a better life than she had known growing up. She had been a tender, bonnie lassie of just nineteen when she was first courted by the muscular, sensuous,

Stevie Dalgleish. When they had married, everybody marked the calendar and bet that Moira would produce her first baby within nine months. Most even suggested that because Stevie was so randy, it would come as no surprise if a blushing Moira were to produce a five-month premature baby of at least ten pounds. Not so. Five long years passed and there was no sign of a baby. In those five years Stevie changed from being a considerate, tender lover to a predatory brute. No one would have believed Moira if she had told them that every night without fail he had to coarsely exercise his conjugal rights in a desperate attempt to make her pregnant. It became such an obsession with him that Moira came to absolutely detest the sexual act. He, in turn, felt that Moira's frigidity was deliberate, and intended to make him look a 'Jaffa'. This was the insulting label attached to men whose wives never got pregnant. Moira was at her wits' end. It was then that her pal Patsy suggested she should demand that her doctor refer her to a gynaecologist for assessment. Moira eagerly agreed, but thought it prudent to forget to tell Stevie.

The very efficient and gentle gynaecologist who examined Moira stated, with no hesitation, that in his expert opinion, Moira was not infertile. In fact, she was extremely healthy in that department. Moira accepted the doctor's diagnosis but knew that there was no way, if she wished to go on living, that she could face Stevie and tell him that he really was as seedless as a Jaffa orange.

The problem was so difficult to deal with that Moira decided to consult her discreet pal Patsy again. Pursing and sucking in her lips, Patsy sensuously and naughtily suggested that the problem could be put right by a visit to her cousin, who worked in the fairgrounds in Blackpool. Her handsome, virile, thirty-year-old cousin could be persuaded – for a small donation to the Travelling People's Benevolent Fund, of which he was the sole treasurer and beneficiary – to assist Moira with her problem and thus save her marriage and Stevie's face.

After her weekend away with Patsy to Blackpool, where for three nights they threw away any inhibitions and just thoroughly enjoyed themselves, Moira felt super. She remembered with relish how she became so mesmerised and intoxicated with excitement that she just joined in all the racy fun that was on offer – especially on the helter-skelter, which Patsy's cousin owned and supervised. Oh yes, she really got her money's worth by having at least two goes every night on that wild and exhilarating contraption.

She was back at the house at seven on the Monday night and before she could even get her coat off, Stevie dragged her into the bedroom. Four weeks later she put a stop to the nightly humiliation, her reason being that she was pregnant and did not wish to have a miscarriage because of overindulgence. Stevie immediately agreed and became the loving, considerate man that she had married. He was so eager to please her that he would have done double somersaults whilst spitting out threepenny bits.

It was true to say that Moira enjoyed her pregnancy. She really did appreciate Stevie's devotion

27

and felt so pleased that he could at last boast that he had put her, his ever-faithful wife, in the family way. That was something that did not matter to her but was so important to Stevie, who worked in the macho coal yard. Naturally, she was very glad to have sacrificed her virtue to enable Stevie to keep face.

Her labour was easy, and when a midwife laid her newborn son in her arms and she looked down at his delicate features, tears surfaced as she became quite overwhelmed by a sense of gratitude and achievement.

It went without saying that Stevie wished at least a hat-trick. Moira, on the other hand, did not wish to become like his beer, which he had to have every night or he wasn't satisfied. To add to that, he got it into his head that if he took her away on a weekend to Ayr during race week, that might be enough to get her pregnant again – after all, hadn't going to Blackpool worked in relaxing her? Unfortunately, watching horses, however sleek and swift, did nothing for Moira. Driven to extremes, Stevie asked Patsy if she would take Moira on another weekend break to Blackpool, to see the Illuminations. Stevie himself would not go. He just couldn't see how people could be fascinated and inspired by electric lights flashing on and off, even if they were in all sorts of designs and colours of the rainbow. However, if looking at these lights somehow lit a spark in Moira, then he was willing to pay for her and Patsy to go down there for the weekend. He would then spend his time in the boozer with his pals, reserving his energies for what he had to do when Moira got home.

'Remember,' he said to Patsy before she boarded the bus after Moira, 'you make sure that Moira has a couple of goes on the helter-skelter.'

Patsy just looked at him and grinned before quipping, 'I sure will, and I might even have a go myself!'

Stevie had shrugged before replying, 'You can laugh, but whenever I ask her why she is not preggers again she replies, "Well, that's because I haven't been on the helter-skelter."'

Unfortunately, Moira and Patsy arrived in Blackpool to discover that the helter-skelter was out of order. Patsy's cousin suggested that they should try the twice as expensive Jungle Ride – his latest acquisition. He even advised that if two spins didn't meet Moira's expectations, he would give her another whirl free of charge. The deal was then struck, not by the shaking of hands, but a sly wink from him and a long sigh from Moira. Four weeks after they returned from Blackpool – where Moira had insisted on having a daily pirouette on the Jungle Ride – she was elated. It had worked again and she was pregnant. Eight months later she gave birth to the most beautiful daughter, who set Stevie's heart a-spinning from the moment he set eyes on her.

There were no more trips to Blackpool, but Moira didn't mind and nor did Stevie. Patsy suggested to Moira that she could go just once more at a discounted rate, as her cousin was offering, but Moira declined. She was not like Patsy and when she had to do things that were not quite ... well, to be truthful, things that would seem shocking to her pals in the Women's Guild, she thought it was time to start keeping to her marriage vows. She did, however, acknowledge that the two trips to Blackpool were necessary and had been, on her part, a sacrifice. She had two beautiful children, but that was all she was prepared to sin for. The temporary laying-down of her religious principles and moral standards had been necessary because Stevie had to keep face in the coal yard. She really did regret that she was unlike her pal, Catholic Patsy, who could confess all, then say four Hail Marys, and all was not only forgiven but also forgotten. That said, if Moira was being honest, did she really wish to forget every single minute of her – completely obligatory – dalliance? Probably not. She giggled every time she thought of it, becoming engulfed in a delightful quiver.

Autumn, their delightful little girl, was everything that Stevie wished for in a daughter. She was beautiful, vivacious, cute, and very, very clever – just like her father, or so he thought. As for Robin ... well, Stevie lived in the hope that adolescence would see Robin develop some masculine traits.

Stevie's concerns about Robin not being the macho kind of son he wished for became an obsession. It put a stress upon his relationship with Moira. Moira felt that she was more than responsible for Robin being gentle, artistic and slightly effeminate. She also found it irritating and conscience-pricking that Stevie was forever claiming that if Robin had not been born in the house, he would have sworn that someone had switched bairns on him.

The constant attacks on Robin and his un-willingness to follow in his dad's footsteps were the start of an irreparable rift between Moira and Stevie. They did still speak to each other, until Stevie, who really only wished to get Robin to 'soldier with him', suggested to Robin that he might like to attend a Hibs football match with his old man. Moira couldn't believe it when Robin said, 'That's very good of you to ask me, Dad, but going to Easter Road would bore me to tears.'

Stevie's jaw dropped. 'Oh my God,' he spluttered, before grabbing hold of Robin and birling him around to face him, 'don't tell me that in addition to you being–' Stevie swallowed hard '–a ... a ... well, you know what you are, you are also a bloody Heart of Midlothian supporter?'

'Apologise!' Moira screamed. 'This is the end. What worse insult could you hurl at Robin than to claim that–?'

'But he blooming well is...'

Before either Moira or Stevie could say anything further, Joey started to chirp and flutter around his cage.

'No wonder you are disgusted,' Moira said to the budgie before running her fingers over his cage.

'Aye, and I am too, Joey,' Stevie butted in.

From then on Moira and Stevie only spoke to one another through the bird.

On the evening following Robin's appointment with Meg Sutherland the mystic, Moira was preparing for Stevie's return home. She said to Joey, 'It will be some to-do tonight, Joey. Aye, there is no point in not taking the bull by the horns and telling my beloved husband that...'

The door opened. Moira turned to find Stevie,

covered in coal dust and looking at the bird's cage. 'What has she got to tell me, Joey? And if it is about a bull then it cannae be about her weakling son.'

'Joey, you tell him it's about Robin leaving school next week and what he would like to work at.'

'Tell the Queen Mother, Joey, that it's all sorted out, as I've got him – against my better judgement – a start beside me in the coal yard on Lindsay Road.'

'Am I hearing right, Joey?'

The bird chirped twice as if to say, 'Yes'.

Moira's cackle resonated off the walls. 'He's finally flipped it! Mind you, Joey, I always knew one day that he would. I mean how on earth does he expect our artistic Robin to carry hundred-weight bags of coal up four flights of stairs?'

'Flipped it, Joey? That'll be the day. But tell her that I've finally come to my senses and from this day on Robin will be known as Rab the Coalman.'

Running her fingers over Joey's cage Moira simpered, 'Now Joey, my bonnie wee budgie, you tell him that our Robin, yours and mine, will not be carrying any coal – not even from our outside bunker – because my clever laddie has gone and got himself an apprenticeship.'

Stevie was so surprised that he nearly spoke to Moira directly. 'Oh, oh, oh, so he's got himself a start in Ferranti's? Oh good, blooming good, because that will at least save my face.'

Joey chirped twice again before turning his back on both Stevie and Moira.

Undeterred, jubilant Moira continued, 'Joey,

you tell Tarzan, who thinks that Robin is going into electronics, that he's got it wrong again and that our creative, sensitive laddie ... oh Joey, come on now, son, turn around and tell him that our Robin's going up town to train as a hairdresser!'

Spluttering, Stevie yelled, 'Joey, is she saying that he's going to work in that Lorimer's, the uptown barbers on South St Andrew's Street? Ye ken, where it costs you a shilling mair than Leith's Joe Galletta's for a short back and sides!'

The bird chirped once to indicate that he had had enough. Fluttering his wings, he dropped down to the bottom of the cage. He instinctively buried his head under his right wing, as though he understood what was about to happen.

'Barber!' exclaimed Moira, 'Joey, you and I both know that our boy is not going to work in a smelly old hovel of a barber's shop. Tell him, Joey – go on, tell him, make my day and tell him – that our Robin is going to be a ladies' hairdresser. An apprenticeship he has won in high society: Stuart's prestigious hairdressing salon. You know, them that keeps the Royal tresses in order when they are in town.'

'Oh,' Stevie uttered with a groan, 'please God no. A ladies' hairdresser. Can't you see, Joey, it will mean me having to throw in the towel and admit that my son is ... is ... a nancy boy.' Stevie was now trying to eat his fist as he continued, 'And Joey, it's no' all his mother's fault. Naw, naw, I am to blame tae. Och aye, you see, when she insisted on calling him Robin and no Rab I should have put my foot down. I mean, Joey, with the poor wee laddie being given a name like

Robin, it's nae wonder he thinks he's a bird!'

Saturday night found the six teenagers monopolising the centre bench of Lochend Park. This was no surprise because the park was special to them. This was the place where they had grown up together, played together, dreamt together...

'So Bulldog Drummond didn't take much persuasion to admit you to his academy?' Molly said, causing Angela to stop gazing at Hannah, who had started to canter down the hill towards the duck pond with a brown paper bag in her hand.

'No,' was all she responded to Molly, who she thought was a bit piqued.

'And how did you get on, Ewan?' asked Robin.

'Well, he just asked me what profession I would like to aim for.'

'And what did you reply?'

'Me? I just shrugged, but my mum told him nothing less than my being a lawyer would be acceptable to her.'

Freda tittered, before starting to run after Hannah.

'What was Freda laughing at?'

'Just your mammy saying that she wants you to study law,' was Robin's reply as he nudged Ewan in the shoulder.

However, Ewan was now staring down towards the pond. He seemed to be completely fascinated by Hannah and Freda, who were enticing the ducks out of the water to get fed. Ewan's captivated reaction did more than unsettle Angela. A feeling of foreboding was suffocating her, because he was looking at one of the girls – but which one? – with an entranced, affectionate gaze. It was a tender look that she had never enjoyed from him; no, never ever had any of her advances towards him sparked such a look of pleasurable arousal. Rising up from the bench, she allowed a possessive smile to light up her face before she slipped her arm through Ewan's and quietly confided, 'Don't mind what any of them say. They are just jealous that you and I are going places ... places that they couldn't possibly even dream of.'

His response was to roughly pull himself free from her grasp. He then started to skip down the brae towards the object of his fascination. Overcome by vaulting jealousy, Angela sank down on the bench again. She wondered which one of her two friends had captivated him. Shrugging, she decided it was of no consequence who he fancied right then, because Hannah was just going to be a glorified clerk and Freda a hairdresser at Janet Briggs's. She gave a little snigger. Oh yes, once her Ewan was climbing he wouldn't wish to be dating either of them. No, no, when she and Ewan got to Leith Academy she would make sure he thought of no one but her. The added bonus was that Ewan's mother would see Angela as a very suitable girlfriend. Angela tittered as she pictured the look of horror on Ewan's mother's face if he ever tried to introduce either Hannah or Freda as his chosen mate for life.

TWO

SEPTEMBER 1966

'Freda, why are we on this bus going up town when I want to go to the shows at Portobello and get a shot on the Jungle Ride?'

Freda did not respond, as she was aware that there was really no answer to that question that would satisfy her spoilt but adored nine-year-old half-sister, Susan. Instead, she stared ahead, her thoughts drifting back four years.

Wrinkling her nose, she acknowledged that now she was – in most people's estimations – a mature, attractive, self-assured nineteen-year-old. How-ever, she conceded that back in 1962, when she arrived half an hour early to Janet Briggs's Hair-dressing Salon to start her apprenticeship, she was a nervous, gawky, immature fifteen-year-old. Vividly she remembered how she had wrapped up, in a brand-new hand towel, the expensive hair-cutting scissors and three combs of various sizes which her grandmother Rosie had bought for her, before packing them into her handbag. Unlike her mother, she was sure that by the end of the day she would be expert enough to cut customers' locks, or at least comb out their perms.

What a shock it had been when, on opening the door of the salon, the owner, Miss Briggs, bid her an offhand 'good morning' as she passed her a tin of Brasso and an assortment of cleaning cloths.

Freda's mouth was still gaping when Miss Briggs pointed to the broad brass doorstep and announced, 'The first of your duties each morning, Miss Scott, is to clean that step, and I should add that I like it gleaming, so that our clients know they are entering a first-class establishment. After that, you should go on to polish up the letterbox. I should make you aware that I just loathe finger marks on letterboxes so any spare minute you have, please check that my letterbox does not require another buff up with the Brasso.'

When Freda finished her chores with the Brasso, she forlornly looked down at her broken and stained fingernails. Only last night Robin had insisted on giving her a manicure so that she would create the right image for starting work at Miss Briggs's. Each nail he had filed to perfection before finishing them off with two coats of clear nail varnish.

She was still looking at her fingernails when Miss Briggs's voice brought her back to the present. 'Well done, Miss Scott. You have cleaned the brasses to my satisfaction, so now could you sweep up the hair from the salon floor?' Miss Briggs was about to walk away when she hesitated. 'Now I think it is only right, my dear, that I point out that I am a fair employer, so I will allow you to choose whether you stay on after closing time to wash the salon floor or come in early in the morning to do it.'

A desire to say that she would prefer not to clean the floor at all had Freda bite her tongue. Forlornly she replied, 'Where are the mop and pail stored, Miss Briggs?'

Miss Briggs's mouth gaped. 'Mop?' she almost screamed. 'Oh no, Miss Scott, I think you should know that I am very particular about the cleaning of the floor, so I expect you to get down on your hands and knees and use a scrubbing brush – a scrubbing brush that I generously supply.'

Having decided to scrub the floor in the evening instead of the morning, six thirty was chiming on her mother's sideboard clock when Freda eventually got home.

'Where the devil have you been?' was her mother's tight-lipped greeting.

'Oh Mum, I would have been better to have taken a job in the filthy Roperie than at the hairdressers. All I have done all day is clean and scrub. I didn't even get a chance to comb my own hair, never mind anybody else's!'

'That right? Then you'll be pleased to know that you can rest all night because I'm going to the Cappy Bingo, so you'll have to stay in and look after Susan.'

Freda was annoyed by her mother's statement, but as it would have taken energy to respond – energy that she didn't have right now – she just huffed, before asking Ellen, 'What's for my tea, Mum?'

'Tea?' exploded Ellen. 'You waltz in here at nearly supper time and you expect me to have kept you some tea? No, no, if you're hungry, just make yourself some toast and cheese.'

Freda scowled in reply.

'And Miss, you can wipe that "who stole my tattie scone" look off your face and think about

38

poor me. Oh aye, with you coming in so late I'll have to get my skates on so I get to the bingo on time. You know that Agnes and I always go together and share out any winnings we get evenly between us.' By now Ellen had donned her coat and as she tied a headscarf round her bottle-blonde hair she added, 'And it would just be like the thing for Agnes to hit the jackpot before I get down and that wee snivel, Jessie Mack, who is longing to be pals with Agnes, to have taken my place so she can swan off with my share of the spoils.'

The outside door banging shut and the quick clip of Ellen's high-heeled shoes on the pathway signalled that she had gone. Suppressing a desire to cry, Freda switched on the television. The television set was rented from Radio Rentals for ten bob a week – ten bob that Ellen continually reminded the family she earned by cleaning up for three hours after a 'clarty bitch' in Morningside. It turned out the 'bitch', Mrs Fowler, really did think that she was too upper class to be doing her own housework and thought she had been put on this earth to write another *Pride and Prejudice*. The other thing that annoyed Ellen about Mrs Fowler was that, unlike everybody in Leith, she owned her television set, which she always reminded Ellen was an indicator of the difference between being poor and working class, like Ellen, and being upper middle class, like herself.

The television had warmed up and *Coronation Street* had just started when Freda started to smile. If there was one thing that could make her feel better about her horrible first day, it was tuning into *Coronation Street*. She, being an avid follower of the soap, knew that even if you had had a pig of a day, tuning into *Corrie* made you feel better. It was just watching how the believable characters – ordinary, everyday people – coped, especially when they were consistently kicked and slapped in the face. She could recall distinctly that when the first episode aired, all the newspaper critics hammered it and predicted that it was doomed. They reckoned that it was just a realistic picture of dreary, everyday working-class life in the North and, this being the case, it lacked the glamour and escapism that was necessary to attract mass audiences. The millions of households who now tuned in each week to watch the goings-on on the street had doomed the predictions of the biased critics.

Freda, while still trying to keep an eye on the screen, dashed into the kitchen to rescue her toast from under the grill. She poured some boiling water into the teapot and it was then she became aware of the strong odour of the Zoflora disinfectant wafting up from her hands. Giggling, she remembered that in an effort to please Miss Briggs she had liberally poured the Zoflora into her wash bucket before starting to scrub the floor. Now, instead of the smell of the disinfectant annoying her, she breathed the lavender aroma so hard that it tickled her nose, causing her to laugh uncontrollably. The scent had reminded her that before *Coronation Street* was the chosen name for the programme, it had been suggested that it should be called *Florizel Street*. However, as soon as it was pointed out to the producers that Florizel was too like Zoflora, the posh disinfectant, it was immediately changed to *Coronation Street*.

She had just returned from the kitchen with her teacup in one hand and toast in the other when she heard the outside door open. Her younger sister Susan bounded in followed by three of Freda's friends: Hannah, Molly and Robin.

'Glad to see that *you* have obviously had a happy day,' snapped Molly.

'Oh, so did working in the gown shop not work out?'

'Well all I did, for the *whole* day, was pick up pins and scraps of material from the floor.' She scowled, adding, 'And when I wasn't doing that, I was continually sweeping that blooming floor or cleaning the lavatory.' She blew out her lips in exasperation, before expounding, 'I wasn't even allowed to put tacking stitches in a hem, I wasn't.'

Freda giggled. 'Oh, Molly, I know how you feel. I had the same sort of day. I felt I was Mrs Mop.' Freda turned her attention to Hannah. 'Now, how did your day go?'

'Well, as you know, I'm working in the city planning office of the Edinburgh Corporation, so when I arrived I was told that the day starts for the office staff with a read of the morning papers and a cup of tea. After that we went over to the town clerk's office to pick up some planning applications that the public had lodged.' Hannah hesitated.

'And?' Freda said in an effort to jolt Hannah.

'Well, we then had to log them all into our system, but I was told that before I did that I had to go round all the offices and find out who wanted what from the canteen.'

41

'For lunch?' spluttered Robin.

'No, they go down to the canteen themselves at lunchtime. I was to go for their morning break rolls – you know, bacon, sausage, black pudding or fried egg. Mind you, some only ordered a plain buttered bap! After my lunch I was told to take a long walk before getting the evening papers, and then to come back into the office to make the afternoon tea.'

Molly and Freda looked at each other before Freda gasped, 'Seems to me, Hannah, that you have landed on your feet.'

Hannah nodded. 'Yeah, and in the afternoon I was sent over to the legal department to see a solicitor and get the court papers for a demolition in Leith. See, when I knocked on the door and a woman's voice shouted, "Don't stand on ceremony ... just get yourself in here!", I couldn't believe it.'

'Why?' queried Robin.

'Because all the bosses are men and the women that I have seen so far are just clerks, receptionists and typists.'

'So, what like was this woman?' Molly tittered. 'I mean was she glamorous like Audrey Hepburn and do all the men in the City Chambers want to go on a "Roman Holiday" with her?'

'Think you mean, roam all over her,' Robin suggested with a wink.

'No, she is a solicitor and she is more a Margaret Rutherford sort of person. Honestly she is – right down to her hair, which looks like it's not been combed for a week. She has a face that only a mother could love, and she continually pulls her tight jumper down over her large, sagging bosom. And her desk! It's just a midden piled up, it is, with all these large sets of papers tied up with pink ribbons.'

Robin, Molly and Freda all exchanged bewildered glances with each other before Hannah continued, 'Her first words to me were, "You a new girl?" and I nodded. She then stared out of her window, which looks over on to St Giles' Cathedral, before turning, looking me in the eye and saying, "Right, to get promoted in here you have to be male, you have to have been educated privately and preferably at George Heriot's, and you have to be a member of the Masonic Order and play golf but"' – Hannah paused for breath and then continued, now wagging her finger in a perfect imitation of the solicitor – '"we women in this Council have to start to change all this nonsense. It is easier for me and Clarinda in the architects department because we have been to university and they wouldn't dare not give us a principal officer's grade, but you can still challenge too – because things are changing. Now to start with, don't clutter up your life with a man. You are not engaged or anything?" To that I just stuttered, "No, I have a problem so I won't be getting married."'

'What problem?' Molly interrupted.

Realising that she had made a mistake, Hannah blustered, 'It's nothing ... just something personal that I don't want to talk about just now.'

'Good grief – surely you're not thinking of becoming a nun!'

Hannah ignored Molly. 'Then Miss Carruthers

43

said, "That is good because you look to me to have what it will take to change things for women here. And the plus is, if you get yourself to night school and up your qualifications, you could do it." Then she became all dreamy and she addressed the wall, "Pity I won't be here to see it, but she will be the first principal officer that has come up through the ranks and not through university." Then she stopped and spoke to me again, saying, "And remember, play your cards right and you will have a job for life here. Oh, and while I remember, get yourself into the superannuation scheme. A pension in old age is really a necessity. A man providing for you just means you are obligated.'" Hannah paused again and took a deep breath. 'And when I got back to my office, I asked about Miss Carruthers and I was told that she might appear like a witch but that she was brilliant at her job – better than any of her male counterparts. Only problem with her is that she doesn't allow the poor cleaners to dust her desk, and to make sure they do not she throws a linen sheet over it when she goes home for the day!'

'Well, all I've got to say, Hannah, is keep at it. Now, do you three lassies wish to know how *my* day went?' Robin cooed, swaggering about the room.

Freda chuckled as she popped the last of her toast in her mouth. 'Darling Robin,' she began as she winked at him, 'I bet that as you, like Hannah, always land on your feet, you were never down on your knees today and no one pushed a sweeping brush into your hand.'

'You're right there.' He gave an elaborate bow to

44

Freda. 'You see, Stuart's is owned by Charlotte Stuart, and her son Billy is a lad that I've got friendly with – he's also training to be a hairdresser – so I didn't have to do any skivvying...'

Freda gasped and playfully punched him in the shoulder. 'Are you saying that you actually got to cut and style someone's hair today?'

'Don't be daft, Freda. Like you I will be at least two years into my training before I am allowed near anyone – that is, anyone still breathing – with scissors ... unless of course my dad drives me into giving him a quick Delilah!' He chuckled before becoming serious. 'But here, Freda, you do realise that most of our hands-on training will be done at Regent Road Night School on porcelain models with wigs?'

'Right enough, we have to enrol and attend there for three nights a week...' Freda's eyes widened and her hand shot to her mouth. 'Oh, but if I do that how will my mother get to her precious bingo?'

'But it's not three nights, it's four.'

'Four! What do you mean?'

'Just that to be the very best at hairdressing, you and I are going to apply for a training place at the Hairdressing Academy, which takes place on a Friday night.'

Sinking down on the settee beside Hannah, Freda's lip began to quiver.

'No use you bursting into tears. If we are to learn how to shampoo and cut with our own brand of style ... mark you, at the start we will also have to be experts at perms, pin curls, marcel waves and flame thinning!' He sank down on the couch and nudged himself in between Freda and Hannah before tucking his arm through Freda's. 'Look, you and I are going places with this hairdressing. So for our particular needs we have to gain modern expertise – and we have to get ourselves hand-held hairdryers that will change the whole idea of how women should have their hair styled.'

'You're bonkers. Yes, stark raving bonkers.'

'No Freda, I'm not.' Robin was now rubbing his fingers together to indicate money. 'As you know, nowadays women have a bit more cash to spend on themselves and they like having a luxury hairdo that is the envy of all their pals. So, that being so, Billy and I are going to be their coiffeurs and you their coiffeuse.'

Disengaging herself from Robin's arm hold, Freda ran her fingers through her hair, stuttering, 'But Robin, last week you said you thought we should be known as stylists... I mean, what do you mean by coiffeur and coiffeuse?

Jumping up from the settee and lifting Freda to her feet, Robin started to dance her around the floor. 'Och, dinnae fash yourself, Freda, coiffeur is just an Edinburgh fancy name for a stylist ... but mark you, stylists in a French way we are going to be.'

Freda chuckled as she became infected by Robin's enthusiasm. He made her believe that their future was so full of promise, she could actually believe that when she and Robin were fully trained they would go on to forge a great working life for themselves. However, all her optimism was shattered when she remembered her mother's bingo nights. She then had to acknowledge that everybody has dreams and her mother's was winning the jackpot at the Capitol Bingo Hall and making all her pals in Leith green with envy.

That was all then back in 1962 and here she was today because Granny Rosie, her dead dad's mum, had put aside her dislike of Freda's mum's selfishness and willingly agreed to look after Susan so that Ellen could go to the bingo and, more importantly, so that Freda could attend night school.

Yes, it was all thanks to Granny Rosie that today she was on her way to suss out the magnificent Assembly Rooms on posh George Street in Edinburgh. She still couldn't believe that in two days' time she would be competing for the prestigious Lorimer Cup, along with the other selected exceptional hair stylists.

Alighting from the bus and holding Susan tightly by the hand, Freda started to mince her way along elegant George Street, hoping that she would not bump into anyone who knew her or – even worse – was aware that she would be competing on Friday night. As luck would have it she heard the clip-clipping of someone's shoes running behind her and her heart sank when she heard the unmistakeable voice of Anne Craig shouting, 'Here, Freda, if you're on your way for a sneaky look-see of the Assembly Rooms then wait for me 'cause that is what I would like to do too!'

Freda's first reaction was to ignore Anne, pass by the Assembly Rooms and head off along George Street. Then she thought 'to hang with it!' and turned around to smile sweetly at Anne, before saying, 'Yes, I think that we should have a quick peek-a-boo of the venue, but as my friend Robin is also a contestant it is not as if any of us others will have a look-in for first prize.'

Anne drew up so quickly that she nearly toppled off her three-inch-high heels. 'Look, a bloke who everybody in the know is proclaiming as the next messiah as far as hairdressing is concerned is not a reason for us to throw in the towel before the competition even starts. The judges don't know him and they may not be into his modern techniques, so let's you and I get in there on Friday night and give the poncy big-head a run for his money!'

'That so?' was all Freda managed to reply before they were standing in front of the Assembly Rooms, where two aproned and turbaned women were down on their hands and knees scrubbing the entrance. 'Excuse me, missus,' Freda began, 'we are in the hairdressing competition that is being held here on Friday, so do you think we could slink past you and have a look at the big hall?'

The taller of the two women stood up, and when she looked at Freda, Anne and Susan, her face just beamed. 'Of course you can,' she twittered, drying her hands on her apron. 'My name's May. Just follow me and try to walk on the dry bits of the floor. Maggie, my pal there, will no' be happy if she has to swipe it clean again.' Maggie just laughed as she sloshed the floor in front of her.

The trio trotted quickly after May into the eighteenth-century Georgian building. However, their pace faltered when they passed through the portals and entered into the great hall. The opulence and splendour was breathtaking and they all just gaped. No way had they expected to see such grandeur. The ornate and magnificent ceiling was adorned with twenty-five sparkling crystal chandeliers – these twinkling lights completely entranced Freda. When she lowered her gaze to note the several elegant old-fashioned fireplaces with huge, elaborate, glistening mirrors she gasped, 'No wonder they say that this is one of the finest buildings in the whole of Great Britain. Oh, Anne, can you believe that little old you and me – hairdressers just past our training – are being allowed to show off our skills in such a grand place? Honestly, I am so overcome by it all that I am beginning to wonder if I will be able to work in here.'

'What do you mean?'

'Well, it's so intimidating and steeped in history.'

'You're right there, hen. I mean, the Queen holds her banquets here when she comes to visit. And not only her but all the other big bugs too.'

Freda's lips were now quivering. 'Oh, dear,' she whimpered, 'you know, for the last three months, ever since Miss Briggs said to me that she had put my name forward for the Lorimer Cup competition, I have been practising on my pal Hannah's hair. And the sessions have been three times a week for the last month.'

'So?'

'Och Anne, it is one thing doing Hannah's hair in Miss Briggs's salon or my mum's living room, but doing it here in this huge hall, where there will be hundreds of folks – including professional photographers – watching...'

'So what? Just think – with Billy and Robin strutting around, who will be looking at us? Oh, by the way, they can't be doing each other's hair in the competition, so who is Robin's model?'

'Angela! And that's another thing! See, with a face like she's got, you could end up making her bald and she would still steal the show.'

'Freda, I thought your pal Angela was training to be a teacher, so why will she be getting her hair done?'

Glancing down at Susan, Freda shrugged. She could have replied that when Ewan had said to Robin that he would take a night off from his medical studies to attend the competition, Angela had there and then offered to be Robin's model – making sure, she was, that Ewan's attention would be on her and not wandering over to Hannah or, worse still, Freda herself.

This reminiscence took Freda's thoughts back to last year, when Ewan had been dux of Leith Academy and the six old school pals had decided to catch up again with a get-together at Alfonso's Italian restaurant on Leith Walk.

Ewan, who was sitting between Angela and Freda, announced that he was not going to study law and that he had applied to and been accepted for medical school. After he made the unexpected statement he put his hand over Freda's, and as she looked at him he winked. Her response was to blush and lower her head, and Angela's was to put her hand on Ewan's face and turn it towards her, before simpering, 'Yes dear, you were awarded the dux medal, but don't forget that I was runner-up and I am always–'

'Chasing you,' Robin quipped.

Angela glowered and snorted before replying, 'No, Robin, I am not chasing him, as I do not have to, but I am visiting his mother regularly and persuading her that our Ewan graduating as a doctor will be as good an accomplishment as him getting a legal qualification.'

'Ooh,' cooed Molly, 'isn't that just dandy? Here, Ewan, any time you wish to take *my* pulse, just say the word!'

Freda's thoughts were dragged back to the present when May said, 'Well, much as I would like to spend more time letting you get a feel of this grand place, I have to get on. Cannae really leave Maggie for too long. You see, she's getting on a bit and right enough she's good at sloshing the water about, but she's no' much use at mopping it dry now.' Freda looked questioningly at May. 'Honestly,' May continued, 'just last week the fellow who was going to lead the Viennese Orchestra's recital thought he had fallen in the Blue Danube when he bounced in the door to do the morning rehearsal... You can laugh, hen, but there was that much water swishing about everywhere that you would have thought that we had just had a flash flood.'

The Maggie tale amused Freda. She liked May and her banter and as she glanced behind her she observed that Maggie must be as old as her granny. Granny Rosie still had the heart to be willing to help out but she could see now that Granny's old bones tired very quickly now.

The trio were out in George Street when Susan

said, 'Freda, have you forgotten that you have not told me why your pal Angela is going to be a hairdresser's model and not a teacher? I mean, is being a teacher not a better job than modelling hairstyles?'

Chuckling, Freda took Susan's hand in hers. 'Well, I suppose it is, but Angela, being Angela, will be able to do both. You see, she is really angling for the top prize, but Susan, life does not always work out the way we plan it.' Freda stopped and hunched her shoulders with delight, before wistfully adding, 'And with a bit of luck that accolade may go to someone else.'

Knitting her brows, Susan sniffed. She was too young to understand what Freda was getting at and too bored now to care.

'Right, firstly, cheerio, Anne, and the best of luck on Friday. Now, Susan, you and I will go and have a snack at a "cup of tea shop", as you call them, and then we will dash home because Molly is coming to give me a final fitting for my dress.'

Susan seemed pleased; however, she had to ask something else, because Susan always did. 'Here, Freda, why do you have to go to this hair thing dressed up in a long frock?'

'Well, darling, it's a very prestigious affair and it has always been necessary for participants to go in evening dress, just in case they are to be awarded the cup. It just wouldn't do to get your photograph taken for the newspapers in a crossover overall and comfy shoes.'

Still not satisfied, Susan then wished to know what Robin would be wearing, because even though her daddy was always saying he was a sissy, surely he wouldn't be going in a frock.

Annoyed at this description of Robin, Freda gritted her teeth before stressing, 'Robin is going in an evening suit with a red bow tie and matching cummerbund.'

'What's a cummerbund?' Susan asked. Freda just smiled as Mackie's tea shop came into view and she knew that she need not answer Susan, as her sister's thoughts would now be diverted on to which sticky bun she would choose to devour.

After months of practising their expertise, Friday came all too soon. Hannah had taken a half-day off work so that Freda could do all her preparations before they took a taxi up to the Assembly Rooms. Firstly, Freda shampooed Hannah's light brunette hair and then she meticulously put in the different sizes of dry hair rollers. She wished to create a modern, slightly less formal style for mature women. She reckoned this approach was the correct one for her because Miss Briggs's clientele were, in the main, financially secure, mature, ultra-respectable women. A sly smile crossed Freda's face when she thought of Robin. She knew that tonight he would not only be joining the revolution in hair styling for younger women in a swinging Mary Quant way, but pointedly starting one of his own.

Once Hannah's rollers were in place, Freda finished the creation off with small pin curls. Standing back, she just was not satisfied, so out came all the small pin curls to be replaced with larger ones.

Finally satisfied that she had done all the advanced preparation that she could with Hannah's hair, Freda then swathed it in a large scarf. Then all that was left for Freda to do was assist Hannah into her sleek lavender evening gown, which naturally Molly had created for her. Standing back to admire her model, Freda became aware that Hannah had matured in the four years since they had left school. For one thing, she had blossomed into an attractive young woman who carried her elegant height and slight form with dignity. However, Freda conceded, there was still an air of mystery about Hannah – something about herself that she kept to herself. This enigma was one of the reasons that Freda had asked Hannah to be her model; one of the things that Miss Briggs had confided to Freda was that the judges did not favour models who tried to outshine their hairdressers by posturing and posing.

The clock chiming the hour made Freda jump and she knew there was nothing else she had time for now but to get herself dressed.

As she passed the tiny purple and white gingham gown over her head, she smiled, because although Molly had fashioned it to perfection, the gown was just so comfortable to wear. Oh yes, in no way would it impede her as she demonstrated her skills, and if – and that was a very big if – she was fortunate enough to win a prize, it would more than meet that grand occasion.

Everyone was more than on time at the Assembly Rooms. A bell was then rung to indicate to the contestants that they could start to work on their models.

On one side of Freda was stationed Anne, and on the other, Robin. Not once in the precious sixty minutes allotted did Freda allow herself to glance at either Anne or Robin. Her full attention was on Hannah's hair, which she was grooming to perfection. The only deviation she allowed herself was to glance at the small clock that she had strategically placed on the table beside her grooming tools.

The signal that the allotted time was up took most contestants by surprise, but not Freda, because she had already laid down her combs and sprayed her creation with a fine mist of hair lacquer.

The stony-faced judges then weaved and meandered their way up and down the hall as they assessed the models. As the minutes ticked by ever so slowly, it seemed to the contestants that the judges were deliberately prolonging their agony. The last duty of the adjudicators was to get into a huddle and then agree on the winners.

When at last the chief assessor called for silence in the hall, Freda felt as if her knees were going to buckle. The chief assessor then pompously announced that he and his fellow judges were in unanimous agreement on the winners, and that the third prize was awarded to Freda Scott of Briggs's hairdressing in Leith.

Startled, Freda started to look about to see who this young woman could be. It was only when Robin patted her on the back and said, 'Well done, sweetheart,' that she realised it was herself. Going forward to receive her trophy from the judge, she began to quiver and tears brimmed in her eyes. Was it true that she, a wee lassie from Leith, had managed to succeed in such a prestigious field?

She was back in her place when the judge gave a knowing bow to Charlotte Stuart, thus indicating her son had been the runner-up. Smugly, Billy saluted Robin. The two lads had discussed the competition and both believed that one of them would be either second or third and that the top prize would be lifted by someone from Greens or Tenfeltz. This prediction was because those two, the most prestigious salons in Edinburgh, took it in turns to be awarded first prize.

Freda, and all in attendance, immediately realised the significance of Billy getting second prize. She just couldn't understand it. She knew that she was an excellent hairdresser, and Billy was as good as she was, but neither of them could match Robin in flair and expertise. She was actually dumbfounded that the judging panel had not seen that Robin was a genius. She was now torn between going to comfort ashen-faced Robin and going to confront the judges to tell them to stick her third prize where – as they would say in Leith – the sun don't shine!

Luckily, before she could do anything, the chief judge called for silence from the now overexcited audience.

As a welcome hush descended in the great hall, the judge said, 'And first prize is awarded to another of the Stuart's competitors, a truly brilliant stylist ... a young man who we predict will go far in his career: Robin Dalgleish.'

To the surprise and amusement of everyone,

not only did Robin pull himself together and begin to march forward for the supreme accolade – the Lorimer Cup – but close on his heels followed Freda, his mother Moira, and his blonde-haired, svelte model Angela, who never missed an opportunity to get recognition and acclaim. Before they reached the judges, however, some stewards steered the three ladies off course and Robin was allowed to stand alone in all his glory. Angela, on the other hand, was parading herself around the audience. When she passed by Freda, Freda just smiled, because it was more than obvious that Angela was the most elegant and best-groomed woman in the hall.

An hour was to pass before everybody was out of the hall and standing in George Street. Ewan, who had been unable to get over to Freda in the hall, started to embrace and congratulate her. Still holding her hand, he then suggested that they all go over to the George Hotel for a celebration drink.

The George Hotel! They had only been awarded hairdressing prizes, not seventy-five thousand pounds on the football pools, thought Freda. Didn't Ewan understand that to go into the George Hotel you would need to be bankrolled by Andrew Carnegie? Granny Rosie immediately sensed her discomfort and pulled her aside. 'Look lassie, you've done so well tonight. Your dad would have been so proud of you.'

Freda automatically placed her hand up to her shoulder, she always did now when she thought of her dad, and tonight it was important to her that she acknowledge that she had felt him in that hall standing beside her, willing her on and wishing the best for her – unlike her mum, who couldn't give up a night at the bingo because it was a special jackpot night.

'Freda, my love, I'll take missy Susan here home to her dad and–' Rosie slipped her hand into Freda's coat pocket – 'that's a wee something so that you can afford to get in there and hold your own. What I am saying is that you mustn't let that stuck-up Angela steal your thunder. What a bloody spectacle she made of herself when she strutted round the room like a demented peacock.'

When it was time to leave the George Hotel, Freda heaved a deep sigh. She knew tonight would always live within her memories – and it was not just because of coming third in such a renowned competition, it was also so good for the six friends to meet up again. To her, the time spent in the George had been wonderful. It wasn't just that she had never been in a first-class hotel before – not even to work as a waitress – it was how Ewan had taken command, and when their first drinks arrived, stood up and toasted firstly her success, and then Robin's.

Angela, of course, had then got up, and as she linked her arms through Ewan's she purred, 'But darling, don't you think that Robin's success was in part due to his model? After all, you cannot make a silk purse out of a sow's ear, and my facial looks and wonderful head of hair meant that Robin was halfway there before he started.'

It was the only time in their socialising in that majestic hotel that Freda cringed. But then

Angela was Angela and she wouldn't ever change, and therefore she would always steal the limelight. However, Robin whispered in her ear, 'Know something ... as far as I'm concerned I did make the haughty pig look not so much like a silk purse, but an unfeeling cow!'

The first to leave the hotel was Hannah, and as she donned her coat, Freda pulled her into a tight cuddle and whispered in her ear, 'Thanks for all you did to help me win that prize. Now, if there is ever anything I can do for you, believe me you just have to ask.'

Hannah began to tremble and Freda instinctively tightened her grasp on her.

'There is something I would like you to do, Freda.'

'What?'

'Go with me to an appointment in the Eastern General Hospital next Thursday.' She hesitated. 'You see, I have something awful wrong with me and they just might...'

'Something wrong? Like what?'

'I don't want to say anything here in case we are overheard... Look, Freda, it's just that I was born with something missing.'

'Well, it can't be your intelligence. Look how well you are doing at your job in the Edinburgh Corporation – already promoted and you are just nineteen, and a woman.'

By now Angela and Molly were looking quizzically at them so Hannah released herself from Freda's embrace. As she lowered her head, she murmured, 'Look, Freda, we will meet up on Sunday after church and I will tell you what the problem is. Tonight I just couldn't bear for Angela to know what is wrong with me. She would just make fun of me and I would become the laughing stock.'

Fifteen minutes later Ewan ordered a taxi and he, Freda, Robin, Molly and Angela piled in. Molly was the first drop-off and Robin was second, but before getting out he whispered to Freda, 'You were just brilliant tonight.'

Her cocky, husky reply was: 'And you weren't too bad yourself.'

The third drop-off should have been Angela, but she told the driver to go past her home and drop Freda off next. When Freda alighted from the taxi so did Ewan, and before rejoining Angela he pulled Freda into his arms. 'You were a star tonight. I don't see so much of you nowadays – too busy studying – but–' he now lightly brushed her cheeks with his lips – 'there is not a day goes by that I do not think about you.'

'Just little old me?' she teased.

'Not exactly... You see, I also wonder every blooming day what my best pal Robin is up to.' He became serious. 'Did you notice that his dad wasn't there tonight. Surely he could have come and supported his laddie?'

Freda giggled. 'They have their priorities – my mum's is the bingo, Robin's dad's is supporting the bar in the Dockers Club!'

Usually when Freda met up with Hannah on a Sunday afternoon she had Susan in tow. If it was fine weather they would go into Lochend Park and feed the ducks; if it was not, they would pass the time away supping on knickerbocker glories in the ice cream parlour on Easter Road. However, on the Sunday following Freda's hairdressing triumph, Freda had to disappoint Susan by saying she had things to discuss with Hannah that would not be for Susan's ears, so she would have to stay at home.

At 2 p.m. sharp, Freda strode into Michael's café. Michael was just about to start making up two knickerbockers when Freda said, 'Coffees today, Michael.'

She immediately got herself into the booth where Hannah was already seated, and as she placed her handbag on the seat next to her she said, 'Right, now Hannah, for years you have hinted that you have a problem where boyfriends are concerned, so no more beating about the bush. Let's get your problem out into the open.'

Hannah's face fired and her breath began to come in short pants. 'Freda,' she slowly began, 'please do not say another word until Michael has put down our coffees and got himself out of earshot.'

'That so... Well, let me tell you, you have got yourself into such a tizzy that you are not aware that the steaming cup in front of you is your coffee ... and as to Michael, he's well out of earshot and is now standing at the front door holding court with the lad that runs Lang's, the pork butchers next door.'

Lifting her teaspoon, Hannah began to lazily stir her coffee. 'Freda, be patient with me. You see, other than my mum, nobody knows.' She quickly added, 'Because I have never told anyone

61

... I am so ashamed.'

'Of what?'

'Oh Freda... Well, here goes ... I am not all there.'

'What? But Hannah, you have arms, legs, eyes, ears, a good brain ... so as far as I can see, you are all there.'

'That's true – I appear all there, but inside I'm not.' Hannah was now pulling at her hair. 'Freda, it's just that...'

'Look, Hannah, if you don't spit out what it is you are trying to tell me you won't be the only one not all there ... I will have joined you.'

Heaving in a large breath, Hannah stuttered, 'I haven't got a uterus!'

Freda sat bolt upright before exclaiming, 'A what?'

'A uterus, Freda.'

'And what in the name of heavens is a uterus?' Freda questioned as she started to titter. 'And know something, Hannah. I don't know what a blooming uterus is and I'm not sure if we really need one.'

'That was the name of what the doctor said was missing when he examined me, back when I was fifteen.' Gulping, Hannah paused. 'It's just another name for your ... womb.'

'You went to see a doctor when you were fifteen to ask him why you didn't have a womb? Why ... and what made you think that you didn't have one then?' Freda stopped to try and make sense of it all. 'Och, Hannah now you have me wondering if I have one, but I most certainly won't be asking anyone to have a look for it.'

'I didn't ask him to look to see if I had a womb. I went to see him because... Remember back to when Angela was the first to get her period?'

'But that's Angela – she is always first to get or do anything.'

Hannah ignored Freda's remarks. 'Well, next it was you, and then Molly, and when I still hadn't seen any sign of mine my mum was frightened I was pregnant, so she took me to the doctor. He sent me to see this other doctor called a gynaecologist.' Hannah's face was now bright red as the memories of that happening were brought to the front of her mind again. 'Freda, it was all so... I hated what he was doing and I demanded that he brought my mum in to hold my hand during his examination of me. Believe me, it was so painful I was screaming. And when he said I would never be able to have a child because I had no uterus to carry it in and that...' She gulped and hung her head, before continuing in a whisper, 'Because I also have an undeveloped vagina, doing what happens when you get married would be very painful for me without...' She raised her head again. 'Freda, are you still a virgin?'

'Of course I am. What made you think that I wasn't?'

'Well, Angela is always hinting that with you and Robin spending two nights a week down in the basement of Stuart's hairdressers, you must be getting up to no good.'

'What? Look, not that it's any of your or Angela's business, we spend that time washing and resetting all the old bald biddies' wigs. Make more than a bob or two doing that, we do.'

'But for why?'

'Because...' Freda leaned over the table towards Hannah and whispered, 'Even though some of the loaded old dears in Edinburgh are losing their hair, it doesn't mean they don't care how they look. So Robin and I have set up a business, through Stuart's, washing and resetting their wigs, which keeps them in tip-top shape.'

'I'm not daft, Freda. I worked that out, but what I don't know is why you are spending all your spare time doing it.'

Firstly, allowing her eyes to dart about the room, Freda inclined even closer to Hannah, who had to cock her ear to hear Freda's even quieter muttering. 'Please, Hannah, don't tell anyone, but Robin and I are going to set up together.'

'Oh, so you are making extra money so you can live together?'

Freda took in a sharp breath. 'No,' she uttered hoarsely under her breath, 'we are not setting up home together and never will. Robin is in love with Billy and Billy adores him. Billy's mother, like most people, doesn't want Billy to love Robin and so she is trying to give Robin the heave-ho. This being the case, he asked me if I would like to go into business with him.'

'Oh.'

'Aye, and thank goodness you've got that straight in your head.' She heaved a long sigh, before adding, 'So all we are doing in the basement is working like slaves to get the wherewithal to buy the equipment we will need. And in the meantime, we are looking about for a shop – a shop in the right location that will get Robin and

I started up on our own. Imagine it: me no longer taking orders from Miss Briggs, and dear Robin not having to dodge the Wicked Witch of the West on her broomstick!'

Pondering, Hannah replied more to herself than to Freda, 'So you are still a virgin? You wouldn't know what it feels like to make love?'

All the response Freda gave was a grimace.

'Do you think Angela is?'

'For heaven's sake, how would I know or even care?' Freda hesitated to contemplate, before saying, 'Right, back to where we were ... you were told at fifteen you had no womb?'

Hannah nodded. 'Yeah, and I also don't have periods like you.'

'Believe me, that's a bonus I would welcome.' Shaking her head, Freda tutted before adding, 'But I'm beginning to think that I'm not all there either, because I can't quite fathom why you have decided to go back to the hospital now.'

'You know how I've just been promoted to a higher clerical job in the city's engineers' department? Well, there is a clerk of works there and I think he fancies me.'

'What makes you think that?'

Addressing the ceiling, Hannah slowly drawled, 'Oh Freda, you won't believe me but every Friday afternoon he brings me in a wee pink French fancy, and he winks at me as he slips it over my desk.'

'Now let's get this straight,' Freda said as she tried to stifle her desire to laugh, 'you are going back to the hospital because some bloke buys you a French cake?'

'Freda, I am only doing what you and Robin are doing – looking to the future. A future day when someone may wish to marry me even though...' Her lip quivered. 'Even though I'm not all there where I should be. Freda,' she babbled on, 'I am so excited. You see, I have just found out that there are now things that can be done so that I could ... not have a baby, but so I would be able to ... you know ... do what lovers do.'

'So that's the real reason you want me to go to the hospital appointment with you and not your mum.' Freda's laughter was now uncontrollable. 'You don't want your mum to know what you are dreaming of doing.'

'It's not funny. Be honest, have you not thought about S. E. X.?' Hannah paused. 'I suppose you might not have because it will never be a problem for you. You're all there where you should be, so you will never have to go and beg for an operation or be shown how to use a dilator before you can...' Hannah was now quite emotional as she blubbered, 'And if a dilator blowing me up won't cause death to romance then I don't know what will!'

A long and uneasy silence fell between the girls. Freda squirmed as she admitted to herself that she had always wondered why Hannah, when in a crowd of young men and women, always seemed to be fretting. She looked over to Hannah, as she wished to meet her eyes and in a look convey to her that she was now beginning to realise what a cruel and bitter blow nature had laboured her with. Shaking her head as tears surfaced, Freda noted that Hannah seemed unable to lift her head. Rising, she wiped away the teardrops from

66

the corner of her eyes before going over to the counter and asking Michael to draw up another two coffees.

When she returned to the table Hannah quietly pleaded, 'Please, Freda, don't tell anybody about my problems. I just couldn't bear the pity or worse still–' she stopped and deliberately held Freda's gaze before adding – 'the ridicule.'

Putting her hands over Hannah's, Freda replied, 'No. You are my best friend and no one will ever hear your secret from me. And Hannah, don't be ashamed of your feelings and of trying to find a solution. We all have dreams... If we didn't, how could we ever know the joy of one coming true?'

Hannah was now wiping her tears. 'Now tell me the truth, Freda,' she wheedled, 'do you ever dream of making love and having babies?'

It would have been cruel to lie to Hannah again, so Freda nodded. 'Aye, I do, and here's something for you to digest and keep secret... Silly me deludes myself by thinking that one day Ewan will see me as a desirable woman and not just a good pal to slap on the back. But when I compare myself with our sexy, sophisticated pal Angela, what hope do I really have?'

More in control, Hannah teased, 'Don't suppose quietly bumping her off is a solution you have ever considered?'

Freda's wicked smile told Hannah that in her daydreams she might not have exactly wielded an axe, but she most certainly had often thought about launching Angela into outer space, or at least the Outer Hebrides...

THREE

DECEMBER 1966

When Freda bounced into Stuart's basement, Robin, who was cleaning out the sink he had been washing the wigs in, looked up.

'You were supposed to be here at half past six, not half past eight.'

'Sorry, I know we had ten wigs to get sorted out … please tell me you managed to get them all done?'

'Aye. But I could have done with a hand.'

'Robin, I just had to go and visit Hannah in the Eastern General Hospital.'

Robin's scowl softened. 'Is she all right?'

'Aye, she was admitted to the gynae for a wee op. The anaesthetic made her a bit weepy so I just couldn't up and leave her.'

'What kind of an op?'

Freda turned away from Robin. What on earth, she wondered, was she going to say? She could hardly claim that Hannah had had her tonsils taken out by a gynaecologist. To keep faith with Hannah she could not tell him the truth, so very quickly she had to come up with a plausible answer. As if by magic, Angela popped into her mind. Last month the poor lassie also had to have a wee op at the Eastern – an op called a D&C, which she quickly said was not because she'd had

68

a miscarriage. No, no, according to Angela when she confided to Freda, the doctor at the Eastern General Hospital had said it was something very unusual ... in fact, he had never come across it before, but not to worry, as a D&C would put it right.

Freda thought that she could say that Hannah's op was something similar to Angela's, but of course not as complicated. 'What kind of an op you ask?' Freda mused, 'Och, just the same as Angela's.' She then turned to face Robin again. 'You know everybody right now seems to be being sent for that kind of operation ... honestly I'm feeling quite left out because I've never been offered one – wonder why?'

Tittering, Robin suggested, 'You've not seen a doctor in years – so that could be the answer! But forget all Hannah and Angela's female problems... Come sit down here opposite me and listen to this.'

Freda had just sat down when Robin made a grab for her hands. 'Sweetheart, in my pocket here are the keys to our dreams coming true.' Robin fished out a set of keys from his pocket, which he then jangled in front of Freda.

'You've found us a shop!' she exclaimed as she grabbed for the keys.

'Aye, not exactly up in a prime site in the heart of Princes Street or the West End but – oh Freda, would you believe it – Elm Row no less! And not only that, but bang in the middle of Valvona and Crolla's delicatessen and the chemist.'

'You rotten liar!' she squealed. 'You are just saying that because I was too late tonight to help with the wigs.'

Crossing his heart, Robin replied with a wink, 'No. It's true, so let's clear up here and get ourselves down to Elm Row so you can see for yourself.'

Breathing in deeply, Freda relaxed her shoulders. 'Does that mean we can also say goodbye to doing these wigs?'

Robin shook his head. 'Not until we are up and running and making a good profit will we be able to say goodbye to cleaning and resetting these hairpieces. But as we are so good at it I am sure Madam Stuart will allow us to do them in our own salon and then deliver them back to her.'

Within half an hour they were standing at the front door of the shop in Elm Row. When Freda looked at the peeling paint and the filthy boarded-up windows, her heart sank and her enthusiasm began to wane.

Tripping over the worn wooden doorstep, her dismay was added to as she looked about the inner shop. True, there was a very large front area that, with a lot of very hard work, could be made into a first-class salon. It needed not only cleaning and decorating, but also fumigating, as there was a foul odour clinging about.

'Well what do you think?' Robin speered when he became aware that she was looking anything but upbeat. 'Now come on, don't look at the dirt … look at the potential!' Freda scowled. 'Come on, Freda,' Robin cajoled, 'I think we can make a go of it here.'

'You do?'

'Aye, you will be amazed at what some soap,

water and elbow grease will accomplish, and don't worry about the drains – see, once some shampoo is poured down them the smell will disappear.'

'Robin, get real. It will take more than a few bottles of shampoo to get rid of the stench of rotting herring guts.'

'Oh, so you've guessed it was a fish shop?'

Freda nodded, and as she looked about the room Robin continued, 'Okay, it was a fresh fish shop but Freda I ask you again not to look at the mess and not to sniff. Now come on ... you can see it has potential.' He grabbed her by the right hand and started to drag her into the back chamber. 'See here how it opens up into another huge space?' He now let go of her hand and as he danced about the room, a scraggy cat jumped out from under a sink.

Freda screamed. The mangy, smelly creature then started to rub itself on her leg, and as she tried to discourage it, whilst also attempting to gulp in some fresh air, she toppled over and landed down on the floor.

Trying hard not to laugh out loud, Robin asked if she was amazed at the size of the room.

Dumbstruck, she nodded. From where she was sitting she could see that the back of the shop was as spacious as the front. Being astute, she knew that not only was the location of the shop important to Robin but also the size of the two areas.

Rising up off the floor, she smirked. 'I hope you are not thinking we could hold wee dances in here?'

Grabbing hold of her and waltzing her about the room, he chuckled. 'Not dances. But Freda, you know how good I am at the make-up. I was thinking that in time we could offer our customers the works. You know ... hair, make-up, manicures.'

Once he stopped birling her she collapsed down on an old wooden chair and her laughter echoed around the shop. 'Robin,' she spluttered through her giggles, 'next you will be suggesting that we take Molly in as a partner and she can create their gowns.'

He stopped abruptly. 'With me getting the keys to the shop, I forgot to tell you that Molly is getting married in two weeks' time, and she and her bloke are emigrating to Canada.'

'Canada?' Freda looked perplexed. 'Right enough, Jack Croft is a first-class telephone engineer, so it will be easy for him to get a well-paid job there. But my pal Molly going to Canada! That's a blow...'

'It is?'

'Yes, you see she has promised Hannah, Angela and me that if ever we were to get married she would make us our wedding dresses.'

'Right enough, Toronto would be a long way to go for the fittings.'

Freda looked about the shop again. She began to think that if you left the door open for a month, got a drainage engineer in to flush out the drains, slapped some paint on the walls and evicted the scabby cat, it just might work. Shaking her head, she grimaced, before saying half-heartedly to Robin, 'Okay, I suppose this dump quite possibly could be the right place for you and me to start up business.'

Robin grinned from ear to ear. 'You're right

there and this old city of Edinburgh is big enough to accommodate me ... and that new boy nipping at my heels, Charlie Miller!'

Robin lifted Freda to her feet and they both started to cackle when the chair toppled over and fell to pieces.

'Hope that's not an omen!' Freda teased.

FOUR

JANUARY 1967

Four weeks later, when bleak January was blowing itself out and a heavy snowfall had covered the already frozen pavements, Robin and Freda were busy doing some decorating to the shop when Robin said, 'Look, the weather seems to be getting worse. I know it's only eight o'clock and we usually work on until ten, but how about we pack up for the night?'

Laying down her paintbrush, Freda grimaced. 'I suppose you're right. I've got Susan to get home and the wee soul must be bored out of her skull.'

Robin had by now stowed away his decorating implements, but before taking off his dungarees – which had more paint on them than the walls – he grabbed one of the wigs that was lying waiting for pick-up. As he donned it he took hold of Freda, who was dressed in Granny Rosie's old crossover overall, and tucked her arm under his own. Susan, who was sitting on the windowsill, stared on in amazement, a huge smile lighting up her face as Robin began to dance around the floor with Freda, singing 'A Couple of Swells'.

When he had finished the caper and let her go, Freda sank down on the windowsill beside Susan. 'We sure do look like a couple of tramps,' she giggled, 'but Robin, just look at what we have managed to do.'

'Well best of all was that drainage bloke, your brother's mate, getting rid of the fishy smell.'

'Aye.' Freda mused as she slipped off her overall to reveal what she was wearing underneath – a tight, skinny-ribbed jumper and a short green miniskirt. 'Wonder if he is any good at getting rid of the smell of gloss paint?'

'Not any old paint, Freda!' Robin protested. 'The very best that Craig and Rose has to offer.'

Fixing Robin, who was now dressed to go out into the night, with a warning stare, Freda mumbled, 'Careful, Susan has big ears.' She was of course alluding to the fact that someone who worked in Craig and Rose had sold them the paint at a giveaway price, because it had obviously been 'acquired'.

Freda put on her white plastic lace-up knee-high boots. These boots were a must-have for anyone like Freda, a fashionable young lassie who just worshipped the designs of Mary Quant. Waggling her legs out in front of her, she said, 'Robin, see all these lassies that can now afford to buy Mary Quant clothes, do you think that as you have now given me a replica of her hairdo, they will flock in here to get the rest of the image too?'

Standing back, Robin looked at Freda's new

hairstyle. It was an exact replica of Mary Quant's – a deep, thick, glossy fringe and short but stylish around the ears. Yeah, he thought, if anyone could go out and advertise the salon, Freda could.

However, before he could answer, Susan piped up with, 'Dad says that your hair looks awful and your skirt is so short that everybody can see what you had for your breakfast. He also says that you will either get pneumonia or something worse.'

Robin was about to put Susan straight, but Freda silenced him with a wave of her hand. Right away he realised that Freda would not chastise Susan, as Susan was too young to under-stand not to repeat things that opinionated adults should not have said. It was also true that Freda and her stepfather only tolerated each other and continually bitched about each other's failings to anyone who would listen.

Placing her left hand up to massage her right shoulder, a sign Robin now knew was her way of thinking of her dad, Freda said, 'Right Missy, you've had a nice tea of fish and chips from Deep Sea – okay, *you* had to go for them – but now it's time to get you home and into a seat by the fire. Sorry, I mean the Gas Miser.' Freda was referring to the fact that her mum, to save herself work, had changed the coal fire for one from the Gas Board. Somehow, Freda thought, gas flames did not seem as cosy or as comforting as the leaping and crackling flames of the old coal fire.

After alighting from the bus on Restalrig Road, Freda bent down and picked up some fresh snow, which she formed into a ball. 'I'm going to get you. I'm going to get you. I'm going to get you, Susan Black!' she chanted.

Susan immediately knew that Freda was going to pelt her with snowballs, so she scampered over the road and down Sleigh Drive, to the four-in-a-block housing where they lived in a front garden flat.

Susan screamed, 'Mummy, Daddy, Mummy, Daddy, please save me,' and this brought Drew Black to the front door.

'What the hell's going on?' he hollered, as Susan toppled over at his feet.

'Daddy, she's battering me with snowballs!'

Freda, unaware that Drew had opened the door, flung one last icy missile towards Susan, but it hit Drew full in the face. As the ice melted and dripped down his nose and on to his chin, Freda became consumed with terror. Susan, on the other hand, thought the whole thing was very funny. She began jumping up and down. 'Freda landed one on Daddy, Freda landed one on Daddy, ha, ha, ha!' she chorused.

Next thing Freda knew, Drew's clenched fist was smacking her full in the mouth. Blood spurted and gushed down her face. As her fingers brushed the warm sticky liquid, the hatred that she had harboured for this man seemed to boil over, and instead of taking flight, she decided to stand and fight. Indeed, her desire to wreak vengeance on him completely overtook her.

Her first vicious kick was to Drew's right leg, which resulted in him lunging forward to grab her by the hair. Cursing and swearing, he dragged her into the house. As his fingers curled further into her short locks she became all too aware of the reality of her situation. For years, Drew had hated her as much as she hated him. She had not made life easy for him since he had married her mother, and she knew that he had waited years for the chance to get even with her and would more than take advantage of the opportunity she had afforded him. A vicious beating was the least she could expect. Putting her left hand up to her shoulder, where she thought her dad would be standing, she screamed, 'Susan, run as fast as you can to Marionville Crescent and get my granny and grandad!'

Susan hesitated, but, young as she was, when she saw her father remove his broad belt from his trousers, she knew that he intended to lash Freda – Freda, her beloved sister and the one person in her young life who she could always rely on. She also knew that any pleading with her father from her would fall on deaf ears, so she bolted on unsteady legs from the house and headed out in the direction of Marionville Crescent.

Marionville Crescent was like its name: a pre-war private housing development made up of rather lovely semi-detached bungalows. Susan always liked going to visit Freda's granny and grandad because she thought they were not only very kind people, but very posh too. Freda had explained to Susan that her grandfather earned a very good wage as he was one of the main compositors in Nimmo's, the printers on Constitution Street in Leith.

Susan had just passed St Ninian's Primary School and was heading towards Kemp's corner shop when breathlessness overtook her. Leaning against the wall of a tenement building, she silently prayed to God to give her the strength to carry on. As if by magic, she felt a second wind starting to flow into her lungs and as she sped away she called out, 'Please, please hold on, Freda. Honestly I'm getting there, and I will, I promise you, get you help!'

Escape from the house was impossible for Freda because to get to the door she had to make it past Drew, who was wildly swinging his belt in her direction. Dodging behind the settee and then manoeuvring herself into the kitchen, Freda hoped to slam the door shut on Drew, but he was too quick for her. Backing herself against the table, she felt around for something to grab that she could use in her defence. She sighed with relief when her hands curled around the handle of a cast-iron frying pan. Then, when Drew lunged towards her, she didn't think twice before she swung the heavy pan towards his head. Momentarily he was stunned and fell back against the door. Freda quickly realised that she had to escape, but Drew was now blocking her exit through the door. She jumped up on the bunker and started to open the window.

Unfortunately, before she could escape, Drew recovered his senses and was now completely set on brutal revenge. The last thing she would remember was him pulling her back by her hair and slapping her viciously on the face. He then flung her down on the floor and began to savagely lash her with his belt. She was still conscious when he stopped the beating and tossed the belt away before throwing himself on top of her. She later remembered screaming, 'No, no, please, don't do that! Daddy, Daddy, please help me! Daddy, Daddy, please save me!' They were the last words she shrieked before merciful oblivion overtook her.

Too often, she would try to remember what exactly happened that night. She did know that she had drifted in and out of consciousness. In her delirium she thought it was her dad that was the first person to come to her aid. She even believed that she saw him attack Drew. There was the glinting of the bread knife in his hand ... or was it being wielded by her, or even someone else?

Then there were the shouts and screams of anger, but above all the commotion she heard the distinctive raised voice of her brother, Stuart.

'Good God,' Stuart had thundered as he wrestled the knife from someone's hand, 'what in the name of heaven have you done? Get a grip, the swine's not worth doing time for!'

Often Freda wondered if she had actually stab, stab, stabbed at Drew – or was it only in her subconscious? She would reason that she couldn't have, because when she awoke in the morning she was in bed. Someone had obviously bathed her and changed her out of her ripped and torn clothes – clothes that she never found again, not even her white plastic lace-up boots. The person or persons who had come to her aid obviously wished to get rid of anything that would ever remind her of her ordeal. She also recalled seeing her mother, grandmother, grandfather and even

79

her father ... but how could that be?

Her head was full of confused thoughts that morning, as she lay in her room bathed in winter sunlight from the window. The bedroom door slowly opened and there stood Granny Rosie.

'You're awake, and how do you feel?' Granny cooed.

Freda's response was to wash her cheeks with hot, stinging, salt tears. 'Granny, he attacked me. I didn't mean to hit him with the snowball and then... Granny, please tell me he didn't?'

Answering Freda's question was hard for Rosie. She could lie and say that when they got there they were in time to save her from the worst, but would that be the right thing to do? 'Look, my dear, what you have to do is put last night behind you. Forget that it ever happened. You have a bright future in front of you ... you will soon be opening your shop and moving your life forward. Brutes like your stepfather are in the minority – most men are good, like your dad was and your grandad is.'

A long silence fell between grandmother and granddaughter. Freda felt sullied and degraded. Inhaling deeply, she knew that she could no longer stay in this house; this house that held such loving childhood memories of life with her father would never feel like a safe haven to her ever again.

'Granny, I would like to get up and dressed and then I would like to leave here. I never again wish to see that man who made my life hell. Nor do I wish to live with my mother, who replaced my daddy with such a brute.'

'No need to worry about seeing him again. Your grandad and brother got hold of him, packed up his belongings and drove him down to Leith docks, where they paid a man on one of the Gibson Line ships that sail to Amsterdam to take Drew with them. Your grandad then warned Drew that if he ever set foot back in Leith he would put the police on to him.'

Freda believed her granny's story because she wanted to believe it. She was further convinced that nothing serious had happened to Drew when she got herself downstairs. The house was in shipshape order: not even so much as a drop of blood or any other upset was visible. Had it all been a dream? It must have been, because her mother was just so calm as she smiled and winked at Freda, before asking if she wanted jam as well as butter on her toast.

The bruising and swelling on Freda's face was so severe that she got her grandad to drive her in his Morris Minor to and from the Elm Row shop. There was just no way she could allow herself the luxury of sick time. The aim was to have the shop ready for opening on All Fools' Day, 1 April. Okay, that day was a Saturday, and therefore not the norm for opening days, but they had decided that that was the date they wished to start up, and they hoped to have their customers begging for an appointment. Oh yes, they had decided that their opening day was to be a grand affair, with all their clients being treated not only to sherry or coffee, but also to titbits.

There was no way that the opening day could or should be postponed. Therefore, the day after Drew's attack on her, Freda, a little better but still shaky and suffering from shock, decided that she just had to go into the shop and try to do as much as she could.

Apprehension overpowered her as she slunk into the shop. Then, when she lifted her bowed head to stutter, 'Good morning,' to Robin, she became confused, because he just smiled and made no comment whatsoever on her bruised and battered face. To any stranger, it would seem like he found nothing unusual in his partner turning up looking as though she had lost a fight with Muhammad Ali. Nonetheless, she knew that he had noticed her battered face because he jauntily – to allay her suspicions, she thought – suggested that she concentrate on the back room redecoration. This, of course, meant that she would not be seen by anyone coming into the front shop.

Whilst working away with the paintbrush, she began to guess that somehow Robin already knew what had happened to her. But how could he have found out? The family had decided that they did not wish to get the police involved, as that would cause further distress and embarrassment for Freda. They had agreed that what had happened in Sleigh Drive when Drew had attacked her was not to go beyond the walls of the house. They had also agreed that if they were ever asked where Drew had vanished to, all that was to be said was that he had decided to go back to sea. They knew this would be an acceptable answer, because Drew was forever telling anyone who would listen to his ravings that the happiest days of his life had been when he was a deckhand on the Gibson Line's SS *Melrose*.

To her amazement, Freda managed to finish the day, and when she staggered out of the shop, she could have cried with relief at the sight of her grandfather's car awaiting her.

FIVE

FEBRUARY 1967

Six weeks later, Grandad Jack was still chauffeuring Freda to and from work. The visible bruises had healed and for two weeks now Freda had been able to eat normally, yet somehow she still felt nauseated and weak. Granny Rosie made such a fuss about Freda consulting the doctor that Freda gave in and made an appointment.

Sitting and waiting to be called into the doctor's surgery, Freda allowed herself the luxury of thinking about how well things were going with the shop. Thankfully, the tradesmen had now finished all the renovation work. The necessary extra electric lights and sockets were in place, and the washbasins were reflected on the other side of the room in the gleaming, ostentatious mirrors. It was almost time to open shop, although up until yesterday Robin and Freda had been unable to agree on a suitable name for the business.

Freda and Robin had been debating possible names for hours and hours when the signwriter arrived to get started. Freda was starting to panic, as they still hadn't agreed on a name. Then

Robin jumped to his feet. 'That's enough,' he declared. 'We are going to be called A Cut Above, because that's what we will be – a cut above all the other hairdressers in town.'

Freda just nodded, because she really did think that Robin was a cut above everybody else in the business.

Without any further consultation with Freda, Robin called out to the signwriter, 'Right mate, you can get a move on now! The name above the outside door is to be ... A Cut Above!'

Freda's romancing about the shop was put to a sudden end by the doctor's receptionist calling, 'Miss Scott, Dr Campbell will see you now.'

Half an hour passed before Freda left Dr Campbell's consulting room. Leaving, it felt to her as though she had entered some sort of unreal world in which she was divorced from reality; she felt stunned and dazed. To be truthful, her emotions were swinging backwards and forwards with such force that she had to quell a desire to scream. If she was being honest, the doctor really had been so good and so patient with her. The information he had given her was very helpful. She would always remember the concerned understanding he showed her, and the time he took to thoroughly examine every bit of her body. He had even taken a look at her mouth, which was, at times, still very painful – he had recommended that she consult a dentist. She would always remember that the doctor finished his consultation with her by taking her hands in his before saying, 'The morning after you were attacked, you should have come to see me.'

He then went on to quietly but positively outline all the options that were available to her. His final recommendation, which he most earnestly urged her to consider, was a consultation with a psychologist or a counsellor. He thought this might assist Freda in coming to terms with what had happened to her.

Leaving the surgery, Freda decided that walking home was the best thing to do. It would give her time to think. On reaching the roundabout at Sleigh Drive, she decided she needed to speak to someone – someone she could trust. Most girls she knew would have spoken to their mothers, but Ellen was so changed from the mum of Freda's early years that Freda no longer felt comfortable opening up to her. Freda wasn't sure exactly when the change had happened, but, if she was being honest, she thought it must have been around the time her dad died. Yes, her mum had lost her way then, and when Drew Black came into her life it seemed as though she couldn't wait to marry him. Perhaps, thought Freda, Ellen had imagined that life would go back to what it was like before Dad died. It didn't. Drew was a brute of a man – a bully – and it was after marrying him that her mother became a bingo addict. Yes, bingo soon appeared to be all that she cared about.

The foregoing all being true, Freda decided to go and visit her grandmother Rosie.

She entered the welcoming, safe house on Marionville Crescent through the never-locked door and lightly called out, 'Granny, it is only me, Freda.'

'Shhh,' Rosie whispered, as she emerged from

the main bedroom. 'Grandad has just fallen over.'

'Hurt himself?'

'No. He's just having a wee nap. But...' She trailed off, looking preoccupied for a moment, before smiling at Freda. 'It's good to see you. How are you doing?'

They went through to the back living room, which was awash with sunlight. Freda always thought that her grandparents' bright, welcoming house complimented their personalities perfectly, but today Granny Rosie looked tired and somehow aged.

'Granny,' Freda began, 'are you feeling all right?'

A spot above Freda's head seemed to catch Rosie's attention. 'Freda, I'm glad you came today. You see, I have something to tell you.'

'What, Granny?' Freda asked.

Rosie was a small, round, cuddly bundle from a long line of fisher folk – the Listons, in Newhaven – and like her mum and granny before her, she was very careful with her pennies and her family *always* came first. Observing Granny Rosie, Freda's concern grew for she knew that her usually cheerful granny's gloomy expression could only mean one thing: someone in the family was in trouble.

'Freda, my dear, I was going to say to you, before that awful night...' Granny Rosie hesitated, hunched her shoulders, and sighed. 'Och, let's not talk about that, it just upsets me, because you are so precious to Grandad and me... Right, now, on to what's concerning us today... Freda, your grandad is very ill.'

'What? He can't be! He was the one who ran

about getting things sorted out when...' Freda began to pant and shake her head.

'I know that. And where he got the strength to do what he did and get everything and everybody...' Rosie grimaced, because she was about to spit out what they all had agreed Freda was never to be burdened with: the truth. Sniffing and nodding, she continued, 'You see, dear, he has lung cancer.' A sharp intake of breath from Freda had Rosie lift her hand, signalling to Freda that she should let her continue. 'Lung cancer it is, and it is inoperable.'

'How long are the doctors giving him?' Freda blurted, as tears surfaced.

Rosie sought for Freda's hand and took it in hers. 'A few months, but with a bit of luck he might hang on a year.'

'Oh Granny, I just can't believe it. You and he have always seemed so indestructible, so dependable... When my dad died, if I had not had you to hang on to–' She broke off to ponder. 'I remember so well that Grandad even took Stuart and me to Lochend Park every Sunday to feed the ducks, just like Daddy used to.'

'Losing your dad was a bitter blow to us. He was our only child. Yes...' Granny Rosie paused to look about the room. 'We were only blessed with your dad, but what a blessing he was. And he left us you and Stuart. In time, you bairns made all things bearable.'

'I know that. You must have been so disappointed when my mum got Drew in tow.'

Raising her hand again, Rosie narrowed her eyes in warning. 'We all have our faults, Freda. It is true that your mum and I have not always seen eye to eye, but she gave me you and Stuart, my grandchildren, and I will be forever grateful to her for that. Oh yes, the sun shone again through you and Stuart after we lost your dad.' Rosie pursed her lips. 'And, therefore, if your mum was ever in need I would do – and have done – whatever it takes to help her.'

Grandad called out from the bedroom and Rosie rose, but before she went to answer his summons, she said, 'It's so good to see you today, Freda, but tell me, is there a reason behind your wee visit to us, or are you just stopping by?'

Freda sighed – how could she further burden her granny today? 'No, Granny, I'm fine,' she lied. 'I just wanted to see you and Grandad.'

By the time Freda had walked slowly home, pondering on the events of the day, she was feeling very lonely. When she opened the front door, her nostrils were assailed by the smell of macaroni cheese cooking. To her surprise, her mother called out from the kitchen, 'That you, Freda, love? Made your favourite tea, I have.'

Before Freda answered, she considered how her mother had changed in the last few weeks. For one thing, she had given up playing bingo – even if there was a big jackpot. She was nearly back to the mum she had been when Freda's father was alive. Back to smiling, singing, cooking and making sure that the home was as welcoming as it could be for her family. Dear Susan was positively blossoming with all the attention she was receiving! It was as if Drew's leaving had had a beneficial effect on Ellen.

'You are never going to believe this pet but–'

'Please, Mum, don't tell me you went to an afternoon bingo session and won?'

'No,' Ellen replied with a chuckle, 'even better than that! Oh Freda, you know I have the two wee cleaning jobs, but they just keep things ticking over now that I haven't got a man's wage coming in?'

Freda nodded.

'Well,' Ellen continued, 'I realised that I just had to get myself a full-time job. And your granny said I was not to worry about Susan coming home to an empty house, because she could keep an eye on her until I was free to pick her up. Oh Freda, I know it was cheeky of me but I wanted to go up in the world, just like you and Robin are, so I applied to Marks & Spencer. Now, be honest Freda, you wouldn't want people to talk about how there's you with your posh hairdressers, and then me, your mum, putting the walnuts on top of the chocolate whips in Duncan's factory!'

Freda began to wonder if she was dreaming. 'Mum...' she faltered, 'I'm a bit lost... What is it that you are trying to tell me?'

Jumping up and down and clapping her hands, Ellen spluttered, 'I got a job at Marks & Spencer! Me! They actually offered me a job. I mean, getting a job with them is... Well, they only take on the crème de la crème, so they do.'

'That right?'

'Yes. And don't you take offence, but they have hairdressers who come in to do your hair, and one of these chiro-something people that come to cut your toenails ... and they have a free staff canteen!'

'You have to be joking?'

'No, I'm not. There is also a staff shop, where you can buy food that's not been sold on the day, at giveaway prices!'

Ellen appeared so excited and happy. But was she? Surely her brave face and excessive joviality was all pretence? Ellen had not been demonstrative towards Freda and Susan in the last few years, so why was she trying to appear so motherly, so in control ... so happy? Drew Black, in Freda's estimation, was a monster, but he was also her mother's husband and he had been banished from everybody's life, including Ellen's. Not only that, he had been banished by Ellen's former father-in-law, Grandad Jack, and her own son, Stuart. Surely that was painful for her? To add to that, could any mother feel so elated such a short time after the violation of her innocent daughter? Freda decided that she was too tired to ask her mum any questions today. It was a pity, because when she had arrived home she had hoped that she might be able to speak to her mum about what was bothering her...

Reluctantly, Freda concluded that there was no way she could talk to Ellen about anything today – especially her main worry – so, smiling, she replied, 'Mum, that's just wonderful. You will make new friends at Marks & Spencer and move forward. Now, how about you dish up your speciality? A nice plateful of macaroni cheese and all the lovely old memories it will awaken is just what I need right now.'

Advancing into the kitchen to dish up the meal, Ellen bit hard on her lip and dared her tears to fall.

Sleepless nights always end with morning coming too soon. That night, when Freda was finally exhausted from tossing and turning and trying to work out what she should do, the alarm clock started to ring.

On arrival at the shop, she was glad to discover that she was the first there. Opening up the back window to allow fresh air in and the fumes of paint and disinfectant out, she sighed. Everything, she thought, had been going so well, but now...

The familiar whistling of a cheery tune put an end to her contemplations. 'Well, if you're not an early bird,' Robin sang, before grabbing Freda and dancing her around the room.

When he eventually let her go, she tottered away from him and sank slowly to the floor in a sort of faint.

'Freda, Freda!' he exclaimed, beginning to massage her hands. 'What on earth is wrong? Have I hurt you?'

Head still reeling, Freda struggled to sit up. Robin, meanwhile, decided to sit down beside her. 'What is it, Freda? What's up?'

Freda's hysterical wailing had Robin take her into his arms.

'Robin, oh Robin, do you know what my step-father did to me?'

'Shhh, my love. Yes, I do know what the pig did, but you have to try and put it behind you.'

'I can't!' Freda cried. 'You see, I'm... Robin,

91

I'm ... I'm pregnant!'

An eerie silence overtook the room. Eventually, Freda whispered, 'Under the circumstances, the doctor says he can help me. Provided I make up my mind to ask before the ... whatever-it-is is under eighteen weeks of maturity, I can have an abortion.'

'That could be the answer,' Robin mused.

'Just now it wouldn't be,' Freda retorted. 'Oh Robin, Grandad is dying, so there is no way right now that I could face killing off a life that is just starting.'

'But if you don't ... will you be able to live with the embarrassment?'

'I could. But could my mother and my granny? Robin, what shall I do?'

'Right now? Get up off the floor and let me give you a hairdo. That will have a double benefit – it will cheer you up but also allow me to make sure that all our equipment is up and running for opening day. Then I think you should call it a day. Go home and have a good rest. Believe me, the answer to your dilemma will be easier for you to come to when you are not exhausted.'

'But we are so near our opening...'

'We are, but I will work on today, and tomorrow is a new day, so we will both get in here by eight o'clock and work our backsides off.'

Lunchtime saw Freda sauntering into London Road Gardens. As a bus passed by, she looked up, and there, waiting to alight, was Angela. On seeing Freda, she waved wildly. When she got off the bus, she rushed over to Freda, and both of them grabbed at each other, excitedly talking over one another.

'Enough!' Angela shouted. 'Yes, we have not seen each other for ages, but let's calm down.' She looked about, before continuing, 'See, there – behind us is a bench. Let's flop down on it and catch up.'

Meekly, Freda did as Angela bid, but, to be truthful, with her mind in such turmoil, Angela was the last person she wished to spend time with.

Once seated, Angela turned to Freda. 'Ewan was saying that he met up with Robin for a pint, and Robin said all is going well with your hairdressing venture. However, when Ewan told me the prices that Robin thinks people will pay to have their hair styled by him, I thought he was being a bit ambitious. Hope an old school pal like me will get a good discount!'

Freda smiled. 'And how is your training at Moray House going?'

'Good. I've had my first taste of getting hands-on in the classroom because I am now able to shadow teachers. You won't believe me but my first work experience was at Leith Academy Primary, so when the day was finished I decided, as I was in the vicinity of Lochend Road, that I should go and visit Ewan's mother. She was so glad to see me, because Ewan is just so busy with his studies that she doesn't see him as often as she would like.'

Angela babbled on, unaware that Freda wasn't listening to her. Freda's thoughts were back to her pipe dream of being with Ewan, which was far-fetched and could never come to fruition, especially now... No, Freda conceded to herself, a snowball being tossed into hell's fires would have a better chance than her winning Ewan's heart now.

When Freda arrived at the shop the next morning, Robin was already there, dressed in paint-spattered dungarees and whistling. 'Hey, Freda,' he called, 'I've been thinking. It's amazing what you can do with a little help from your friends...'

'That right?' commented Freda, taking her coat off and hanging it up.

'Sure is. Freda, come and sit yourself down whilst I tell you what I think we should do.'

'Well, I don't know about you, but after an hour of having my ears bent by Angela yesterday afternoon, I'm now considering suicide.'

'You'll forget that when I tell you that I have the solution to your problem.'

Chuckling, Freda stuttered, 'What, other than jumping off the Scott Monument?'

'Yes. It is all so simple. You and I are partners, so why not go the full hog... Let's get married!'

Choking laughter overtook Freda. 'Robin, my dear friend, being partners in a business is one thing. Marriage is for two people who love each other... Yes, we are good pals... Best pals... But...'

'We are all that from nursery school days,' Robin butted in, 'and that is why I think – no, I *know* – that it would work.'

'Robin, you are romantically in love with Billy, and I am in love with–'

'You are in love with someone? I didn't know

94

that. Who?'

No way did Freda wish to tell Robin that she fantasied about Ewan, so, gulping in an attempt to come up with an answer, she hurriedly replied, 'Paul Newman. Honestly, whenever I look at him I think I become the cat on the hot tin roof.'

'Look, don't reach your decision about marrying me right now. Ponder it until early afternoon and I'll do the same. Then, when we stop for a cuppa we can talk again. And Freda? Stop thinking about what happened yesterday and stop worrying about tomorrow – it will take care of itself. It's the here and now that you should focus on.' He stopped to take her hand in his. 'All I'm offering is to look after you, with no strings attached, just like your father would have done... And not only will I look after you, I'll also take care of the baby.'

The tea had just been poured when Freda took a deep breath. She needed it, because she was going to say to Robin, 'Thanks for your kind offer, but no thanks.'

'Robin,' she began, 'I appreciate what you have offered to do for me, but–' She got no further, because the door opened.

'Yoohoo! It's only me,' Hannah called out, 'and I see I am just in time for a bite and a cuppa.'

'You are!' enthused Freda. 'Now, what brings you here today? It's your lunch hour, isn't it?'

Hannah nodded and hunched her shoulders, before saying, 'It is, but I needed to see you, Freda.' She glared pointedly at Robin.

'It's okay, Hannah,' Robin said, as he got up

and vacated his seat for her. 'I can eat my sandwich in the back room.'

Hannah grinned. Once Robin was out of earshot, she sat down and leaned in towards Freda. 'I've just come to ask you what you think.'

'About what?'

'Freda, do you remember that I told you about the nice fellow who was buying me wee French fancies?'

Freda nodded, wishing a wee French fancy was all *she* had to think about today.

'Well, now he's upped it to a fresh cream chocolate éclair!'

'Look, Hannah, I'm not quite following where this is going–'

'Well, as an éclair costs more than a French fancy, don't you think this means he is trying to date me?'

'I would need to know more about this man ... I mean, has he ever been attached to anyone else?'

'No, that's just it! You see, he's always had a mother.'

'And has she died or something?'

'Not quite, but she is very ill.'

'Which hospital is she in?'

'Oh, she is still at home. But I think that when he looks at me, he feels that he should be planning for the future.'

Unfortunately, with all that was going on in Freda's life, it was not the day for her to be anything but blunt with the very clever, but very naïve, Hannah. 'Hannah,' she began, 'don't be a stupid fool. You haven't said how old he is but I am betting he is twice your age.'

'Not quite twice,' Hannah replied defensively.

'Okay, maybe not quite twice, but listen to me and listen good. He is not quite anything more than a man looking for another mother because his birth one is on her way out. He's looking for someone like you, who he thinks will be grateful for a wedding ring.'

Hannah's lip started to quiver. Tears were not far away, but Freda was now in full swing so she continued, 'You are good-looking, clever and desirable. You deserve better than old age creeping over you. Hannah, can't you see that he only upped you to an éclair because he now has his grubby little paws on the housekeeping money? For goodness sake, you deserve someone who will look after you, provide for you, put himself out for you ... and, finally, someone who will grow old with you.'

'Freda, you are forgetting that I cannot be choosy, because I am not all there.'

'And if you don't get a grip and stop selling yourself short you will be another bit missing, because I'm going to part your head from your shoulders!'

Both girls had now raised their voices, and Robin decided that they might require a referee. He emerged quietly from the backroom and simpered, 'Problems?'

'No,' Freda replied, 'Hannah was just saying to me that she has decided to get a hold on her life and, from now on, every Friday night she is going to be dancing up at the Plaza with some blokes her own age!'

Hannah shrugged, her eyes downcast. She

nodded to signal consent, before mumbling coldly, 'I had best be off. I have to be back in the office in twenty minutes.' She hesitated. Freda was her best friend, who she trusted completely. So, with her hand on the doorknob, she turned back to face Freda. 'Will you be going to the Plaza with me on Friday?'

Freda nodded. 'I sure will be. And Hannah, if you get back to the office and there is another éclair on your desk, I trust you know where to stick it?'

The door had just clicked shut when Robin asked, 'What was all that about?'

'Nothing that a little gumption from Hannah won't put right.' Freda paused and bit on her thumb. 'I hope to heavens that before we get to the Plaza on Friday the slimy toad doesn't get desperate and offer her a fresh cream meringue!'

Robin laughed. 'You sure have a great turn of phrase. Now, before Hannah came in, you were just about to–'

'Yes,' she interrupted, 'I was just about to say that, if you are sure that you can settle for a marriage in name only, then I am pleased – no, delighted – to accept your offer.'

Robin was perplexed. He was so sure that Freda was planning to say thanks but no thanks. What had changed her mind? Obviously it had something to do with what she had discussed with Hannah.

'And, Robin,' Freda continued, 'before we get carried away, we have to think of the problems ... the obstacles...'

'Like what?'

'Where would we live?'

Robin just shrugged in reply.

'Under the circumstances, if we lived with your mum or mine, don't you think they would find our relationship ... a bit weird?'

Robin replied with another hunch of his shoulders.

'Edinburgh Corporation housing department has a waiting list as long as your arm. We can't afford private renting and there are no single, furnished rooms up for rent in this area.'

'How do you know all that?'

'If you had lived with my stepfather, you would also have made all the enquiries necessary to get a new home. It wasn't just for me – I also had Susan to think of.'

Robin nodded. Then, strolling into the back room, he called out, 'Know something, all we need in here is a bed, a settee, a dresser and a wardrobe. There's already a table, chairs and a small cooker.'

Freda joined him in the back room. 'Yes,' she mumbled hesitantly, 'you and I could live here ... but what will we do when the baby arrives? You do know that they take up a lot of space with their prams, cots, nappies...? Not to mention the room will always be full of washing!'

'I know all that, but by the time the baby arrives I am hoping that I will be able to open the back shop up as a beauty salon, because we will have–'

'Just stop right there, Robin. Look, we saved hard for years to set up our business, but I have to tell you: we are just about stony.'

'Where did all the money go? I mean, we still

have an income from the wigs.'

'Don't be so daft – doing this place up has just eaten money. Next week I will have to go over and bite Granny Rosie's ear.'

'You mean to ask her for a loan? But where will she get it?'

'From her bra.'

'Her bra?'

'Aye, her bra... Surely you know that's where all old fisherwomen keep their money?'

Robin had grown quite crestfallen. Then, as if touched by a wand, he brightened. 'You are forgetting that the special prices I will be charging on Thursday, Friday and Saturday will bring in a fortune.'

Freda sighed. 'Robin, I accept that the money my old dears will bring in at the beginning of the week will pay for the running of the shop, but I am still to be convinced that your clients will be daft enough to pay over the odds for one of your hairdos!'

'They will. Take my word for it. The more they have to fork out, the more they will be convinced that they're going to get exclusive attention. That was what I was trying to tell you. Oh aye, within six months we will have stashed away the deposit for a house of our own.'

The desire to argue with Robin over his ambitious claims ebbed from Freda. She flung down a towel and said, 'Right, we will see what six months brings in. But let's get back to what we have to do now.'

'Right enough. Firstly, we have to get down to the registry office and book a wedding. I suppose we will need our birth certificates.'

'Yes, and I can only hope, Robin, that they will not ask for a certificate about your sanity.'

'Then we will tell our mums.' Robin stopped, and Freda could see that his thoughts were far away. What she didn't know was that he was thinking of his mum, Moira, and how, when some of her pals were digging the dirt about the latest scandal – some poor soul whose lassie had got pregnant without being churched, or got some of the milkman's double cream and paid for it in kind – she never got involved. She and her best buddy Patsy would just exchange knowing looks, before exhaling and shaking their heads.

'You in a private dream world of your own, Robin, or, as we are getting married, would you like to share your thoughts with me?' Freda asked.

'Just thinking about telling my mum we are getting married, because ... you do know we will have to tell everybody that it was me who got you into trouble?'

'Yes I do, but my mum – and indeed my granny – will not be deluded.'

'I know that, but will they say anything?'

'No. They will be the souls of discretion. So we just have to worry about Billy and how he is going to feel.'

'Billy will be fine with it because it will get his mother off his back. Tired, he is, of her insisting that he gives me the heave-ho. The only person we have to worry about is Joey, when my mum gets him to tell my dad!'

The first person to be told that Freda and Robin

were to be married was Ellen. Freda told her on Wednesday night, when she came in from her new job at M&S. She had just got in the door and started to unpack her bag of knock-down-price goodies when Freda said, 'You liking your new job, Mum?'

Ellen nodded. 'Believe me, it is just what I needed ... a right boost to my confidence, it is. You see, Freda, there is no use in worrying about your problems – you have to *do* something about them.'

'Yes, I know. And, Mum, I think you should sit down, because I have something to tell you.'

Ellen slumped down on a chair.

'Now, don't worry,' Freda said.

Ellen's response was to gulp, and swallow hard. From past experience, she knew that when someone was going to tell you something but firstly told you not to worry, then they were almost certainly about to impart bad news – or, at the very least, something you'd prefer not to know.

'It's just that–' Freda broke off, before continuing in a happy-go-lucky tone. 'Believe me, it will work out fine. Mum' – she paused to inhale – 'Robin and I have decided to get married in two weeks' time.'

Slumping back against her chair, Ellen gasped. 'No, Freda! Please, don't tell me you are...'

Freda dropped her head, so that her mother wouldn't see the pain in her eyes. This was all the confirmation Ellen needed.

'But Robin is not the father?' Ellen murmured.

Still with head bowed, Freda whispered, 'Not the natural father, but Robin will be a better father than that sod ever was, or could be.'

'Dear God,' Ellen cried, throwing her arms up and addressing the ceiling, 'is there no end to the torture you put me through? Yes, I have sinned, but my Freda hasn't so why has she to pay?'

'Mum, you are not to blame. Please, I need you to understand why Robin and I are doing this. You see, we have always been pals who share everything, so our getting married is just taking our partnership a stage further. As for the baby, who is not even here yet, please don't tell anyone what you ... well, what you only *suspect*.'

Rising, Ellen went over to Freda and took her in her arms. 'Darling, what a price you are going to pay to give the child of a monster a name. You do know that Robin is–'

'Homosexual? Yes, I do. Knowing that – and I have always known that – makes it all the easier. As I have already said, he and I are mates, partners ... we support each other through thick and thin.'

'I know you accept that he loves Billy and that because of attitudes they cannot come out and tell the world that they love each other, but Freda, what will happen if you fall in love? Would you be prepared to be just a bit on the side or, worse still, to dump Robin?'

As expected, Robin had an easier time telling his mum. Moira was no fool, and she quickly worked out that her son was not the father of Freda's baby, although she did wonder who was. Nonetheless, her son saying he was getting married to a lassie because she was in trouble didn't upset Moira. She liked Freda and somehow she knew that, whatever else happened, their marriage would be a success. The problem, as she saw it, was this: what was Stevie going to say when Joey told him?

Looking over to the birdcage, Moira smiled.

The smile became a broad grin as Moira thought back to a short while earlier, when Robin had been round to tell her the news. They'd been quietly chatting, when Robin turned to her and said, 'Here, Mum, am I wrong, or is there something different about Joey boy?'

'In what way?' she replied.

'Well, last week he was half the size he is today and not only that, he also had a blue-feathered chest. Now he has got a sort of green one, and the feathers on his head have turned white.'

'You are very observant, dear,' Moira whispered. 'You see, Robin, I don't know what I do wrong, because my budgies never live longer than nine years. When the first one died, I bought another one to replace it and nobody seemed to notice. And that was strange, because the first dead Joey, God rest his soul, was green-feathered, whilst the new one was a brilliant blue. And today, when I realised the second one had died...' She stopped, folding one hand over the other and tittering. 'I just had to go and get another one. After all, if we do not have a bird, your dad and I can't communicate with each other.'

'That makes sense, but is that budgie not a parakeet?'

'Aye,' Moira agreed, as she went over and tweet, tweet, tweeted to the bird. 'But they are the same kind of thing. You see, Robin, son, I was so upset about Joey, which was understandable – he was my mouthpiece over the past few years – that I got my pal Patsy to chum me to the pet shop. On the way there, she asked me if I had ever thought of getting a bigger budgie – a parakeet. She told me that parakeets are very sociable birds that like to chat. Then, when I got to the shop...' She ran her fingers over the bird's cage and spoke, rather than tweeted, to the bird, 'I saw you, and we fell in love with each other – no other bird in the whole wide world would do me.'

In response, the bird chirped and fluttered. Robin just shook his head. Often he had wondered if any other bairns he knew had been brought up, as he had been, by such completely off-the-wall parents.

As soon as Robin left that afternoon, Moira began to confide in Joey. 'You see, Joey, my Robin is a sensitive, creative laddie, and when you meet my husband, Stevie, who is big and coarse in every way – especially his mouth! – you'll be wondering how he fathered such a gentle, thoughtful boy.' She chuckled, lifting a duster and starting to polish the birdcage. 'I never said to Robin that I know he didn't get Freda into trouble. He wouldn't, because he loves Billy and Billy loves him. Freda, bless her, is his business partner. Although, to be fair, they have loved each other, in a very affectionate way, since they were toddlers. See, the first time Robin, Freda, Ellen and I were down at the Portobello shows, we allowed the kids to have a go on the helter-skelter. When they whizzed down, Freda, the poor wee soul, was shaking with terror. But Robin ... well, Robin was laughing and singing! Ellen, as she wiped Freda's tears away, joked that she thought Robin must have been born on the helter-skelter. I never corrected her. You see, Joey, Robin wasn't exactly born on the helter-skelter, right enough, but he was certainly conceived near one! So, now you'll be wondering about Autumn, my darling daughter. Well, with the way she throws herself here, there and everywhere – and not just when she's dancing – it's easy to guess that there is a bit of the Jungle Ride in her...'

Thirty minutes later, Moira was still chatting to Joey when the door opened and Stevie barged through it.

'I've no' had a bad day, Joey boy,' Stevie began. 'Aye, and like always, I've been working my tripe out so that your lazy mistress can stand and admire you with a stupid gaze on her face.'

'Joey, tell our lord and master that his tea will be another half-hour and that a week on Saturday he has not to volunteer to work overtime.'

'And you tell her, Joey, that if I wish to overtax myself by working overtime for slave wages, that is my concern and has nothing to do with her. And tell her that if I do go out and work overtime, her grubby paws will no' be seeing any of the extra dosh.'

'Tell him, Joey, go on and tell him that I'm not interested in his dough – aye, not even if Hughie Green invites him on to *Double Your Money!* But, a week on Saturday he will be unable to work, because he'll be at the registry office, watching his son getting hitched to Freda Scott.'

'Robin is marrying a lassie, Joey?' Stevie stuttered, eyes bulging and mouth gaping.

The bird nodded its head and chirped twice.

'I dinnae believe it. No, I dinnae believe it,' Stevie spluttered in reply.

'Joey, you tell the Brain of Britain that he'd better believe it because, at the present time, you are only allowed to marry a member of the opposite sex.'

Stevie's demeanour was beginning to change. He started tapping his feet in time with his ranting. 'Here, Joey, see, when I looked at you just then, I could have sworn you were a different bird from yesterday. Aye, and it's not just that the feathers on your wee heid hae turned white, you are also now sporting a chest yon Marilyn Monroe would have been proud to say was all hers. And if that's no' enough, it's so swollen that it looks a different colour. Now, I think I was wrong. You're the same wee bird. Honestly, son, I think you, like me, are just over the moon that oor Robin is going to marry a lassie!'

Moira was just about to tell Joey to inform Stevie that he *was* a different bird, when Stevie squealed, 'Now, Joey, tell her that if our son is getting married, I want to invite some folks.'

'Joey, you tell him that they are getting married in the poky wee registry office on Junction Place, so there's only room for the immediate family,' Moira gasped. 'And if he's thinking of trying to squeeze another couple of bodies into Freda's mother's house for the wedding tea ... well, he can think again.'

'You tell her, Joey, that if my laddie is getting married to a lassie, then it's no' going to be a hole-and-corner affair. I want – no, Joey, I *insist* – that we invite all my pals who think my son is a nancy boy. Then, when they are tucking into a steak pie at the Kintore Rooms on Queen Street, they can eat their words along with it.'

'Steak pie at the Kintore Rooms on Queen Street, Joey? Has he lost his marbles?'

'Naw, I havenae, and you tell her, Joey, that as it's the cooperative function suite, she might even get a dividend when I give her the dosh to pay the bill. Yes, Joey, I am so over the moon that I will not only pay the bill for the meal but also put on a free bar!'

'Naw, naw, Joey, you tell him he already has a dividend, because Freda's ... pregnant. That means we have a grandchild on the way and we need all our spare cash to buy a pram!'

Stevie began to dance about the living room. 'Freda's preggers and Robin's to blame! Oh, oh, that's my boy! Oh aye, Joey, that's my boy!' he chanted. 'How could I ever hae thought that a laddie I sired would be... Wait until the morning, when I tell all my mates at the coal yard that my boy – yes, *my* laddie – has got a lassie into trouble, and he's going to be a dad. What a boyo, what a boyo. A right chip off the old block, is he no'?'

In the past, Moira had never been tempted to tell Stevie the truth about Robin – and indeed Autumn – but today, as Stevie pranced about the room, she knew for certain that she had done the right thing in keeping him ignorant about his infertility. How could she ever burst his balloon, especially today? He had worked so hard to give her and the children a nice home; he did all that he could for them so that 'his' children would never want as he had done. Moira looked at Joey and, as she ran her fingers over his cage, she smiled, because she knew that a father was not just someone who slept with your mother. No, no, a father was a man who worked every hour he could, to bring home a decent wage. He was also a man who stood by his children through thick and thin. Moira chuckled as she recalled how Robin and Autumn just had to ask, and Stevie would put his hand into his pocket and willingly finance their dreams.

If Freda had not promised – and felt it was her duty to keep her promise – to go with Hannah to the Plaza dance hall on Friday night, she would have stayed at home. At home, in the peace and quiet, she would have thought about what she was going to do next week. She was never free from wondering what kind of marriage she and Robin would have and, to be truthful, she was having second thoughts...

They had just arrived at the dance hall when Hannah gasped. 'Freda, I thought we wouldn't know a soul here, yet look over there!' She pointed at two well-dressed, attractive young women, who were leaning on the wall at the far side of the hall. 'Those two lassies work in pay control at the Corporation, where I work.' Hannah started to chuckle. 'Here, Freda, look! They are waving at me to join them – do you mind?'

Even if Freda *had* minded it would not have mattered, because Hannah had already skipped over to be with the two girls. Freda smiled as she watched the trio grinning and gossiping. Their smiles then changed to giggles when three young men asked them if they would like to dance.

Freda didn't really wish to dance with anyone so she took herself off the floor, where you waited to be asked to dance, and got herself seated out in the foyer. She was pleased that Hannah had met up with two work colleagues because it meant that her plan had been successful. Yes, Freda knew that Hannah needed to make some more friends of her own age, who she could go out and have fun with. Hannah definitely didn't need Freda as her only pal, because Freda would soon be, as she saw it, a downtrodden wife and mother. Freda allowed her thoughts to drift back to her dilemma: should she go for an abortion – an abortion that would allow her to be carefree and enjoy the rest of her youth – or should she go ahead and marry Robin, who she knew would always take care of her? She thought about the future. She didn't think she would be able to go through with an abortion, but what if she was unable to love a baby that was conceived in such degradation? Furthermore, would Robin be able to love the baby that wasn't his own? She was still contemplating, lost in thought, when she became aware that a handsome young man was standing in front of her. When she realised who it was, she felt the desire to cry out in protest. It was none other than Ewan. Her breath was now coming in short pants and she could only nod to him. The very sight of him had made her throat contract, leaving her speechless. To be confronted by him at this difficult time was a cruelty beyond endurance.

'Now,' Ewan tersely began, 'with what Robin told me today, you are the last person I would expect to meet here tonight.'

Swallowing hard, Freda stammered, 'I only came to keep Hannah company.' She gestured towards Hannah, who was on the dance floor having an animated conversation with a rather dishy young gentleman. 'She is still very shy and unsure of herself, so I am her moral support.'

An uneasy silence fell between Freda and Ewan, but he did sit down on the bench beside her. Bending over and rubbing his hands together, he seemed lost and forlorn.

When Freda could stand the silence no longer, she quietly asked, 'Is there something worrying you, Ewan? I mean, I know how hard your course is – qualifying as a doctor takes such a long time.'

Slowly, Ewan raised his head. 'Yes, it takes years to train as a doctor, but somehow I thought that you understood that ... I thought that you were waiting for me, but obviously not!'

'Waiting for you? But Ewan, I met Angela recently and she was full of how you two will be marrying once you are qualified to practice. She has tea with your mother every week; they even go out to the pictures together!' Freda was now crying profusely.

'Believe me, Freda, I have never ever given Angela, or my mother, any reason to think that I would consider marrying her. You...' He trailed off, his voice cracking. 'You were always the girl of my dreams, Freda. See, today, when Robin asked me to be his best man and told me that he is going to marry you, because you are pregnant...' He was

111

bent over again, and the floor was getting his full attention. 'Good heavens, Freda, how could you allow yourself to be made pregnant by Robin? Were you that desperate?' He faltered, shocked by his own anger. Beginning again, he tried to speak more calmly. 'Robin is homosexual – or so I thought! He will always be my friend but I accept that he is different to me, in that he prefers to be romantically involved with *men*. Surely you know that too? Can you be sure he will be a faithful husband?'

Freda wished to scream out, 'Ewan, do you know how dirty and completely humiliated I have felt since my step-father, the beast that he is, violated me? I probably should have had an abortion and cleansed myself of his filth but I can't do it!' There was so much Freda wished to tell Ewan, but the words wouldn't come out. Inwardly, she was crying because even if she'd known that her darling Ewan felt the same way about her as she did about him, she knew she could never have faced him. Where would she have found the courage to tell him about her shame at being raped by a monster? Knowing him so well, Freda knew that Ewan would have insisted on calling the police and making sure that Drew was charged for his crime. Freda knew that involving the police was the right thing to do, but there was something about the way that her family had handled everything that night that made her think there was something they were not telling her. She wasn't sure that she fully believed Drew had been exiled to Amsterdam and she feared that if she went to the police, someone in her family – someone that she loved, and who loved her – might end up in big trouble... Freda shook her head and gave Ewan a sideways glance. No, she thought, a price has to be paid to keep my family safe and I have to pay it. Without uttering another word or even glancing at Ewan, she got up and left, leaving not only the dance hall behind but also her shattered dreams.

Robin asked the taxi driver to stop the cab at the end of Montgomery Street and after he paid the fare, he and Freda headed towards their shop. As he struggled to get the key into the lock, Freda started to laugh uncontrollably.

'Glad you're amused,' Robin, who was still having difficulty finding the keyhole, muttered.

'Sorry, it's just that I have never seen you the worse for drink before. Here, give me the key and I will open up.'

'No, I will manage.'

'Look, Robin, see those lights twinkling over on Gayfield Square? That is the police station. Now, if you don't get the door open soon, someone from there will come over here because they will think we are trying to break in, and we could end up spending our wedding night in a cell.'

Tossing the keys towards Freda with a grunt, Robin said, 'It's all thanks to my dad that I am–' he hiccupped.

'Drunk and incapable?' interjected Freda, as she opened the door and switched on the light. 'But, know something, my dear,' she mused, 'what a wedding we had! It was all so unreal and not what I expected at all.'

113

Robin filled the kettle and spooned Nescafé into two cups. 'They say strong coffee helps you sober up.'

'Maybe so, but don't bother with any for me. I haven't had a single drink, unless you count umpteen cups of tea.'

'Right enough, you were lucky that my dad didn't keep slapping you on the back and saying "Well done, son, I never doubted you", before setting another dram down in front of you.'

'It was some do, right enough. And Billy did just great as your best man.'

'Aye, he did. Mind you, if Ewan had got more warning he would have done it, but he is away south for a couple of days...' Robin stopped to ponder. 'Thought, I did, that he would have taken the luscious Angela away with him, but she evidently preferred to come to our wedding. I wonder when they will tie the knot.'

'Never,' Freda mused. 'She's not his type. And our reception in the YWCA didn't suit her to-night.'

'It didn't?'

'No, just a bit too working class for her – even though your dad had those upmarket caterers, Crawford's, supply the buffet!'

Now it was Robin's turn to giggle. 'See, when I saw that old guy come tottering into the hall–'

'Which old guy?' Freda looked puzzled. 'There were just so many of your dad's old pals there, and they all seemed to have trouble staying up-right!'

'Come on, Freda. You know who I mean! The one who staggered in, carrying an accordion.'

'You mean the old guy that supplied the music for the evening?' Freda was laughing again. 'But, give credit where it's due, when he eventually got started on the box, he gave Jimmy Shand a run for his money!'

'Yeah, it was just a pity that during the Scottish country dances, he stopped if anyone wasn't doing them properly.'

Sniffing back happy tears, Freda looked lovingly at Robin before saying, 'Thank you for all you are doing for me and for giving me such a lovely day today.' She stopped to giggle. 'It was so different from what we planned, but when your dad got involved all sanity and reason took a back seat!' She paused again and nodded. 'Know something, despite it all going everybody else's way but ours, I will always have such fond memories of our wedding day. Now, let's go through to the back and get the bed settee down and ourselves off to sleep.'

Robin pulled down her bed for her and then removed a folding camp bed from the cupboard.

'Who's going to sleep on that?'

'Me. Remember, Freda, I did promise you that there would be no strings attached. In order to keep to that, separate beds are a must.'

By now, Freda was out of her evening dress. It was the gown she had worn on the night of the Lorimer Cup, and today it had served her again as a wedding dress. She could have said more to Robin but exhaustion was overtaking her, so she slipped between the crisp new sheets on her bed and was asleep before Robin had even switched off the light.

After Robin and Freda left their wedding reception, the guests began to dwindle away. Soon, only Ellen, Moira and a very drunk Stevie were left. Both women sat down at a table and laughed as Stevie, who had valiantly tried to hold out, began to slip down the wall, before landing in a drunken heap on the floor.

'Will I go out and see if there is a taxi passing for you?' Ellen asked.

'Aye, Ellen, in a minute,' Moira replied. 'You know, my Stevie did so enjoy this day. I thought it was a pity though, that when he asked everybody to rise and toast the bride and groom, he also felt the need to say "and my grandchild, who is on his way"!'

Ellen tittered. 'Well, I suppose there is no use in hiding the fact that Freda is pregnant. She's not the first to find herself in that position and she most certainly won't be the last!'

Strumming her fingers on the table, Moira had something to say but was hesitant to say it. Eventually, leaning over the table and covering Ellen's hand with hers, Moira looked her straight in the eye and whispered, 'Ellen, I just want you to know that when the baby arrives, it will be, as far as the world is concerned, our grandchild. What I am saying to you is this: I do not know who the father of Freda's baby is, but I do know that it is not my Robin. And furthermore, that knowledge is safe with me.'

Ellen had always liked Moira and admired how she coped with Stevie's eccentricities and indeed her own. Curling her free hand into a ball, she decided that she owed it to Freda to tell Moira the truth – not the whole truth, but enough to make sure that Moira knew Freda was no tart.

After haltingly telling Moira about Freda's shameful, brutal rape, she stopped. As much as she trusted Moira, she did not dare tell her about the happenings after the attack. No one was to be privy to the knowledge of those happenings, except for those that were there that night.

'Ellen,' Moira began, but before continuing, she looked over to make sure that Stevie was still comatose. 'Ellen, say no more. Let me just say to you, it is a wise child who knows his own father.'

When she was home and safely tucked up in her bed, Ellen went over and over the cryptic words that Moira had spoken to her. She was sure that Moira had been trying to tell her something – but what exactly?

SIX

APRIL 1967

The number 16 bus, which Stevie had boarded at the foot of Leith Walk, had just arrived at Elm Row when Stevie said to himself, 'Nothing else for it then, but to get myself off the bus and...' He sighed as he alighted at Elm Row. He just had to walk three steps down, pass through a hole in the hedge and cross over the road, and then he would be at the door of his son's shop.

He had never visited the shop before, but he

soon spotted it – the balloons and streamers hanging from the door and window caught his eye. To be truthful, he and his son had never really soldiered together in the past, but ever since the laddie had got married, Stevie had tried to build bridges. He knew that today was a big day for Robin and his wife Freda; indeed, every day for a week now, Joey, the font of all wisdom, had told him that if he did not turn up to this event, then he would probably never see his grandchild, who was due late September or early October.

This grandchild had changed the way that Stevie's mates viewed his son. He knew that, behind his back, they had often sniggered and hinted that Robin was a nancy who would never father any offspring ... but that was then. Now, Freda being three months pregnant stopped that subject of gossip dead in its tracks.

Stevie had just entered the shop when someone handed him a Pimm's – a cocktail sort of thing with bits of fruit floating in it. He wasn't quite sure whether to eat it or drink it! As he gazed down at it, he thought that it certainly didn't have the same appeal as a pint of McEwan's Export beer. Nursing the glass, he looked about the hairdressing salon. His heart sank. It was, to his eyes, like something out of a French brothel. Everywhere there were mirrors, lights and people talking loudly and bawdily, smoking cigarettes through long, pretentious holders. Then he espied Robin. Robin was now a fully-trained hairdresser – okay, ladies' hairdresser – but his own locks had obviously not seen a pair of scissors in a month and had been expertly brushed into a Beatles-style bob. A wicked wee smile came to Stevie's face, as he remembered how he had remarked to Joey that he wouldn't be surprised if Robin ended up in a yellow submarine! Joey had replied that Robin was only following – and enhancing – the Liverpool look, which all the trendy young men had adopted. Shaking his head, Stevie thought that the Beatles, a band of four lads from Liverpool who had taken the world by storm, had a lot to answer for. In Robin's case, it was not just the mod hairstyle (a heavy fringe that drooped over his eyebrows, and side lappers that Dracula would have been at home with) it was also his apparel. Today he was sporting a long, tunic-like coat with stand-up lapels. However, as 'Strawberry Fields Forever' blared out from the record player, Stevie conceded that, on the plus side, Robin was also wearing a royal-blue bow tie. This, in Stevie's opinion, was a more acceptable accessory than the swinging medallion Robin had worn last week to compliment the bohemian style of his open-neck shirt.

When Robin disappeared into the back shop, Stevie's attention was taken over by the young women. He just wasn't prepared for the amount of bare flesh that they put on display! The 'in thing' for fashionable women was to ape the model Twiggy. This meant that they all wanted to look as though they were in need of a good feed, and all dressed in the shortest, brightest and gaudiest skirts they could find. Stevie shook his head, observing that the only thing of decent size that the girls were wearing was their tall 'go-go' boots...

'Hello, Dad!' A voice broke into Stevie's thoughts and put an end to his ogling.

119

'Hello to you too, Freda,' he managed to stammer, before guiding her over to a hairdryer. Pushing the hood up, he indicated that Freda should sit down on the seat. Looking down at her, he noted that she was wearing a bright crimson shift dress, multi-coloured tights and a pair of flat Mary Janes. He grimaced. He had thought that, by now, she would be covering herself up in a smock – a smock that would indicate to the world at large that she was pregnant.

'Nice that you could make it today,' Freda observed. 'It will mean so much to Robin.'

Just then, a young lassie with a tray of small cakes appeared and asked if they would like one.

Stevie's mouth gaped as Freda put her hands on to her stomach and started to shake it, spluttering, 'No, thank you. Just look at the way I am putting on the beef!' She giggled. 'Think it's a heifer I'm having, not a baby. What do you think, Dad?'

Stevie was now staring at Freda's bump, transfixed. He was awash with delight to see that it had ballooned, even since he saw her last week.

Moira sidled over to him and said, 'You're learning. And, as my mum used to say, it is never too late to do that.'

Stevie was about to say that yes, he had, under duress, put in an appearance, but she should know that half an hour of all this flashy swanking was about as much as he could take. However, he was so overcome at the sight of Freda's bump that he remained dumb. He looked about the salon for some sort of help, but he couldn't even see a birdcage, never mind a bird, so he was unable to reply to Moira. This being the case, he decided to make a quick exit. As he bounded over to the outside door, two things happened.

Firstly, Moira shouted to him, 'Stevie, did Joey tell you that I will be home in time for your tea? It will be your favourite ... a white pudding supper from Elios on Duke Street!' Stevie was about to turn and signal that he wanted plenty of muck sauce on it, when the second thing happened: he collided with a young couple coming in.

The young lassie, who had fallen over at Stevie's feet, looked up at him and smiled. 'Nice to see you here, Mr Dalgleish,' she said as he helped her up.

Stevie grunted in reply.

'Freda's been telling me how over the moon you are about the baby,' the lassie continued.

Stevie nodded vigorously. 'Aye, Hannah, and I'm sure you are looking forward to being the wee soul's godmother.'

Now it was time for Hannah to nod.

'Look, lassie, I'm heading aff. I dinnae want to seem rude, but this is no' ma scene. No' exactly the Dockers Club on Morton Street, is it?'

Hannah put her hand up to her mouth so that Stevie wouldn't see that she was stifling a giggle. She knew that Stevie was referring to the Leith Dockers Club on Academy Street, formerly known as Morton Street. Stevie, who thought that the Council had no right to change the name of the street, always referred to it as Morton Street. As to whether it was Morton Street or Academy Street, Hannah knew that did not matter to him really. What mattered to Stevie was that it was the home of the Leith Dockers Club, the working man's hostelry that many of his mates, like himself, were dedicated members of.

Before Stevie could be stopped, he rushed out the door. He was sure that if he got his skates on, he would still be in time to get a decent pint at the Dockers.

Hannah was still chortling, watching Stevie's fleeing figure, when Freda said, 'Thank goodness you've got here. I was beginning to think that you'd forgotten about our big day!'

'I would never do that! I know it's not usual on a Saturday, but I had to work overtime at the City Chambers.'

'Why?'

'I just had to dig out some files that are in the archives, about the now-closed Hammond fire-work factory at the old quarries in Craigmillar. Required urgently, they are, as there are plans to clear the site and any chemicals still stored there will need to be safely disposed of.'

'Okay, but did you have to get them out *today?*'

'Well,' Hannah began, with a wink to Freda, 'Tom – Tom Davidson – is up to his eyes in work, and the files are stored in the vaults at Mary King's Close. He is responsible for those vaults and everything that is in them, and he could only take me down there today.' She tittered, continuing, 'So, what else could I do?'

Freda looked beyond Hannah and smiled at Tom Davidson. She was pleased to see that he was a tall, handsome man, probably about six years older than Hannah. Like Hannah, Freda was captivated by his engaging smile and twinkling, deep blue eyes.

Extending her hand to him, Freda smiled, but the smile died on her face as she watched him move the walking stick he was carrying from his right hand over to his left in order to shake her hand. However, his handshake was firm and his hand, like himself, exuded warmth.

After the initial introductions, Freda had Robin engage Tom in conversation whilst she steered Hannah through to the back room. As soon as the door was closed behind them, Freda spluttered, 'What is the story here? Is Tom disabled?'

Hannah just nodded. 'Yes, he's like me.'

'Missing a part, is he?'

'Don't be facetious.'

'Now, there's a word you didn't learn at Norton Park Secondary School!'

'What's wrong with you, Freda? Why are you being so horrible? Tom had polio as a child and was left with a limp – yes, a pronounced one. But he has a kind manner and he is an able, intelligent young man who is very good at his job. And he doesn't have a mother, which I know matters to you very much!'

Freda's face fired. She wished she could take back the hurtful words she had just hurled at Hannah. Hannah's welfare was so important to her, and she was always concerned that Hannah would accept a proposal from the first man that asked her.

What Freda did not know was that Hannah was also anxious about *her*, and had been ever since Freda told her about the baby's true parentage. She did think that Freda deciding not to abort the baby was the right thing to do, but marrying

123

Robin... Surely that was a sacrifice too far?

The girls stared at each other, both unsure what to say. The awkward silence was finally broken by Robin, who knocked on the door and called, 'Right, you two, time for the raffle! With a bit of luck, Hannah, you might win not only a special hairdo, to be done by moi, but also a manicure!'

SEVEN

SEPTEMBER 1967

'Are you feeling all right?' a concerned voice asked.

Freda attempted to sit up further in her chair. 'It's just the heat,' she gasped.

'Well, true, it is warmer today and there's been a blink of sun, although you could hardly say that we're having a heatwave with sunshine morning until night. And just think, as we had typical sodden August weather up until two weeks ago, there is no shortage of water!'

'Thank goodness for that.' Freda gave a short laugh. 'You know,' she began, as she tried to get comfortable, 'last Friday night I was sweating like a pig, so I just went out and sat in London Road Gardens and let the rain lash down on me.' She paused. 'Oh, it was just so wonderful. Wish I could do that right now.'

'You do?'

'Aye, no kidding. Don't you think that I look

like a bloated, stranded whale?'

Jessie didn't need to look at Freda for confirmation of her description. She had seen many pregnant women in her time, but never one so cumbersome and out of shape as Freda was. Indeed, when Freda had waddled into the early-afternoon antenatal clinic at the Eastern General Hospital earlier that day, she had felt sorry for her. That being so, all she said in response to Freda was, 'My name's Jessie, Jessie Spence, and I know you've been coming here for as long as I have.'

'Nice to meet you, Jessie,' Freda replied, holding out a mottled, swollen hand. 'Yeah, I have noticed you once or twice.' She giggled. 'In fact, up until three weeks ago I thought you were here under false pretences, what with you being so slim!'

'No. My mum says my baby is lying all to the back.'

Freda tittered. 'Lucky you, because as you can see, mine is sprawling all over the place.'

'What are they saying here about all the weight you've put on?'

Freda pursed her lips. Before she could answer, a nurse came out and called, 'Jessie Spence!'

Freda felt relief wash over her as Jessie was ushered away. She would not have liked to lie to this woman who had, after all, tried to be friendly to her, when she knew she must look like a bit of a fright.

Once Jessie had left, Freda's thoughts went back to her last visit at the hospital. It was then that the doctor had placed her stethoscope on Freda's bared stomach, a puzzled look coming to her face.

125

Removing the instrument, she called over to the sister in charge and asked her to have a listen for the heartbeat of Freda's unborn child. It was not until another two health care professionals were summoned to listen to the heartbeat of the baby in Freda's womb that Freda realised that there was something wrong – very wrong. This problem was probably the reason why Freda had so much water retention. The female doctor said, 'Mrs Dalgleish, I think that you should prepare yourself.'

'Prepare myself?' Freda inwardly screamed. 'How exactly will I be able to do that, when I am stretched out here on this trolley bed like Moby Dick, with everyone in the vicinity having a listen in to my stomach rumblings?' To add to her discomfort, she became awash with guilt, because she couldn't help wondering just how many times she had wished that the baby she was carrying would just die. And then, when she was sure that she was about to be told the baby was dead, she hoped that she would be able to say, 'Oh no, please don't say that!'

That was one wish she was granted. Taking her hand, the doctor then said, 'Mrs Dalgleish, I am delighted to tell you that you are expecting twins. Yes–' she had looked at her colleagues for confirmation – 'we have all heard two hearts beating. For final confirmation, we would like you to have an abdominal X-ray.'

After the X-ray confirmed that twins were on their way, the doctor went on to advise Freda that her babies would probably arrive early – possibly as early as six weeks. If Freda had been perfectly honest, she would have said, 'Look, as that is just about right now, how about I stop waddling about and just stay here until it's all over?'

That would have made sense, but she had to go back to the shop and give Robin the news. This thought made her lower lip tremble, because the two of them were already living on top of each other in the back room; honestly, they were really anything but comfortable there. However, they did bend over backwards not to make things too difficult for each other. Freda knew that it was mainly down to Robin that they muddled through. He was such a gentle, kind soul who, because he valued her as a friend, had made such sacrifices for her. They had already discussed how impossible life was going to become when a baby also shared the space, so how in the name of heavens would they make room for *twins?* It was true, their business had flourished beyond their wildest dreams, but they were still a couple of hundred pounds short of a deposit for a house. Freda wailed then, because she realised that she would also have to fork out for a twin pram, instead of using the single one that her mum had ordered. Dumbfounded, she slunk out of the side door of the hospital, which bordered Craigentinny golf course. She looked about to make sure that there was no one within hearing distance, before throwing a tantrum – a real humdinger of one, which included foot-stamping, fist-shaking, and screeching to a decibel level that could have awakened the dead.

When the tantrum had exhausted itself, Freda headed home, and as the bus trundled along London Road, she rehearsed and re-rehearsed what she was going to say to Robin. She was grateful that it was past closing time when she arrived at the shop. After opening the door, she drew up quickly. She had hoped that Robin, and Robin alone, would be in the shop. However, there, standing beside him, was her mother.

'How did you get on, dear?' Ellen crooned, as she advanced towards Freda.

'Fine, Mum,' Freda lied. 'They said everything was hunky-dory and I have to waddle back there next week.'

Robin just nodded, before going into the back room to fill the kettle. Switching off the tap, he called out, 'Freda, are you hungry? If you are, I could open a tin of soup for you.'

Freda and her mother headed through to the back shop, and as Freda slumped down on a chair next to the table, she replied, 'Aye, soup's okay, but you know, I have a feeling that you need to be telling me something...'

Her mother turned to look at her, her expression anxious. 'Freda... Look, Stuart came into Marks this afternoon to tell me that your grandad's health has taken a real bad turn. He is now on the F ward at the Eastern General. Granny Rosie is with him, and Stuart said that he would go down to the hospital to be with her.'

'Good grief,' Freda wailed, 'you all knew I was down there, so why on earth did no one come and tell me? I could have gone and visited him!'

'We thought that you would be on your way home. We didn't know you were going to be this late,' her mother explained, as she glanced at the clock.

'Oh, where on earth am I going to get the energy to get myself back to that blinking hospital tonight?'

'Here, dear, dry your tears and drink this,' Robin pleaded as he handed her a mug of soup. 'And don't worry about getting back to the hospital because once you've had a rest, we will order a taxi and get you there.' Robin stroked Freda's hair. 'And, darling, I have a wee bit of good news for you.'

Slamming the cup of soup down on the table, Freda shrieked, 'Good news! Ah, so you are going to tell me that the mess I am in, carrying this baby elephant about, is all a bad dream, and that I am going to wake up from this blasted nightmare and skip down to Marionville Crescent to find my grandad pottering about in his back garden?'

'No,' Robin soothed, as he took her hand in his, 'but remember how we looked at that deserted, broken-down garden flat on Brunton Place?'

'The one just by the bus stop, before the Easter Road turning?' Freda's mum asked.

'Yes Ellen, that one. Well,' Robin lifted Freda's hand and kissed it before continuing, 'it's just come on the market and, because of the state it's in, I think we could – just maybe – afford it.'

If Robin had expected Freda to be excited, he was in for a disappointment. She dragged her hand from his and started to pull at her hair. 'Look,' she screamed, 'right now, I couldn't face cleaning up the tea dishes, never mind renovating another dump! Can't any of you see that I'm tired ... completely whacked... All I want to do is go and see my grandad.'

Both Ellen and Robin nodded, before Robin said, 'Fine, dear, but we do have to find somewhere suitable to live, and pretty soon at that.' Freda was about to yell at him again, but he put up his hand, lowered his voice and quietly stated, 'But that will be my worry. All you have to do is look after yourself and the baby.'

Freda should have told Robin and her mum there and then that it was not a baby, singular, but *babies*, plural. However, as getting back to the hospital to see her grandad was her main priority, she kept the news of the twins a secret.

Seven long days had passed since that night, and still she had told no one, because grandad was somehow holding on. It was as if he was waiting for something, or someone.

Freda was pulled out of her memories of that day by the sound of the nurse calling to her. Hearing that the doctor was ready to see her, she stood up, feeling unsteady as she did so. Next thing she knew, she was hyperventilating, because water had started to cascade down her legs and on to the floor.

'No need to panic,' the nurse said kindly but firmly, 'you haven't wet yourself, your waters have broken. That, Mrs Dalgleish, is a sign that your labour has started. Your babies are on their way.'

'But I can't give birth to them right now! You see, I promised my grandad I would visit him today, so it is not convenient for me to give birth even to one baby right now, never mind two!'

'That right?' the nurse replied.

Freda nodded, but as the first labour pains gripped her, she found herself grabbing hold of the nurse's wrist and digging her nails into the back of the nurse's hand. As she recovered, she managed to squeal, 'Well, maybe at this moment I can't visit Grandad! Hope he'll understand and hang on.'

Wrestling her hand free from Freda's grip, the nurse replied, 'Yes, he will, and much later on today you may be able to pop in to see him, bringing two nice surprises with you!'

An over-sized bouquet hid the face of her visitor, but when Freda heard the voice behind it say, 'Well, aren't you a dark horse!' she knew that the dulcet tones belonged to Hannah.

'In what way?' Freda replied as she indicated to Hannah, who was trying to press the flowers into her hands, that she couldn't take the flowers as she had a baby in her arms.

'By not telling a single one of us – not even Robin, your *husband* – that you were expecting twins!' Ignoring Freda's shrug, Hannah continued, 'And I hear that they're not identical.'

'No, they're not. But then,' Freda scorned, 'I'm pretty sure they have to be the same sex to have any chance of that...'

Hannah, as per usual, did not take offence. Instead, she looked earnestly at the baby in Freda's arms. 'Which one is that? You see, I cannot tell if a baby is a boy or a girl until I see their bottom!'

'Here's a clue: this one is wrapped in a pink blanket...'

'So she is!' Hannah tittered. 'And where is your wee son?'

Looking lovingly down at her daughter, Freda

responded, 'Wee is the operative word for him. Jackie, here, weighed in first at five pounds, five ounces, but her brother, who I have not thought of a name for yet, could only tip the scales at four pounds, fifteen ounces. He has to stay in an incubator until he gains weight and is a healthy five pounds.'

'How long will it take the wee soul to gain that weight?'

'A couple of days at least – mind you, I could always spit on him before the next weigh in.'

'Freda! Surely you wouldn't do that?' Hannah sighed. 'Oh, God bless the wee soul. Here, Freda, has anybody apart from you seen him?'

'The duty sister on the labour ward phoned Robin to say that I had gone into labour, and he got a message through to my mum in Marks and then his mum. Those two, in turn, became a bush telegraph, and then the race was on to see who could get here first! You can snigger all you like but, honestly, more people turned up at this maternity unit than attended the last Hibs and Hearts derby!'

'May I hold her?' Hannah pleaded. Freda nodded, before passing the baby to Hannah.

'She's so tiny ... and her brother is even smaller?'

'Yes, but according to Stevie, my bullish father-in-law, Jackie is the living image of him.' Freda quickly looked up at the ceiling whilst she stifled a laugh. 'Please God no. Two of him in the world at the same time would be just too much!'

Now it was Hannah's turn to cackle. Freda continued, 'Then Stevie said that the boy is the living image of Robin. "Oh aye," he muttered to me, "there's no way my laddie could deny them!"'

Before anything further could be said, a porter arrived with a wheelchair. 'Mrs Dalgleish,' he hollered, 'your taxi has arrived!'

Hannah looked quizzically at Freda, who explained, 'Grandad is quite poorly, so the sister said that she would arrange for me to go up to F ward to see him. I'll get into the chair and you follow with Jackie. I just wish him to see her.'

Before Hannah could say that Grandad would probably like to see the little boy too, a sister arrived, holding a diminutive baby wrapped in a yellow blanket.

'I am very sorry,' the sister said, 'I would have liked to pass your son to you, Mrs Dalgleish, but he is a wee bit frail. He's wrapped in a yellow blanket so that all of my staff know he is to be handled with care. Now, off we go, and after your grandfather has seen his great-grandson, I will return the wee baby to the nursery immediately.

Seven days, very long in some ways and very short in others, had passed since the birth of the twins, and Granny Rosie and Freda were sitting in the living room of Granny Rosie's Marionville Crescent home, each of them bottle feeding a baby.

'That was some send off your grandad got yesterday. Never in my life have I seen such a...' Granny Rosie seemed stumped for words.

'It was certainly different from what I remember my dad's being like. There were just so many tears at Dad's,' Freda mused.

'Aye,' Granny Rosie agreed, 'but then your dad's going was tragic, because he left us well before his time... But my gentle Jack, your grandad, well ... it is heartbreaking for me, but most would say that he had one year more than what the Bible promises – you know, threescore and ten.'

Freda, who was still very emotional about the loss of her grandad, just sniffed in response.

'Wasn't God good, allowing him to stay until he saw these two little beauties?' Rosie continued. She had removed the bottle from the mouth of the baby she was holding and as she gently rubbed his back, she smiled. 'And you and Robin coming to live here with me until the house on Brunton Place is habitable will help me come to terms with losing Jack.'

'Granny, we will be here for years!'

Rosie chuckled and hunched her shoulders with delight.

'You can laugh,' Freda went on, 'but that house is so ramshackle it will cost more to make it habitable than it would to repair Mary, Queen of Scots' broken-down Craigmillar Castle!'

Rosie was now speaking to the baby. 'Hear that, Harry, your mum was just saying that you will be staying here with me until you are at least walking.'

'Yes – and you too, my darling Jackie.' Freda looked down at her daughter's face. 'I can bet that you will have to show your brother how to do that.'

This statement had Rosie stiffen. It was evident to her that Freda had bonded, or was wishing to bond, with Jackie, but she showed little interest in bonding with Harry. Rosie feared that because Harry was a boy and would mature into a man, and therefore possibly – God forbid! – a man like his father, Freda was rejecting him. In her seventy-one years, Rosie had seen this happen a few times. As she certainly did not wish it to happen to her precious wee great-grandson, she knew that she had to say something to Freda. Being astute and not wishing to ruffle Freda's feathers, Rosie knew that she would have to be foxy, tactful and, most importantly, sensitive.

Just then, Freda turned and laid the sleeping Jackie down in her Moses basket. As she turned, she placed her left hand over her shoulder, which indicated to Rosie that she was thinking of her dad.

Rosie lifted Harry up on to her right shoulder and lightly pressed her cheek to his. She crooned, 'There, there, my bonnie boy. Och, you are just so like my Fred was.' She stopped to fish for a handkerchief and wipe her eyes. 'You know, Freda, your grandad and I would have liked more bairns, but we were only blessed with your dad.' She gulped a short breath before adding, 'Premature, your dad was. Just a delicate wee bundle like Harry here. Your Harry is the living image of my Fred – I think that your dad has been given back to me in Harry, and we must look after him and treasure him.'

Freda now looked earnestly down at Harry. She knew she had to really look at him to be sure that he did not look like his father, Drew Black. As she scanned Harry's tiny, crushed-up face, he opened

135

his eyes and – did she imagine it? – smiled up at her. She could once more see that smile of her dad's... Yes, Harry's smile was identical to her dad's, his right upper-lip crooked up.

Rosie nodded. She knew that Freda would try to love Harry as much as she did Jackie, but she was also a realist. She knew that if Harry did resemble his grandfather, Fred, then things would work out just fine. However, she also acknowledged that it would be hard for Freda to bond with Harry if he did end up resembling his brute of a father. She was about to say something to Freda, when her eye was drawn over to the window. Moira and Stevie were pushing a brand-new twin pram up the garden path.

'Oh, Harry-boy,' she said. 'I think your granny and grandad Dalgleish will be hoping to take you and your sister out for a walk in the brand-spanking-new pram they have bought you!'

Freda was a bit reticent about conceding to Moira's wish that she pack a bag with two feeding bottles and some nappies, and let Moira and Stevie look after the twins for the afternoon so that she and Rosie could have a rest. Freda knew that the babies would not be going directly to the park; no, they would be taken along Great Junction Street and paraded up and down so that the populace could admire them. In Stevie's case, it would also be an opportunity to show off the living proof that Robin was not homosexual.

Moira, Stevie and the babies could have only been gone about ten minutes before both Rosie and Freda stretched themselves out on the sofas and fell asleep. However, only a half hour later they were awakened from their slumbers by the ringing of the doorbell.

'It's all right, Granny,' Freda muttered, getting to her feet, 'you snooze on. I'll see who's at the door.'

Stumbling into the hall, she was surprised to see that the visitor had already opened the door and was advancing towards her.

'Hannah, it's good to see you,' Freda said, 'but what brings you here today? Is Saturday not the day that you spend with Tom Davidson?'

'Mmm,' Hannah replied.

By now, the young women were back in the lounge, where Granny Rosie was getting to her feet. 'Oh, it's you, Hannah,' Rosie said. 'Now that I have the chance, I must thank you for coming to Jack's funeral. You were such a great help to Freda.'

'It was nothing, Mrs Dalgleish. I was just so pleased to help with the babies. Where are they today?'

'Holding a peep show down in Leith!' Freda chuckled. 'But Hannah, I get the feeling—'

Before Freda could say anything further, Rosie interrupted. 'Look, I'll go through to the kitchen and make up some tea and sandwiches – that will let you two lassies get up to date with all your tittle-tattle.'

Rosie had just quietly closed the door when Hannah sank down on to an easy chair. 'Freda, I'm sorry to bother you, especially right now with all that you are coping with.' She exhaled deeply. 'Freda, I need some advice.'

'On what?' Freda asked, before she too took a seat.

'Well, the good news is that Tom has suggested that he and I get engaged.'

'That's just wonderful! What's the problem? You are both single and–' Freda chuckled – 'very much in love.'

'That's all true. It's his religion that's the problem. Freda, he's Roman Catholic.'

'So? You either change your religion, or you agree that any children of the marriage will be brought up as Catholics and educated at Catholic schools – although that will not matter in your case.'

'That's just it. You see, when he asked me to marry him, I felt that I had to be honest with him. So, I told him about my problem. I thought that, as he loves me, it would only be a slight inconvenience to him – something he could cope with.'

'Are you saying that he is being squeamish about the dilator thing?'

'No, not that.'

'What, then?'

'It's his mother.'

'But you told me he didn't have a mother.'

'Of course he has a mother! She just doesn't live with him.' Hannah looked pleadingly at Freda before saying, 'Please, Freda, this is all very difficult for me, so don't interrupt until I tell you the whole story. Here goes. Tom told his mother that we were going to get married but there would be no grandchildren for her because of well, you know what. His mother said that was a price she was not prepared to pay, so–'

'Just a minute, Hannah. You, like me, are twenty-one and Tom is – correct me if I'm wrong – seven years your senior?'

Hannah nodded.

'Here is what I think. Tom is a man who has always done his own thing. As soon as he was able to, he left his mum and set up on his own. He is therefore his own man. Deciding not to marry you because of your problem is *his* decision.'

Hannah began to shake her head as tears welled and her lips quivered.

'Believe me,' Freda continued, 'he is a hypocritical coward who is not brave enough to say to your face that he wants to call it a day because of your problem. Hannah, get real, his mother objecting to no grandchildren suits his purpose and he is delighted to hide behind her skirts!' Freda paused. 'Hannah, did you come here today to ask me what I think you should do?'

Wracking sobs shook Hannah's body. 'Freda,' she spluttered. 'I love him so much that I don't wish to live my life if he is not in it! Is it not bad enough that I will never cradle my own children? Must I go through life a lonely, bitter old maid, too?'

A few minutes elapsed while Freda contemplated. 'Hannah,' she quietly began, 'he has made up his mind and you have to accept that. But, on the plus side, you are a very good-looking, intelligent woman and, more importantly, a selfless, loving, caring one too! Hannah, I can tell you that you will live to be grateful that Tom Davidson left your life. You were wrong about him being all there! He is not all there, he is truly disabled: he

139

is missing a heart!'

Hannah's sobs began to abate and Freda knew that she had to say something positive – something to help Hannah get back on track with her life. A sly smile crossed her face; she knew how easy that would be. She whispered, 'Hannah, I hope – no, I *know* – that someday soon Mr Right will come into your life and he, like me, will know that he is so, so lucky to have you by his side.'

Freda went over to Hannah. Hannah, her dear friend. The friend who had been there for Freda, through all her trials and tribulations. As she stroked Hannah's beautiful, silken hair, Freda was overcome by a desire to do Tom Davidson an injury. With her left hand, she squeezed her right shoulder tightly and gulped. She was back to wondering if the dreams she frequently had about the night of Drew's attack were really dreams at all. *Did* she ruthlessly stab her stepfather? Today, as she thought about doing Tom Davidson actual bodily harm, she was certain that she had had that uncontrollable urge before and she knew that she was capable of violence. She tried to relax. Surely, the desire to care for her babies, which was growing so strongly within her, would stamp out any violent urges? Indeed, she was so overwhelmed by love for her children that she knew she would always think twice before taking revenge. Besides, was a louse like Tom Davidson really worth doing a prison sentence for? No. As Granny Rosie was always saying, God – well, her God – always evens the score. Therefore, Freda thought, she and Hannah should just sit back and wait for Tom Davidson to get his comeuppance…

EIGHT

JULY 1970

Hannah had just finished giving Jackie's details to the receptionist and was about to sit the children down in the waiting area of the Royal Hospital for Sick Children's Accident and Emergency department, when three-year-old Jackie decided to throw a tantrum. As per usual when having one of those exhibitions, she flung herself down on the floor and appeared to be trying to kick her legs off her body.

'Jackie,' Hannah began, but she was drowned out by Jackie's blood-curdling screams and deafening shrieks, which echoed around the room.

'You are not my mummy! I want my mummy!'

Trying to give the impression that she was in control, Hannah bent down and fruitlessly tried to haul Jackie to her feet. She very quietly and pointedly said, 'Jackie, your mother is just parking the car and she will be here in a minute. Now, stop this nonsense. Come on and sit nicely, like Harry is doing, until someone comes to see your sore arm.'

Hannah's lecture only seemed to infuriate Jackie further, as she started to haul at the bloodied bandage on her right arm.

Just then, a group of four young junior doctors came into the waiting area, along with a consultant who was showing them around the hospital. To Hannah's surprise, the tallest of the group came over to her. Glancing up at his face, she was delighted to see two familiar dancing eyes and a pair of generous lips forming a welcoming smile.

'Ewan!' she shrieked. 'What on earth are you doing here?'

'We–' he indicated to the rest of his group, who were now leaving the room – 'will be starting our two-year hospital training here next week, so we are just having the geography of the hospital pointed out to us. What brings you here? Well, you and the children...' Ewan was now playing a silent peek-a-boo with Harry who, as per usual, was trying to make himself invisible by wrapping himself in the folds of Hannah's skirt.

Thankfully, Jackie had now spent all her fury and was sitting up on the floor.

'Jackie, here,' Hannah explained, 'decided to throw herself off the garden wall. She bounced off the path and cut her arm. Then she landed in the rose bushes, which resulted in grazed legs!'

'I wouldn't have hurt myself if Harry had done as I told him to and laid himself down on the ground so I could land on him!' Jackie retorted.

Ewan started to laugh. Before completely controlling himself, he grabbed Hannah and encircled her in a strong embrace. 'Hannah, this chance meeting was so great. I take it that the children are Freda and Robin's?'

Hannah was so overcome by Ewan's loving actions that all she could do in response was lightly pat him on each shoulder and nod. However, before anything further could be said, Freda came rushing into the room.

'Sorry, Hannah,' she began, 'I just couldn't find a place to park!' It was then that she became aware of Ewan. She hadn't seen him for more than three years, and she blushed when she remembered the last words they had spoken to each other. Bitter words that, even today, had the ability to make her feel cheap and dirty. Today, seeing him in person after so many years, she became awash once again with her futile feelings for him. She was, however, pleased to note that he had matured into a slim but athletic build of nearly six feet, and his eyes seemed to dance when he looked at her. Was his bewitching gaze, she wondered, trying to tell her that he was genuinely delighted to see her? Or was he just thrilled to be meeting up with Hannah again? Before she could ponder further, she was taken aback as he swept her up into his arms.

She felt his lips brush against her hair as he said, 'Good to see you, Freda. How are you?'

'Doing well. And, as you can see, my children are...' She was about to say 'just wonderful', when she remembered that her mother had enlightened her that she and Robin looked at the twins through rose-tinted glasses.

Two wonderful minutes elapsed as they held each other – time that allowed him to breathe in her intoxicating feminine fragrance. He gulped. The desire to hold her closer and never let her go overwhelmed him, but he knew that he must reluctantly release her – she was, after all, the wife of his best friend and therefore 'out of bounds' to him. Dragging his thirst for her back under control, he turned his attention to Jackie. 'Miss,' he said, lifting her bandaged arm up, 'what is the matter here?'

Before Jackie could reply, Harry slunk over to her side and lifted his little face to stare into Ewan's eyes. He mumbled, 'Please, Mister, don't hurt her. She cries when she gets jagged.'

'It's okay, little fellow. I won't hurt your sister and, know something, you are just so like your dad.' Ewan straightened up. 'Remember, Freda,' he said jauntily, 'how, when we were at primary school, Robin never liked anyone to get hurt? I think he must have gone through hundreds of hankies wiping up our classmates' tears and the gushing blood from their scraped knees. By the way, every time I try to persuade Robin to meet me for a catch-up at the weekends, he says he is busy.' Freda looked perplexed, prompting Ewan to add, 'Believe me, he does! Only last week I asked him to come on a night out to celebrate my graduation, but he said he couldn't make that either.'

Freda didn't reply immediately, because she was trying to fathom why Robin had not told Ewan about his routine visit to London every month. The London visits had begun after Billy's mother announced that she was opening up a salon in London's Mayfair. Both Billy and Robin had been shocked when she went on to declare that Billy would manage the London venture. This ploy was the latest of Mrs Stuart's efforts to break Billy and Robin up. She was convinced that if she could get Robin out of Billy's life, Billy would no longer be homosexual. Therefore, she reckoned all she had to do was put miles between them.

Unfortunately for her, like all her other dodges, it failed. There was just no way that Robin and Billy could live happily without having some kind of relationship with one another. So now, every four weeks Robin took off for London on Friday night and did not return until Monday afternoon. Thinking about London, it dawned on Freda that Robin had not told Ewan about his arrangements with Billy because he did not wish it to be known that his marriage to Freda was just a convenience. This desire was even stronger now, because Robin just loved being Daddy to Jackie and Harry. Freda shuddered at the thought that one day she might have to tell her children the truth about their parentage. Not only would that be devastating to the children, but also to Stevie, who took Jackie and Harry out every Saturday afternoon – being told that his precious grandchildren were really not his lineage would be a blow too cruel for him to endure.

Freda knew that she had to respond to Ewan's question about Robin, but she was struck dumb. She was remembering her schooldays with Ewan, Robin and the 'fabulous four'. The six of them had been so happy ... but that was then, and today was today. Gathering up all of her courage, Freda managed to offer Ewan her hand, before saying, 'Congratulations, doctor.' To release the tension, she blabbered on, 'Angela was in the shop this morning, getting her hair done for your graduation tomorrow. She is over the moon that you are now qualified!'

'Yes, she would like to be in the hall to see me capped, but you are only allowed two guest tickets and naturally my mum and dad were my first choice. Here ... why was she getting her hair done today and not tomorrow?'

Hannah and Freda exchanged a knowing glance, before Freda said, 'Angela will have no other but her very own Mister Teasy-Weasy, my Robin, doing her styling but as he is away in London this weekend, he won't be available tomorrow.'

'Are you saying that Robin goes to London regularly? Why?'

The young women exchanged another quick, anxious glance. They both thought that Ewan should be told exactly why Robin went to London. However, ever cautious, Freda decided that by doing that she might create more problems. Fortuitously, a nurse saved her from deliberately lying to Ewan when she called out, 'Jackie Dalgleish? We are ready for you now.'

Once Hannah and Freda had settled the children in bed, they sat down to have a glass of wine. As the wine began to relax them, Hannah said, 'Know something, Freda. See, when we met Ewan today, I thought that it was really no wonder that all the girls at school, including you and I, were hopelessly in love with him.' When Freda shrugged in response, Hannah sensuously licked her lips and simpered, 'Come on, Freda, admit it – as Ewan matures, he becomes even more desirable!'

'Yeah, you're right there, but we also know that he is Angela's personal preserve!'

It was eleven o'clock when Hannah eventually left, leaving Freda alone with her memories. Pouring herself another small glass of Blue Nun, the must-have German wine for the modern woman, she thought back ... back to three years ago, when she had first come to stay in this house, this lovely home, this safe haven.

She was only supposed to be Granny Rosie's guest until the house on Brunton Place was habitable, but the renovations had taken much longer than expected and it was eighteen months before the tradesmen moved out of the house. However, before Freda, Robin and the children took up residence, Freda realised that they could not move out of Marionville Crescent after all, because Granny Rosie had grown too frail and dependent to live alone. Freda's brother, Stuart, who also lived in the house at the time, had just qualified as a fireman. Through an introduction of Hannah's, he had met a lassie named Edith and fallen hopelessly in love with her. Naturally they wished to marry and set up home together. The wedding had been arranged, but a week before the happy event, Granny Rosie was struck down by a massive stroke that claimed her life. Granny Rosie, being Granny Rosie, had left her affairs in order. Her home was gifted to her two grandchildren. Freda was overcome when she was told that she had been left half of her beloved Marionville Crescent home. It was the place where she wished to bring up her children. Stuart and Robin knew how she felt about the house and the wonderful memories that it held for her, so they decided that Freda should buy Stuart's share of the Marionville house, and Stuart would then buy the Brunton Place property from Robin. Both houses, of course, still required mortgages, but very small and manageable ones – all thanks to Granny and Grandad Scott.

Sipping her wine, Freda's thoughts turned to Ewan. She sighed. Since the children had been born, she had occasionally thought about him and wondered how he was getting on. But as time passed, she had realised that any future they might have had together was now impossible. Indeed, she was so busy with her babies and the building up of her hairdressing business that she had stopped fantasising about him. Meeting with him face-to-face again had upset her. Just standing beside him had made her heart race and that old black-magic spell that only he could cast over her had surfaced again. Common sense told her that it was useless to pursue these dreams – after all, hadn't Angela, just this morning, confided to Robin that Ewan's mother had hinted to her that by Saturday she would be displaying a diamond solitaire on her ring finger? Freda chuckled, remembering how Angela had raised her voice to tell Robin the news, knowing that Freda was in the back room and would – even with the washing machine humming away – be able to hear every heart-breaking word.

The University of Edinburgh's graduation cere-monies were held in the iconic McEwan Hall: a magnificent, imposing building which was gifted to the university in 1897 by William McEwan who, at that time, was the owner of the largest breweries in the city.

When Ewan arrived at Teviot Place for his graduation, he and the lads that he had spent the last five years studying medicine with were stunned to silence. It was true that they had passed the amazing McEwan Hall many times before but today, on their special day, they took the time to really look at the building, which had been built in the Italian Renaissance style. As they passed through the hall's portals, the lads gazed up at the dome above. Ewan only had time to read the beginning of the dome's inscription – 'wisdom is the principal thing, therefore get wisdom...' – when he was reminded by John, one of his fellow students, that it was time for them to take up their places in the great hall for the graduation ceremony.

There are days that stay within our memories always, and the day that he graduated as a Doctor of Medicine would always be one of Ewan's. As he waited to be called forward and capped, he thought back to the day at Hermitage Park School when the results of the Eleven-plus Qualifying Examinations were announced. He chuckled as he recalled how the headmaster had told his class teacher that only five in her class had passed and were eligible for a senior school education. The five did not include Ewan; he was one of the many remaining that was asked to pick up the rubbish in the playground. Pick up the rubbish! Was that all that he and Robin were thought to be capable of at the tender age of eleven? What a load of nonsense that was, because he was about to be capped at the University of Edinburgh, and Robin had built up one of the most successful and lucrative new businesses in the city. Ewan was grateful that he was called forward before he could think about how well the girls he had gone to school with were doing because that would, of course, mean thinking about Freda – Freda, who would always be beyond his reach.

As he proudly strode up to receive his honour, he knew that his mother would be crying and his father would be gazing at the mural decorations and works of art on the walls, because he would not wish people to know that he was overwhelmed by the occasion. Ewan thought about the differences between his life and his father's. Ewan, even though he was from the working class, had been given the opportunity to have a privileged education, unlike his dad. His dear father, a man from the Pru who collected customers' premiums for their death policies or endowment plans, was as bright as Ewan – or even brighter – but he was denied the education that would have allowed him to reach his full potential.

It was four o'clock in the afternoon when Ewan and his parents met up with Angela for high tea at The Wee Windaes restaurant on the Royal Mile. There was no doubt about it: when Angela sat herself down in front of the stained-glass windows of the restaurant, she outshone their brilliance. Her hair had been styled by Robin to look natural, soft and flowing. The expensive, emerald-green satin blouse she was wearing complemented not only her blonde hair, but also her soft skin tone. Ewan knew he should compliment her on looking so good and he would have done had his head not been left a mess after an uncomfortable incident with his mother on their journey to the restaurant.

They had been heading down the Royal Mile to

the restaurant, when his mother had started trying to push a wad of notes into his hand. 'Son,'
she had whispered, 'your father, Angela and I are
all so proud of you. Now, I know that you would
like to ask Angela to marry you, but you cannot
afford the engagement ring. So, here, take what I
have been saving up for you, and put the icing on
the cake today by buying Angela a ring!'

Ewan had pushed the money back towards his
mother. At the sight of his scowl, she'd grown
embarrassed and confused. 'What's the matter
son?' she had continued. 'Nobody, especially not
Angela, will know that it is my money that bought
the ring.'

Ewan had drawn up abruptly. 'Mum,' he had
hissed, 'at the present time I do not wish to ask
anyone to marry me, never mind Angela. Now,'
he had continued through gritted teeth, turning
to face his mother straight on, 'try and understand that it will be difficult enough for me to
cope with two long, hard years of slog as a junior
doctor in the hospitals, without complicating my
life further with a non-starter of a romance!'

Mrs Gibson's lips had quivered as she looked to
her husband for support, only to find that he was
doing what he always did in awkward situations
between his wife and son: pretending that he was
looking elsewhere. St Giles' Cathedral and the
Heart of Midlothian stone sculpture had his full
attention.

By the time they had arrived at The Wee
Windaes, Ewan had cooled down. Sitting at the
table with his family and Angela, he now regretted
his outburst. He knew that he was right to reject

his mother's offer of cash, but this was a big day for her and his harsh words had wounded her and blighted her joy. He also knew that she had told Angela to expect a ring, so Angela was going to be bitterly disappointed too. In addition to this, he feared that his mum felt she had not gone all out for him in planning a celebration, because she had not booked the upmarket Caledonian Hotel for dinner. He would never forget how her face had fallen when Pippa Gladstone's mother, who had travelled up with Pippa's father from their estate in the Borders, had matter-of-factly announced, 'We have booked into the Caledonian Hotel and invited twelve others to join us there for dinner.' Somehow, prawn cocktail, steak and chips, followed by Black Forest gateau, no longer seemed to be the upper-class nosh his mum had always thought it was.

Once the waitress had cleared away their coffee cups and Dad had settled the bill, Ewan announced that, as regrettable as it was, he would have to leave. Angela took this as a signal that she should join him but as she rose to take her jacket from the coat stand, Ewan continued, 'Five of the lads I studied with are dragging yours truly on a well-earned pub crawl. Don't wait up, Mum, but if I am not home by noon tomorrow, call the police!'

As Ewan left, Mrs Gibson bowed her head. She could not bear to look at Angela, because she was afraid to tell her that it would be at least another two years before Ewan would think about settling down.

Undaunted, Angela smiled sweetly at Mrs Gibson, before saying, 'I must be off too. I'm meeting up with some friends to go and see a re-release of *Gone with the Wind*. I've seen it so many times before and I do believe Vivien Leigh is just wonderful in her part.' She then seemed to retreat into a world of her own. Almost inaudibly, she whispered, 'And tonight, when it appears that Scarlett has lost Rhett forever, I will take strength from her as she utters those unforgettable words ... after all, tomorrow *is* another day.'

NINE

JULY 1972

The smartly-dressed young man sprinted towards the train, which was just about to be cleared for take-off. 'Guard!' he shouted. 'Is this the London to Edinburgh Waverley train?'

Yanking open the first carriage door, the guard replied, 'Yes, it is. In you go!'

Ewan leapt aboard, landing – thanks to the guard giving him a hefty push – on the floor. The carriage door banged shut behind him and, after one final whistle from the guard, the train began its journey northwards.

Before Ewan could pick himself up, a fellow traveller emerged from the first carriage to assist him. 'Can I give you a hand up?' he asked Ewan, before they both started to laugh.

'You sure can,' Ewan breathlessly replied. 'Believe me, I was just so desperate to catch this train and get home to Auld Reekie that I sprinted to the station! And now I am doubly pleased that I made the effort, because it means that you and I can catch up, Robin.'

Assisting Ewan to his feet, Robin replied, 'Aye, it's been so long... It's two years at least since we last had a pint together.'

'Will we look for seats together?'

'No need. I am the only traveller in my carriage, so we have it all to ourselves – unless, of course, someone gets on at any of the following stops.'

'That's a surprise. The train I came down on yesterday was so busy that some poor sods had to stand in the corridor for the complete journey.'

Once they were settled in the carriage, Ewan was again surprised – this time because of the carriage's superior seating and spaciousness.

Robin got himself seated and Ewan took off his coat. Robin couldn't hold his curiosity back any longer, so he asked, 'Ewan, what took you down to London?'

Flopping down on the couch opposite Robin, a pensive Ewan replied, 'Well, I know you know through Angela that I survived the two years working in hospitals – that said, only just! Honestly, you would not be worked as hard in prison after committing murder!' Robin nodded, and Ewan continued, 'Then, it was time to decide what branch I wished to specialise and serve in and I, being me, decided to become a GP.'

'Good for you.'

'There is an opening coming up at a practice at the foot of Leith Walk and there's another in

Musselburgh, but I'm not sure I want to go for either. A lad I graduated with got in touch with me to say that he is in London working as a GP, and there's a vacancy at his practice.'

'Are you saying that you will be leaving Edinburgh? Would that suit Angela?'

'The answer to your first question is no,' Ewan replied emphatically. 'No, I will not be leaving Edinburgh, because on my way down to London last week I was overcome by homesickness before we'd even passed Newcastle!'

'Homesick? Before Newcastle?'

'You can laugh, but back home in Edinburgh, and in particular the place where we were brought up, there are people that mean too much to me to leave behind! Besides, London is too big, too noisy and too...' He hesitated. 'Too smug and pretentious.'

'Does that mean that, at long last, I can hear wedding bells for you and Angela?'

Ewan shook his head but did not respond to the question. 'And you, Robin, why are *you* on this train?'

'I come down every four weeks to spend three hap-hap-happy days with Billy. Usually I come back on Mondays. But on this Sunday I am homeward-bound because our twins are starting school tomorrow and she-who-must-be-obeyed – my Jackie – would be piqued if I was not there to see her off on her first day.'

Ewan sat quietly and pondered. Why, he was wondering, did Robin go down to London every month to spend time with Billy, when he had a wife and children at home? It didn't make sense to

Ewan, so he quietly said, 'Robin, I do not wish to pry, but this arrangement you have with Billy–' He stopped. He knew what he wished to say, but the words seemed to stick in his throat.

Sensing Ewan's unease, Robin said, 'Are you asking if Billy and I are in a "gay relationship" as they call it nowadays? Yes, we are and we have been since we met as teenagers.' He stopped to allow Ewan to digest what he had just said, before continuing, 'Billy is now based in London, because his mother is attempting to break up our relationship.' He chuckled, before adding, 'And, believe me, opening a London salon was a good thing for her to do, because it is outdoing her Edinburgh one!' He winked. 'Oh, by the way, she knows nothing about my trips to London, so if you meet up with her ... button your lip.'

'But what about Freda and the children?'

Even although they were alone in the carriage, Robin looked furtively about to ensure that what he was about to impart to Ewan would not be overheard. Satisfying himself that they were alone, he leaned over and rubbed his hands together before whispering, 'Ewan, knowing you, I am sure that you will keep to yourself what I am about to confide to you.' Ewan nodded his agreement and Robin continued, 'You see, there would be more people than just Freda and I hurt if all and sundry were to find out the truth. Especially my father, who is besotted with Jackie and Harry – honestly, he would literally curl up and die if he knew. The truth is, I am not Jackie and Harry's biological father. But, regardless of their true paternity and no matter what comes along, I will always be their father by choice.'

This news rocked and shocked Ewan. He had always hoped that Freda's pregnancy was not the result of a sordid little affair, as gossip had suggested. He remembered how he had cringed when his mother told him that Angela was upset to discover that Freda was pregnant. According to his mother, Angela had respected Freda, so was disappointed to find out that she was 'little more than a tart'.

He was brought back from his memories by Robin, who said quietly and seriously, 'Ewan, what I am trying to tell you is that Freda was brutally assaulted and raped by her stepfather. Freda, being Freda, decided that abortion was not an option for her, so I suggested that we get married. She agreed, and it has worked out very well.'

Ewan wanted to ask, 'Very well for who?' but instead he said, 'When did you first know about what happened to Freda?'

'Almost immediately,' Robin replied. 'You see, Freda and I were doing up the shop at the time. On the day of the attack, she left the shop early to take Susan home. After she left, her brother, Stuart, arrived to drive her and Susan home. But the girls had already gone, so Stuart and I went for a pint at The Artisan Bar instead. We only had the one as the weather was getting worse, and we fancied a game of pool. So, we decided to take his grandfather's car back to Marionville Crescent and park it, then go on to the pool hall. However, when we arrived at Granny Rosie's house, Susan was on the doorstep crying that Freda required help. Granny Rosie told Susan to stay put at

Marionville, and then the rest of us got into the car and Stuart drove like a maniac down to Sleigh Drive. When we got there, both Freda and Drew were unconscious. Freda's mother, who was already in the house, was babbling incoherently as she kicked Drew's body, over and over again.' Robin grimaced. 'She also had a bread knife in her hand and it was smeared with blood. Granny Rosie and Grandad then took charge. Freda was attended to first and once she was in bed, they decided that we should dispatch Drew—'

'I hope this means that Drew is dead – that someone had the guts to kill him!'

'I am not saying that he is still alive, but he was when we dumped him.'

Before anything further could be said, the conductor opened the door and called, 'Tickets please!'

Both Robin and Ewan immediately handed over their tickets for inspection. Looking down at the two tickets, the conductor frowned before saying, 'This is a first-class carriage, but this—' the inspector waved one of the tickets in the air – 'is not a first-class ticket.'

Ewan, who had stood up when the conductor had entered, flopped down on the couch and started to laugh uproariously. 'Now does that not just say it all?' he spluttered. 'Here I am, with a degree from the University of Edinburgh and certificates to say that I am qualified to practise medicine, and I can only afford a third-class ticket, whilst my oldest friend can afford to travel first class.'

'Yes sir, I accept that, but as you are occupying

a seat that you did not upgrade to, I will have to issue you with a fine.'

Robin was now on his feet. 'Look,' he said to the conductor, 'you know me. I travel this route regularly. My friend jumped on board the train as it was leaving King's Cross, and I pulled him in here.' He took his wallet from his jacket and pulled out a note, which he pressed into the conductor's hand. 'You take this, and I can assure you that in half an hour's time my friend and I will be in the dining car. I imagine we will finish our journey to Edinburgh there.'

The conductor nodded. 'No offence, Mr Dalgleish, I didn't know the gentleman was a friend of yours. But even if I did, I was only doing my job.'

When the excited conductor had closed the door behind him, Robin began to laugh again. 'Well, at least that took our minds off Freda's...'

The mention of Freda's name caused the smile on Ewan's face to die. He was awash with guilt, because there had been times when he had thought badly of Freda. He gulped, thinking back to an incident he had dealt with as a junior doctor. He had attended to a young girl in Accident and Emergency, who had been brought in after a rape. He would never forget that lassie's anguish and pain, and the way that she screamed in terror when any man, even a male doctor, came anywhere near her. And now, to discover that Freda had been through the same thing! He felt awful. On the plus side, at least she and Robin had made a go of things. He pondered. There were elements of the story of what happened to Drew that made him question whether

159

Robin had imparted the whole truth. Exactly how badly hurt had Drew been, and who had inflicted the injuries on him?

'Mummy, we are going to be late and it is all Harry's fault,' Jackie, who was standing at the outside door ready to go to her first day at school, moaned.

'Harry, we have to get a move on!' Freda shouted through the open back door to Harry, who was down at the rabbit hutch.

'I know, Mum, I was just reminding Bugsy that I won't be here to let him out to play today but he will get a long, long run about the garden when I come home.'

Freda put her hand over her mouth and sniffed as tears welled. How, she wondered, could I have rejected Harry when he was first born? There was nothing of his biological father in her gentle, sensitive boy. Today he was going to school. Freda was so glad that both he and Jackie had passed for Leith Academy Primary School. This was not because it was a fee-paying school – after all, you could hardly say that the token fees of twelve pounds a year were onerous – it was because their intake number meant that they had two classes starting today. This being the case, she had asked that Jackie and Harry be put in separate classes. She knew that if Harry were in a class with Jackie, he would never get out from under her domination. Freda squirmed as she remembered when they had gone to sit the test for admission. The infant-school mistress had floated down the corridor, her black academic gown flying around

160

and scaring Harry, who had whimpered and tried to hide himself away in Freda's skirt. Today she hoped that the infant-school teachers would not be dressed in black gowns, so that Harry would be able to see that they were human beings and not Wicked Witches of the West like he thought the infant-school mistress was.

Robin had already said goodbye to the children, assuring both of them that they looked so very smart in their royal-blue blazers. He had hesitated when leaving, because he wished to go with them to the school, but Freda had said, 'No. The other children will only have their mothers there and we don't wish to seem overprotective.'

That all being so, there was nothing left for Freda to do now but, as she was now a competent driver, get the children into the car and drive down to the school.

On arrival at the school gates, Freda was surprised to see Hannah there. But then again, why should she be? After all, Hannah had played such a big part in the children's lives from the day they were born.

'Why are you not working today?' she asked Hannah.

'Told my boss that I had an early appointment with the dentist,' Hannah teased, waggling her tongue around her lips.

Freda playfully nudged her. 'You're a lying hound.'

'Not really. I didn't actually tell him I was going to the dentist. I told him how much I would like to see the kids going into school on their first day and Jim, being the sweetie he is, said I could come into work about eleven.'

'Here,' Freda began, as she tucked her arm through Hannah's, 'I meant to ask you about this Jim Baxter that you seem to like so much... Has he a mother?'

'No. He did, but she is dead now.'

'Good. So, now that you have transferred to the personnel department, is he a possible...?' Freda pulled a face, widening her eyes.

'No. He hasn't a mother alive, right enough, but he does have a healthy and breathing wife!'

'So what's the attraction?'

'He encourages his staff to get on and he's a nice guy to everyone.' Now, it was Hannah's turn to tease. 'In my case, he has given me day release so that I can go to Napier College and study for an IPM.'

'What's that? I hope it's not infectious!'

Hannah gave a smug smile. 'It's a qualification. Institute of Personnel Management. When – or if! – in two years I am awarded that qualification, I could become the personnel manager for one of the departments in the Edinburgh Corporation.' She chuckled. 'Imagine it! I would be the first woman to be employed in such a role.'

Before Freda could reply, she looked beyond Hannah and gasped. 'Well, well, if it isn't the dynamic duo.' She turned Hannah around, to show her what she was seeing.

'Oh Freda, isn't that just lovely?' Hannah said. 'Your mum and mother-in-law have come to see the children off.'

If the sight of the two women was not enough to make Freda sigh in exasperation, spotting Stevie and Robin trailing behind them certainly was.

Hannah pointed. 'Look, Freda, their grandad and dad have come too.'

Freda slumped against the wall, her body shaking with laughter. 'Methinks,' she drawled, 'I should have sold tickets for this event – I could have made a fortune, so I could.'

Four weeks later, when Freda was cashing up the shop on Friday evening, she was surprised to hear someone knocking on the door. Being wary, she slammed the till shut and, before she advanced to open the door, lifted one of the handheld hairdryers. Swallowing hard, she put the security chain on the door before opening it just a fraction.

'Freda, please take the chain off and open the door wider,' a male voice pleaded. A foot was placed in the small opening, preventing her from closing the door. The voice said, 'It's Ewan. I wish to talk to you.'

'There's nobody else here, so you will have to come back tomorrow,' Freda responded hurriedly.

Ewan sighed and winced as the door was pushed harder against his shoed foot. What was he to do? He now realised that he had been stupid. He should have telephoned Freda last night to tell her that he would be calling on her this evening. Ever since Robin had told him of her ordeal, Ewan had been unable to get her out of his mind. He kept seeing her battered face and in his sleep he would hear her cry out in agony. He reckoned that her reluctance to allow him into the salon was because she was nervous now to be alone with any man.

A police constable on the beat arrived on the scene, putting Ewan at a further disadvantage.

'Problem, sir?' the bobby asked. As if by magic, upon hearing his voice Freda took the chain off the door and opened it wider.

'Oh, it's you, Constable Smeaton. Why don't you come in and have a cup of tea or coffee?'

Ewan did not wait to be asked in. Before Freda and the constable had time to stop him, he settled himself in one of the chairs.

'Now, is it tea or coffee?' Freda asked the constable.

Constable Smeaton shook his head. 'It's my break-time right enough, Mrs Dalgleish, but one of the other cops brings in a fish supper and we divide it between us. But, before I go, do you wish me to see this gentleman off the premises?'

'Oh!' exclaimed Ewan. 'Are you saying that you do not recognise me?'

The constable peered at Ewan, before exhaling and holding out his hand to him. 'Sorry, Dr Gibson, I didn't recognise you. Mrs Dalgleish, no need for you to worry – this is one of the doctors we call out to test our drunk drivers.'

The door had just closed shut on the constable, when Freda said, 'I know you mean no offence, but could you just leave? Anybody passing by could look through the window and get the wrong impression.'

'Freda, just calm down and relax. You know that I mean you no harm. It is just that since I travelled up from London with Robin–'

'My blabbermouth husband had no right to tell you what he did.' Freda was now running her fingers through her hair, her lips quivering. 'It is my sorry tale to tell and mine alone. Believe me, I have only trusted one person with the sordid details.'

'Hannah?'

'Yes, Hannah. When we were naïve nineteen-year-olds, she confided in me about her own painful secret, which built a special bond between us...When I required a shoulder to cry on, who else could I possibly have turned to?'

'You could have come to me! I would have helped you all I could.'

Freda's derisive laughter echoed around the room. 'Now, let me guess ... you would have recommended a good gynaecologist so I could abort my children?'

'Perhaps. I may have suggested that as one possible solution, but I could also have offered to ... to marry you.'

'Marry me? And what would Angela and your mother have said about that?'

'It would have been none of their business. I love you, I always have,' Ewan said emphatically.

'I am sorry about that,' Freda retorted, 'but at that horrible time I hated every man I knew. I loathed myself – and I still do, because I wasn't strong enough to stop what happened to me!'

'You hated every man?'

'Well, obviously not my grandad, my brother or Robin,' she grudgingly conceded.

Time ticked slowly by. Ewan still sat in the chair whilst Freda stood rigidly, supporting herself against the far wall.

When he could stand the silence no longer, Ewan pleaded, 'Freda, I am here tonight to ask you if you think we have any future together.'

'How could we? I am married to Robin, who was my rock to cling on to when I was in a rough sea and drowning. We made a pact to wed and stay married to each other no matter what. My children think – no, they know – that he is their supportive, loving father. I refuse to do anything that might put their trust in Robin and I in jeopardy.'

'Couldn't we even have an arrangement like Robin and Billy? No one knows why he goes to London once a month.'

Before he could go on, Ewan was interrupted by the crash of a hairdryer bouncing off the large mirror behind him, thrown at him from across the room.

'That insulting proposal has just helped me better understand what poor Hannah has had to endure. Men only think about getting women into bed. Well let me tell you, Hannah and I have reached the age of twenty-five and we are still virgins!' Catching sight of Ewan's confused expression, Freda continued, 'Yes, I know what you're thinking, but when I was raped I was unconscious. Never have I made love to someone who loved me. To someone who valued me.'

'I can understand why you do not accept anyone's advances, but what about Hannah?'

'Beautiful, graceful, elegant, intelligent Hannah is like me, in the sense that she was short-changed.'

'Short-changed? Surely she wasn't also–'

'No, not that – although it has been traumatic for Hannah too, in its own way. You see, she was short-changed at birth. Nature decided not to give her a uterus and, as if that injustice was not enough, it also threw in an undeveloped vagina. Now, since you are a high and mighty doctor, I'm sure you will agree that such an affliction often results in death to romance.' Freda's voice was cracking with emotion. 'Do you know how many times I have had to wipe away Hannah's tears after a courtship that seemed to be going right ended up with her being dumped because she could not easily ... well you must know what?'

The clock slowly ticked the minutes away. Ewan was in a dilemma. He had come to Freda in the hope that he could persuade her to develop a relationship with him. A relationship that he hoped would, in time, see her and Robin divorcing so that she could marry him. He now knew he must accept that Freda was damaged by what had happened to her and no longer trusted any man who made advances to her. She had also made it very clear that she would never break her arrangement with Robin. Theirs was a bond that could not be broken. Freda was willing to sacrifice the possibility of a happy relationship with Ewan, because it would endanger the feeling of security that the children enjoyed with her and Robin as their parents.

Rising up from the chair, he accepted that he must go. He had made a complete mess of trying to tell Freda that he loved her, that he wished to marry her and spend the rest of his life with her, that he would have accepted anything – even an arrangement like Robin and Billy's – just as long as she was in his life. He saw now that it could never be. Freda had her standards and her loyalty was to her children – and indeed also to Robin, who had picked her up when she was broken into pieces and put her back together again. For Robin, their arrangement meant that he was safe-guarded from intolerance and bigotry. Ewan knew that his hopes were futile: Freda and Robin were a solid and unbreakable partnership.

Eight weeks later, Ewan had still not accepted that he and Freda had no future together. Her rejection left him feeling awful, and he found his thoughts turning to Angela – Angela, who for years had waited so patiently for him to show even the slightest interest in her. Ewan decided that he would contact her and invite her to partner him at a friend's wedding the following week.

At the reception, Angela was so eager to please Ewan that she outshone the bride. Naturally, Robin had done her hair and make-up and he had excelled. Her fuchsia-coloured dress and match-ing coat screamed class and were evidently from a designer shop on George Street. However, it was not the make-up or the fancy clothes that made Angela glow... No, it was the belief that Ewan had finally realised he should be courting her.

It was true that Ewan went out of his way to woo Angela at the wedding; she couldn't believe that at last her dreams were coming true. When the dancing stopped and it was time to head home, Ewan, being the gentleman that he was, escorted Angela all the way to her front door. However, when she winked sensually at him and invited him in for a nightcap, he seemed to be repulsed at the idea.

'Eh, eh,' he stammered, 'I'll pass this time.'

Angela's face contorted and Ewan felt awash with guilt because he had obviously hurt her, just like Freda had wounded him. He hurriedly added, 'But, you know, things change... Maybe sometime in the near future, when I have got my mind sorted out, we can catch up again and we'll...' He stopped to meditate, before adding, 'Que sera, sera.'

It would have been kinder to harshly slap her on the mouth. In response to his rejection, the colour drained from Angela's face and her breath came in short pants, profuse tears splashing down her cheeks. She was so gutted that she made no attempt to cover up her distress. She finally realised that the dream she had pursued since the age of eleven would never ever come to fruition. Finally she mumbled, 'Catch up again, Ewan? Now why on earth would I wish to do that? No, my dear, as far as I am concerned you are yesterday's dream – or should I say nightmare!'

She turned and, moments later, Ewan had another door kicked shut in his face.

TEN

OCTOBER 1973

Freda had just returned home from the Royal Infirmary of Edinburgh when Hannah, who had been babysitting the children, asked, 'How is your mum?'

'She has broken her right femur. They said they would take her into theatre tonight to set the bone, and then in a few days' time she will be allowed home.'

'Mmm,' Hannah replied, before cautiously asking, 'and what about the cruise that you two are due to go on next weekend?'

'Well, she won't be able to do that, will she?'

'And you?'

'I suppose I will have to forget it too.'

It was just then that Robin arrived home. 'How's your mum?' he asked Freda.

'Robin,' Hannah interjected, 'listen to this. Ellen can't go on the cruise around the Canaries because she will be in plaster–'

'Which is all thanks to her getting plastered on a Marks night out!' sniped Freda.

'And,' Hannah continued, ignoring Freda's gripe, 'Freda, here, says that means *she* can't go either.'

'Well, wouldn't it be stupid for me to go?' Freda replied. 'I mean, the only reason I was going on the cruise in the first place was because my mum did not wish to go on her own!'

Hannah shrugged.

Robin turned to Freda. 'Know something, love? I think you should go. Here, Hannah, would you like to go with her?'

'I would be delighted to but as I have just started my new job as the principal admin and personnel officer in building control, I'm afraid I can't.'

Before anything further could be said, Jackie and Harry came bounding into the room. 'Mum,'

Harry wheedled, edging closer to Freda, 'have you thought any more about the puppy?'

'What puppy?'

'Last week, when Bugs went to be with his mother in heaven, you said that as rabbits don't live that long and I cry when they die, I would be better off getting a puppy dog.'

Freda was about to protest when Jackie said, 'Yes, you did say that, Mum. And Daddy, didn't she promise that she would think about getting him a Labrador?'

'A Labrador?' shrieked Freda. 'Within months it would be pulling Harry off his feet.'

'I don't know about that,' Robin responded. 'They say that Labradors are good-natured dogs and very good with children.'

'I think I will go back to bed and try getting out on the other side to see if this day could go a bit better!' Freda cried.

Robin laughed. 'Look, love, you go on the cruise and I'll see about getting a Labrador puppy for Harry.'

'No. There will be no dog in this house right now.'

'But Mum...' whimpered Harry.

'Harry, please try to understand that you are too young to take on the responsibility of a dog,' Freda said gently but firmly.

'But I have experience! I chum old Mrs Sloan when she is out walking her dog.'

'Yes, dear, but Mrs Sloan's dog is a Chihuahua, and when he gets tired she lifts him up and puts him in her handbag. Now, think, Harry, what would you do with a Labrador if it needed help?'

Harry looked at Robin, his eyes imploring him to help.

'Remember, Dad,' Jackie, who knew that Robin would not break Harry's heart and therefore a dog would be joining the family in the near future, butted in, 'I like *brown* Labs the best.'

'It's not going to be your dog, it is going to be mine and I like... I like...' Harry stalled as Jackie was scowling at him. 'I like the bla–' He broke off as Jackie threw him a further glower. He bowed his head in resignation. 'I like the brown ones too.'

Raising her voice several octaves, Freda chanted, 'Jackie, it will be Harry's dog and therefore he will choose the colour he wishes it to be, and so it can be golden, black, brown or even tartan – I don't care, as long as he is happy with it! And, again, must I remind you to allow Harry to think for himself?'

Jackie's response was to toss her hair and hunch her shoulders. Harry, on the other hand, bounded towards his mother. Throwing himself at her, he stammered, 'Oh, thank you, thank you, Mummy, I will love you and the puppy dog forever!'

As it dawned on her that she had just agreed to Harry getting a dog, Freda looked over to Robin in the hope he would overrule her, but his face was a picture of merriment.

Robin spluttered with laughter. 'Walked yourself right into that one didn't you, sweetheart?' When his laughter subsided, he looked directly at her. 'Now, about your cruise on the *Black Prince...*'

Freda stared long and hard at him. She knew that he was feeling guilty because last year he and Billy had managed to spend two weeks sunning themselves on the Costa Brava, which costa plenty! Then even more money had been splashed out in March earlier that year on a ten-day Fred Olsen cruise around the Canary Islands. By the time Robin returned home, he had fallen in love with cruising and the Canaries and he insisted on booking Freda and her mother onto a similar cruise in October. The small ship, he assured them, had an intimate feel to it and would in no way overwhelm them. He was also anxious to point out that it was renowned for its friendliness, and the food was excellent and would appeal to their Scottish palates. He just knew that they would fall in love with the ports of call – he was willing to bet that they would wish to stay on longer at Madeira. Freda had been reluctant to even consider going on holiday without the children, but when Robin told Ellen of his plan she was delighted. Oh yes, she just couldn't wait to go, especially since Robin would be footing the bill! The following day she had floated in to M&S to tell all her workmates that she was going on a cruise. Not wishing to disappoint her mother, Freda had then grudgingly conceded. And now here they were, just four days before their departure day, and Ellen had managed to book herself into the Royal Infirmary.

If she was being truthful, Freda did think that she could benefit from a holiday, especially as she would soon be left to run the Elm Row salon singlehandedly when Robin opened up his dream designer hair studio uptown ... but was it realistic to be going on a cruise right now?

'Robin, dear,' she began, 'I think we have to

accept that my going on this cruise alone would be sheer lunacy! I know we will not be covered by the insurance for my cancellation, but we will get my mother's expenditure back.' Then, to try and get him to accede, she wheedled, 'You have committed yourself to opening up this exclusive shop on the lower part of Frederick Street... Now, before you start, I know that we make a very comfortable living from the Elm Row shop, but where will all the money be coming from to finance this extravagant adventure of yours on Frederick Street?'

'No problem. The bank is going to roll us, because they can see that we are more than good at making a go of things.'

'That's what I mean! Wouldn't it be more prudent to use my mum's refund from the cruise to help finance the shop, and take a smaller, more manageable loan from the bank?'

Robin was now chortling. To the delight of the children, he grabbed Freda and began to dance her around the room. 'I have it all under control and I have worked everything out. Come on now! Do you really think that I would put the well-being of you or the children in jeopardy for a new venture? Look, as Billy says—'

Freda managed to get herself free before she spat, 'I should have known that Saint Billy would have something to do with all this.'

'Yeah, it was Billy who said we should be expanding because we are meeting a market need! People have more money now to spend on themselves. They want to look good, and we are going to give them what they want! This is just the beginning. When our kids are ready for the big bad world, they will be able to come into a business that you and I have built up. Freda,' he enthused, 'can't you see that we will have set them up for life?'

Before Freda could argue, her brother, Stuart, arrived.

'I've just been to the Infirmary to see Mum,' he said as he came through the door. 'She's gutted that she won't get to go on the cruise with you. But she did ask if you could arrange for her to get a refund. She and one of her workmates want to go to Benidorm on the Costa Blanca. Apparently, her and this Anne-somebody are planning to spend a week there in a first-class hotel next May, and the refund will more than cover the expense for both of them.'

Freda just gaped. Robin was biting his lip in an effort not to laugh out loud.

Eventually Freda, still looking as if she had been hit by a ten-ton truck, said, 'Know something? Mugsy here is going to go on that cruise, and I intend to have one whale of a time!'

'Good for you,' Robin replied. 'Now, don't forget that you have three days booked at a five-star hotel in Tenerife before you board the ship...'

Robin had just enough time to drop Freda off at Glasgow airport before he had to head home. The turnaround was quick because Freda had insisted that he was on hand when the children returned from school, so he had to hurry off to get back in time. However, this meant that Freda, who had never been outside Scotland before, had to get herself through check-in and passport control independently.

Although she always gave the air of being completely in control, Freda suffered from an inferiority complex. She also found it difficult to be in environments where there was not a single face that she was familiar with. This feeling of unease turned to panic if a strange man came towards her, and she lost control completely if he blocked her view.

She was aware that the time had come to face her demons. She could still feel the thrill she had experienced upon opening up the official envelope and removing her precious passport from it. It had signalled to her that she was starting a new phase in her life. It would, she hoped, open up new avenues for her – and for the children, because if she managed the holiday she was now embarking on, then it was her intention to arrange a sunshine holiday in Spain next year for herself, the children and her ever-faithful Hannah.

Once all the official procedures were behind her, she located the departure lounge. She was sitting enjoying a cup of coffee when a little girl, who she judged to be about five, sidled up to her.

'Are you just with you?' the little girl asked.

Freda smiled. 'I suppose I am.'

'Did you not even bring your teddy?'

'No. You see, I haven't got a teddy, but my little boy, Harry, does.'

Before the child could respond, a tall, charming man arrived on the scene. 'Jodie, did I not tell you not to wander off?'

'I didn't wander off. I just came here to say hello

to the lady and ask her if she needed a friend.'

The man frowned. 'Sorry if Jodie bothered you,' he said to Freda.

'She was no bother! I have a son and daughter just a wee bit older than her.'

'They are not travelling with you?'

'No. Everyone at home thought that I was in need of a break, so here I am going off on holiday.'

Before he could reply, the overhead Tannoy system announced that the Tenerife flight was now boarding.

Putting her half-drunk coffee down, Freda got up and smiled. 'That's my flight, so I must go.'

'No rush. We are travelling on the same flight.' The man now looked down at Jodie. 'Aren't we?' He turned back to Freda. 'Eh, I didn't catch your name.'

'Freda, Freda Dalgleish.'

'Tommy, Tommy Winter,' he replied, offering her his hand. 'Now, Freda, as Jodie and I travel back and forth from Tenerife at least four times a year, we know that there is a big rush for the departure gates. But, if you don't wish to be crushed in the stampede, just hold back.' Freda frowned and he continued, 'Honestly! As your seat is already booked, you will find that it is still vacant when you get on board.'

'Thank you for saying that.' Freda paused. She didn't wish to seem like a lonely, lost soul, so she smiled brightly and quipped, 'This is my first trip on my own, but I am a quick learner!'

Tommy smiled. 'Then sit back down and finish your coffee. I will signal to you when it's time to get moving.'

They were the last to get on the bus that taxied them to the aeroplane. When they alighted, Tommy pulled Freda back as the crowd surged forward and stormed towards the steps of the plane.

Once they were aboard, she could see that he was right. Her seat A in row 2 was still vacant, as were seats B and C. She got herself seated and had just obeyed the instruction to fasten her seat belt when she was pleasantly surprised to find that her travelling companions were Tommy and his daughter, Jodie. A smile crossed Freda's face as Tommy took his time to see that Jodie was strapped into her seat before he sat down and fastened his own seat belt.

Within ten minutes they were air-bound and the 'Trolley Dollies' had started their rounds, offering drinks and, a little later, providing a meal – well, if you could call the dried-up chicken and the sorrowful pudding dish edible.

Before the attendants had gathered up the refuse, Jodie fell asleep.

'Does she often just drop off so early in the day?' Freda asked Tommy.

'No, but we had an early start, you see. My home is halfway between Inverness and Aberdeen, but Glasgow has the most flights to the Canaries.'

'And you travel four times a year?'

He seemed to hesitate before replying, 'Yes, I know that it is time-consuming, but Jodie's mother and I are divorced and she now resides in Tenerife with the new man in her life. I think – no, I *know* – that it is important that I spend as much time with my daughter as I can.'

'I'm sorry about your divorce.'

'No need to be. It was best for both of us. We had married young – too young! – and five years later we discovered that we had nothing left in common, so we called it a day and moved on.'

'So you will be flying back to Glasgow tomorrow?'

'Usually I return the next day, but this time I have booked myself onto a *Black Prince* cruise which will eventually land me back in the good old UK!'

Freda couldn't help but chuckle. 'Know something, I think we are on the same cruise! Although I am spending three nights in a five-star hotel at the Playa de las Americas before I board.'

It was now Tommy's turn to chortle. He winked at Freda and said, 'Snap.'

The following morning, after breakfast, Freda decided that she would just laze around the pool. However, when she arrived to get herself positioned on a sunlounger, she discovered that they were all covered with towels, as were the plastic chairs and small tables. She squinted at a notice that stated in three different languages, including English, that you should not reserve a sunlounger unless you were ready to use it. Freda was coming to the conclusion that the hotel guests – the majority of whom were of German nationality – were all illiterate, when a voice behind her said, 'Now, Freda, if you were thinking of doing a bit of sunbathing, you should have been up at five o'clock this morning to put your mandatory booking-towel on a bed.'

'Are you allowed to remove someone's towel if they are not here?' she queried.

'You could, but as we are still recovering from World War II, it is not advisable to annoy our fellow German residents.'

Freda shrugged.

'But how does this sound?' Tommy continued, as Freda raised her eyebrows in expectation. 'I've hired a car, so let's go sightseeing!'

Freda gulped. Terror, her old enemy, boiled up inside her, reminding her that Tommy was a man that she didn't really know. 'And what if he tries to...?' she silently screamed, breathing deeply.

Tommy sensed that she was ill at ease with his proposal. Sniffing and raising two fingers of his right hand to his forehead in a mock Boy Scout's salute, he chanted, 'I promise to be a good boy and nothing but a good boy, if you will only say "yes" and come with me. I also promise to get you back in time to do battle in the restaurant with our German friends, who seem to think that they are entitled to six sirloin steaks from the buffet table whilst we are entitled to none.'

Freda looked at him and as her countenance softened, Tommy knew that he had won her over.

Truthfully, Freda was lonely, very lonely. She had never really been on her own before. Thankfully, Tommy was so charming that the thought of spending the day being entertained by him was very inviting – although a quiet voice of caution inside her kept saying "be careful, be careful". However, she decided to throw caution to the wind and happily climbed into his car.

The next three days seemed to whizz past.

Tommy took her to places she had never been, nor seen anything like before. He paid close attention to her needs and was ever so patient with her. He made her think of her father, as he was the first man since her beloved dad to take her on adventures and show her something of the world. It was true, her dad had not actually taken her to see the sights and wonders that Tommy did, but through his magical storytelling he had taken her into the magical land of make-believe.

On the day they were to join the *Black Prince* cruise ship, Freda was so eager to get on board that she was showered, dressed and packed well before necessary.

After breakfast she sat in the foyer, as eager as a child waiting for Santa Claus. Her dancing eyes were sparkling like diamonds and her tongue kept licking her lips.

Tommy's voice brought her out of her excited reverie. 'Are you going to fly by yourself to the ship, Freda, or do you think you could come back down to earth and travel on the bus with myself and a few others?'

Rubbing the fingers of her hands together, Freda quietly squealed, 'Tommy, I am just so excited! I've never been sailing before...To be truthful, I have never been on a holiday like this. I wish Hannah, my best friend, could have been here with me. She deserves a treat like this.'

The bus arrived and the staff loaded the luggage into its boot. Freda sighed with relief. She had been told that she did not have to worry about her luggage as she would not see it again until it was brought to her cabin.

Freda would think back many times to what happened next. When they boarded the bus, they discovered that there were passengers from another hotel already on board. Thinking that Tommy would wish to sit with her, Freda walked halfway up the bus to a vacant double seat. Whilst she was making her way up the aisle, she became aware of a rather attractive, overly made-up, mature woman, who she reckoned was probably fifteen years older than her. She smiled, noting how the woman's stance seemed to say 'this is my space, do not intrude'. To make sure that no one would dare to sit down beside her, the woman had occupied the inside seat and placed her rather large handbag on the outside seat. Freda had still not yet settled herself down when she saw Tommy get on board. She waved to him and smiled. However, the smile died on her face when he merely saluted to her in acknowledgement, turning instead to the older lady. Lifting up the lady's handbag, he not only sat himself down beside her but also leaned over and gave her a long, passionate kiss.

The *Black Prince* set sail. Freda, now dressed in flared trousers and a matching top, headed up to the deck to enjoy the view. It had been two hours since she had alighted from the bus and boarded the tender that had shipped her and the other passengers out to the cruise ship. This had been a nerve-wracking experience for Freda. She had struggled to keep her dignity whilst boarding the tender in high-heeled shoes and a skirt that had been donned because it showed off her svelte figure. Unfortunately, the garment was so tight that it did not allow her to jump from space to space, and she was left blushing when she had to hitch it so high that her underwear was visible.

She closed her eyes and drank in the heat of the sun on her face. She was somewhat put out to soon have her peace disturbed by a female voice asking, 'Are you on your own?'

Freda opened her eyes and was surprised to find that the voice belonged to the woman who had met up with Tommy. 'Yes,' she replied. 'I am alone, but I am not lonely.'

The woman then proffered her hand to Freda. 'I'm Alana Gowks and I hail from Glasgow's Kelvinside.'

'Pleased to meet you. I am Freda Dalgleish.'

'Yes, I know that, and I also know that you reside in Edinburgh. If you are wondering how I know that well, Tommy told me.' Freda just shrugged, and Alana continued, 'Now, be honest and tell me, are you hoping to bag yourself a rich widower husband on this cruise?'

Freda just gasped.

'Now, if you are, don't waste your time on Tommy Winters,' Alana went on. 'He hasn't a penny; *I* paid for his trip on this cruise and, Freda, I should warn you that I like value for my money.'

By now, Freda had recovered from her surprise. Her hackles were up. 'Alana, I am not here to find a wealthy husband. Why would I do that when I have a husband at home, who may not be stinking rich by your standards, but is very comfortably off? And even if I didn't, I am no pauper myself.'

183

'So, what do you do to be in such an agreeable position?'

'I am sure you will have heard of A Cut Above, the hairdressing salon of some renown. Well, I have the pleasure of informing you that it is owned by my husband Robin and I.'

Alana looked perplexed. 'But is Robin Dalgleish not the ... err, let's say "special friend" of Billy Stuart?'

This statement wrong-footed Freda, but she was determined to hold her own with this woman, so she sweetly replied, 'Yes, he is a friend of Billy's but, more importantly, he is married to me and our union has been blessed with two children.'

'You do surprise me,' Alana replied, making no attempt to hide her disbelief.

However, before Freda could continue, she noticed that Tommy was making his way towards them. Alana had her back to him and he signalled with his hands to Freda, mouthing that he would call on her later.

Not wishing to prolong the meeting with Alana, which had been uncomfortable, Freda smiled and said, 'Ah, here comes Tommy now. However, you must excuse me. As they say, two's company, three's a crowd.' She lifted her hand and waved a happy goodbye to both Alana and Tommy.

Arriving back in her cabin, she decided to have a shower and a rest before she went up for afternoon tea. She had a look at all the meal and snack times and groaned – if she indulged herself at all of them, she would be going home looking like Two Ton Tessie from Tennessee! A little giggle escaped her as she recalled how after the twins were born, it had taken her nearly a year of utter starvation and exercise to get her figure back. She had to look good, as she did today, because she and Robin were running a business that depended on women paying good money to look glamorous and their customers would hardly feel inspired to spend more if their locks were done by a scruffy, overweight has-been.

As the refreshing water cascaded down on her, Freda decided to linger in the shower for a while longer than she normally would. However, all good things must come to an end and when she eventually got out from under the massaging spray, she felt so relaxed that she literally purred. Leisurely, she got herself into her dressing gown, before swathing her wet hair in a towel. Then, to her dismay, a gentle tap sounded on her door. She reckoned that the cautious rapper would be gigolo Tommy. She knew Alana would have told him that Robin was gay, so she suspected that he was eager to find out if Freda was a better meal ticket than Alana. Now, how was she to deal with him? The best way, she reckoned, would be to not open the door. However, after three rat-a-tat-tats, she wrenched the door open in sheer exasperation. She was overcome by terror and panic when the caller forced her back into the cabin. Then, to stop her from screaming out for help, he placed his hand, albeit gently, over her mouth.

Taking his hand away from her mouth, but still holding her firmly to him, he gently murmured, 'There, there, stop gasping and take deep breaths. Believe me, you have nothing to fear. It's only me, and you know I would never hurt so

185

much as a hair on your head.'

Freda tried to calm down but the walls of the small cabin seemed to be closing in on her. The height of the man and way he was standing with his back to the door, barring her escape, was so intimidating. Swallowing hard, she decided that she would have to look at the gate-crasher. When her eyes met Ewan's, her legs buckled. Still firmly holding on to her, he guided her over to the two-seater couch. Once they were both seated, he took her clammy hand in his.

'Come on now, love,' he pleaded. 'I'm sorry to scare you and push my way in, but I knew you wouldn't let me in otherwise. Try and pull yourself together and at least say you are pleased to see me.'

Slowly but surely, Freda felt her old fighting spirit begin to surge within her. Her vital inner strength flowed back. As soon as she felt capable of retaliating, she grabbed her hand from his grip. '*Love,*' she hissed, 'you break in here, clamp your hand over my mouth and nearly suffocate me, then have the audacity to demand that I say I am pleased to see you? Well, I am blooming well *not* pleased to see you!' Tears were now brimming, and she sniffed long and hard in an effort to keep them from spilling over. 'For a start,' she continued, as her voice cracked with emotion, 'what on earth are you doing here? And please don't insult my intelligence by saying that you were only passing by and thought you would look me up!'

'No, I won't say that because it would not be true.' Ewan tried to take Freda's hand in his again, but she responded by tucking both of her hands under her legs. 'Freda, I came because ... I have to ask you to forgive me. Look, I know I got it all so wrong when I came to the shop and asked you if there was any way that we could have a relationship.' He put up his hands to show surrender. 'Now, don't worry, because I have accepted that you will never allow that. I am just a crazy fool chasing rainbows, but when I heard that you were alone on this cruise, I just thought... Freda, wouldn't it be wonderful for us to spend ten days together? Ten days out of a whole life-time, just you and I... Is that too much to ask? While you are thinking about that, might I suggest that you lay your hands in your lap? They will be more comfortable there.' Her reaction to this statement was to sit up straight and push her hands further under her legs. Ewan shrugged. 'Have it your way. I am here to tell you that I love you and I wish to have you all to myself, just for ten days. After all, what harm would that do anyone, especially Robin?'

Jumping to her feet, Freda began to thump him on the shoulder. 'And what exactly do you mean by that?' she shrieked. 'Surely you cannot think that Robin, your friend, who was willing to hold out a hand and assist me when I was in deep trouble, is some sort of lesser human being and deserves to be... Don't you understand? Without Robin's self-sacrificing help, I might not be here! Suicide seemed like my only alternative.'

Ewan nodded.

Tears were cascading down Freda's face, and she stood back from Ewan before continuing, 'Know something, you are supposed to be a doctor – someone who helps and heals his fellow mortals – yet you have dared to come here with a crass and stupid assessment of my relationship. For goodness sake, Ewan, get a grip, and stop taking lessons from your mother!'

Bowing his head, Ewan accepted that he had been an insensitive ass, but he had come here with a purpose: he had to try and salvage the situation between himself and Freda. Raising his head, he whispered, 'I'm sorry. I know that I, too, should be grateful to Robin for all that he has done for you–'

'And my children, who have never been cold or hungry and have never doubted that Robin and I love them and work hard to provide the best we can for them.'

Ewan nodded again. 'Right. I will tell you the truth. I love you and I always have. It is true that I believed that you had ... well ... I knew, or wished to believe, that Robin was not the father of your twins, and I thought that–'

'I was a tart, as your mum and darling Angela both said?'

'No. I thought that you may have got carried away with someone...'

Freda laughed scornfully, shaking her head.

'Please, Freda, this is all so difficult for me, so don't interrupt again until I say what I have to.' Freda nodded, and Ewan went on, 'Look, I think that you feel the same way about me as I do about you...'

Freda inhaled deeply and nodded. However, still being wary, she raised her hand to indicate that he should keep his distance.

Ewan continued, 'When Robin told me that

188

you had come on this cruise by yourself, I thought this could be a gift for us... Ten days might be all we will ever have together, because your first priority is your children. As hard as it is for me to accept, I know that you will never leave Robin. Freda, please try and understand that I just... I jumped at the chance to spend time with you. And I promise you, I most solemnly do, that there will be no strings attached. Please, Freda, for ten short days allow me to just be with you... Allow me to play make-believe with you.'

'I trust you are not suggesting that you share my bed?'

'No. I have a single cabin of my own – true, you wouldn't be able to swing a cat in it, but I have booked and paid for it. Don't you see? I just wish to spend precious time with you. Dance with you, go on the excursions with you... I promise you that I will not ask for anything more than to be in your company.' Ewan's eyes met Freda's, beseeching her. He sought her hand again, and this time she allowed him to take hold of it. He raised it to his mouth and tenderly kissed her open palm. 'Freda,' he whispered, 'please, please let us grab this chance at happiness.' Freda started to shake her head. Quickly, in order not to lose the momentum he had gained, Ewan added hopefully, 'Let me reiterate that nothing will happen between us on this holiday, unless the advance comes from you.'

A long silence fell in the cabin. Both were thinking about just how much they had always desired that the other would love them. Freda knew that she would never know the joy of being Ewan's wife, so would it be so wrong to steal the next ten days and make them their special time? Indeed, who would ever know? Most importantly, who would it actually hurt? The only problem for Freda – and it was a big one – was that before the attack and ever since, she had not been intimate with anyone. Now, the very thought of allowing anyone, even Ewan, that close to her filled her with revulsion and self-loathing.

Lifting her eyes to meet Ewan's imploring gaze, Freda began to weaken in her resolve to reject his proposal. She had always loved and desired him, and he had made a promise that she knew he would keep. There would be no strings attached, and he would only cross the line if she gave the signal.

She was surprised to hear herself say, 'Okay, let's give it a try. But you have–'

She was interrupted by another soft rat-a-tat-tat on the door.

'Who will that be?' Ewan asked.

'Well, unless one of us opens the door, we will never know,' Freda retorted.

Freda had the door only slightly ajar when Tommy stuck his foot over the threshold. 'Freda,' he hurriedly began, 'I just wanted to explain about...' His words died in his mouth when he became aware of Ewan's presence.

'Tommy,' Freda began blithely, 'please let me introduce my very good friend, Ewan Gibson. He is going to be my companion for the rest of the cruise. Now, is there something I can do for you?'

'No. Not really,' Tommy blustered. 'I only wished to make sure that you knew that afternoon tea will be served in the bar area in half an hour.'

Then, without uttering another word, he did an about-turn and fled from the cabin.

'Who was he?' Ewan asked.

'Just a gigolo that kept me company for a couple of days, until his first-class meal ticket turned up and I was–' she started to laugh – 'saved from telling him that I am not that kind of girl!'

The memory of the Canaries cruise would stay with Freda always, because it was like living in a dream.

On day one, Freda said goodbye to Santa Cruz de Tenerife and the island of Tenerife itself, and hello to ten days of having Ewan all to herself. For the rest of her life she would, with affection, recall their trips from the ship to Lanzarote, Fuerteventura, Gran Canaria and Lisbon. They spent wonderful days strolling hand in hand, sometimes sightseeing and sometimes just sitting together, enjoying being a couple. Sipping a coffee or a cooling drink at a wayside café, they would watch the world pass by and wish the day would never end.

However, it was Madeira and its laid-back capital of Funchal that Freda would never, ever forget. Looking back later, Freda had to admit that she had been intoxicated by the perfume of the beautiful and exotic subtropical flowers and fruit that grew there. As the magic of mystical Madeira seeped into her being, she began to wonder what it would feel like to make love to the man she loved. She became so exhilarated by the thought that she could even picture herself slowly awakening from sleep to find him lying beside her. She still experienced a sickening feeling whenever her old demons surfaced, but when they did they were soon banished by the sight of Ewan's wonderful smile, which stretched the very cute dimple on his chin. Freda accepted that magical Madeira had completely bewitched her and perhaps, just maybe, it was time for her to satisfy her longings...

To be truthful, they were both reluctant to leave Madeira – the two wonderful days in that port were enough time for it to get under their skin. However, when they got back on board the *Black Prince*, a steward reminded them that it was the special Captain's Dinner that evening. For the event, you had to put on your very best glad rags and have your photograph taken when being welcomed by the captain.

Freda was still so relaxed that she enjoyed every minute of the evening. The entertainment was just superb and as they had been taught dance at school in Leith, as well as at the Palais de Danse in Fountainbridge and the Eldorado Ballroom in Leith, she and Ewan were both accomplished modern and Scottish country dancers. Indeed, when they took to the floor for 'Strip the Willow', they were the champions. As Ewan birled and twisted Freda up, down and through their partners in the reel, the sensual longings she had experienced in the morning began to resurface.

Arriving back at their table, Ewan asked Freda if she would like another soft drink, as she did not drink alcohol. To his surprise, she did not sit down again. Trying hard not to look directly at him, she said, 'Why don't we have our nightcaps in my cabin?'

Ewan's response was to put the index finger of his right hand in his ear and waggle it. 'Tell me that I am not dreaming and that you really have just asked me to a pyjama party.'

'Pyjama party?' Freda almost shouted, looking quickly about to make sure that no one was listening. 'I am just asking you to have a private goodnight drink with me.'

'Oh, so I shouldn't go back to my cabin and collect my nightclothes?'

'No,' Freda replied tersely.

The music started up again and as Ewan swept her onto the floor to enjoy a waltz, Freda leant in close to him and murmured, 'Ewan, please don't walk from your cabin to mine with your pyjamas in your hands.'

'Would it be okay if I ran and collected my toothbrush? I promise you, I will hide it away in my dinner jacket pocket.'

'Before you get carried away, there are things I have to make you aware of.'

They had only just opened the door to her cabin when Freda began to get cold feet. She couldn't believe that she had actually led Ewan to believe that she would allow him to... As they began to run their hands over one another, Freda flared up with embarrassment. Her face was on fire and as scarlet as her lips, and she began to back away from Ewan.

'Changing your mind?' Ewan asked as he closed the door behind them.

'Please try and understand that because of what happened to me, I find it difficult to even be alone with a man. As for love-making, I have–'

she was now crying softly – 'no experience.'

'Okay. Now, here's what I propose. We will take it slowly, step by step. Tonight we will just laugh and talk. Then, when we get into bed together, we will just cuddle.'

Freda relaxed. The plan seemed so sensible. However, plans do not always follow the path that they should; by the rosy dawn, Freda was no longer afraid to be alone with Ewan, and her demons had been well and truly slain.

The rest of their holiday was like a honeymoon. True, they had not been churched, but as far as they were concerned they had grabbed the chance to experience what life could have been like. They were so besotted with each other that they were oblivious to everyone else on board with them. The three-day sail to Southampton more than fulfilled the dreams Freda had once had of what being loved by Ewan would be like. He was a gentle, considerate lover, and he gave her a sense of healing and well-being. For Ewan, their union was so perfect that it filled him with the desire to try and persuade Freda to leave Robin and marry him. This was now his burning objective but, as he did not wish to break the magic of the spell that seemed to be surrounding them, he decided not to broach that subject until they were off the ship and homeward-bound.

Long train journeys – especially if you're travelling in the barely-occupied first-class compartments – are a great time to think things through, make plans for the future or promise yourself that you will take the bull by the horns and get things sorted out once and for all.

Travelling home to Edinburgh, Freda was in a semi-awake state thinking about how, when she got home, she would reorganise her life so that she could spend more time not only with her first priority, her children, but also with Hannah. She truly loved Hannah and now, after the awakening of her own sexual pleasure, she realised what they had both missed and she wished to help Hannah experience the same fulfilment.

She had just started to work out a master plan for Hannah, when Ewan snuggled closer to her and placed his hand on her knee. In the past, her reaction to such an intimate gesture would have been to brusquely brush the hand away, but she was so relaxed with Ewan, and so very much in love, that she just smiled and covered his hand with hers.

'Freda, let's talk. Let's make plans,' he said softly.

In response, Freda sat bolt upright. She knew what he was going to ask. She accepted that this would be a 'Meg Sutherland' moment in her life – Meg Sutherland being the clairvoyant mystic she had consulted when she was fifteen. Meg had been truthful and told Freda that no one could really predict a person's future, as we are all given choices in life. Sometimes, Meg had warned, Freda would find herself at a crossroads in her life; on those occasions, it was Freda, and Freda alone, who would decide which road to follow.

Ewan was now holding Freda's hand in his. He turned her face towards him with his free hand and pleaded, 'Freda, we love each other, so what would be so very wrong with us being together?

If you are worried about the children, don't. I love you so much that I will take them on and we can become a family.'

Derisive laughter echoed around the carriage. 'Ewan, Ewan,' Freda moaned, 'if it was all as simple as that, wouldn't it be wonderful? But it is not as simple as that – it never was and it never will be. Can't you see? The children would be devastated. They would have to cope with losing their–'

'But at this present time they are too young to understand.'

'Ewan, don't be a fool. Children are more sensitive than you think.'

Ewan leant forward and entwined his fingers, trying to think of a positive argument that he could persuade her with. He was so engrossed in thought that he didn't hear her say, 'There is not only the children to think of. Have you thought of what my leaving would do to Robin? He was the rock that I clung to when I was sinking. Then there is my mother, and Robin's parents. Dear, helpful, discreet Moira and rough-diamond Stevie – are you aware that my children absolutely adore them? Now, be honest with yourself. If I was selfish enough to break all those trusting, unquestioning hearts, would I be the person that you fell in love with?'

A long silence fell between them. All that could be heard was the rhythm of the train as it click-clacked its way northward.

When she could no longer stand the mounting tension between them, Freda said, 'Ewan, you must forget me and what could have been.' She was surprised that he did not react to her plea,

196

but Ewan had very reluctantly accepted that there was no way that he could win. Blundering on, Freda said, 'You know that Angela has spent her life waiting for you to show some interest in her. She loves you. Like Robin and I, it wouldn't be a perfect partnership but it also wouldn't be intolerable. And the bonus for you is that you would make your mother very happy – Angela is her choice for you.'

Ewan shook his head. 'Honest to goodness,' he expounded, 'is it not bad enough that my mother is always throwing Angela in my face, without you joining in too? As I have explained over and over again to my mother, I am *not interested* in Angela. She runs after me and I have never, ever given her any reason to think that I am interested in her.'

Freda was taken aback by his emotional outburst. 'But,' she replied gingerly, 'have you ever told Angela how you feel about her?'

'No, not exactly. I'm not a sadist. But let me tell you this: you, and you alone, are the love of my life and as long as you live, I will never marry anyone else. Freda, don't you understand?'

Freda was now crying profusely as she pleaded, 'Ewan, please, please don't make it any harder than it already is for me. Remember, the bargain was that we would steal ten days. Yes, they were a blissful ten days of wine and roses. Lovely days that I would not have missed for anything, but we both knew from the start that they were always going to be short-lived.'

When all the pleas and rejections had been made, there was nothing left to do but agree that at their journey's end Freda should alight first from the train, as she was being met by Robin. Ewan would then wait on board the train until Robin and Freda's car had left the station.

Summoning a porter to assist her with her luggage, Freda sprinted up the platform. She reached the foyer and was met by faithful Robin, who smiled and called out to her that he had missed her.

During the car journey home, Robin and Freda kept interrupting one other, as both wished to know how things had gone for each other in the last two weeks. Freda said that her holiday was so wonderful that she intended to treat the children and Hannah to a Mediterranean holiday the following year. She asked Robin how things had been while she was away, and he replied, 'We had our moments and you are in for a surprise.'

The hour was late when she arrived at her front door, but as soon as she was over the house's threshold she started to sprint up the stairs.

'Freda, the children are asleep,' Hannah called after her from the front room.

Freda already knew that Hannah would have put Harry and Jackie to bed, as they had school to attend tomorrow, but she was desperate to see them.

Now it was Robin's turn to say, 'Hang on a minute, Freda, there is something I have to explain to you first.'

His plea also went unheeded. Freda opened the door of her daughter's bedroom. She could see by the light of the hall that Jackie was sleeping peacefully, and that she looked well. Freda leant over her daughter and brushed her lips across her forehead; in response, Jackie gave a slight shrug but did not awaken. Tiptoeing from Jackie's room, Freda headed for Harry's, but before she could enter, Robin grabbed her arm.

'Look, sweetheart, two of Harry's baby front teeth got knocked out when he fell down the back steps.'

Without waiting for an explanation, Freda bounded into his room. At the sight of Harry's head, she almost shrieked. 'Robin, never mind him losing his baby teeth – after all, they were long overdue to come out – what on earth is that crowning his head?'

'It's just a–'

'Puppy!' she squeaked. 'But why is Harry wearing the mongrel like a hat?' She almost laughed when she saw that the pup's legs were dangling down over Harry's ears.

'She's not a mongrel,' Robin retorted defensively. 'She's a Labrador. She's just seven weeks old so is still pining for her mother.'

The light from the hall was a bit on the dim side, but as Freda squinted at the pup she couldn't make up her mind what colour her fur was. Then she remembered that Jackie had told Harry he was to have a brown-coloured dog.

'Now, how much did that brown Labrador pup cost?'

'She's not brown, she's jet black. When Harry saw her, he asked the breeder why they call it jet black instead of just black. The breeder explained that it was just a way of saying that something was very black. That being so, Harry decided that the pup should be called Jet, so we would all know that she was black – *his* choice.'

'And what did Jackie have to say about that?'

'Nothing. You see, my dad went with us to the breeders. He knew that Harry really wanted a black dog, so he told Jackie that the black ones were much cheaper than the brown ones and that if they got a black pup, he could probably afford to buy Jackie a couple of additional tap-dancing lessons.'

Emotion began to choke Freda. She had only just got home but because of a black pup, her son, her daughter, her doting father-in-law and Robin, who was the best daddy a child could ask for, she already knew that her decision to reject Ewan's proposal was the right and only one she could have made.

ELEVEN

DECEMBER 1973

The grand opening of Robin's exclusive hairdressing shop on Frederick Street was on Thursday, 5 December. All those that Autumn thought should be invited, were. She also asked some of her personal friends along too, because she wished them to know that she was going to be the administrator and chief receptionist of the establishment.

Freda did not raise any objections to Autumn being appointed at the new shop, whilst she remained at Elm Row. The Elm Row shop was where they had started out and it was where her long-standing customers – or 'clients', as Autumn referred to them as – felt most comfortable. It was also the shop that had exceeded all their expectations and one of the main reasons that Robin thought they should be branching out. Freda, on the other hand, had always been more cautious – a steadying hand on the tiller. She would have liked them to have further established themselves on Elm Row before they started up in opposition to the big boys.

She did, however, concede that Robin had trained up four exceptional hairdressers for the new salon. However, they could leave at any time and with just one month's notice. Freda feared that, despite being grateful for their excellent training, they might do just as she and Robin had done and start up on their own or – and this was perhaps more likely – Robin and Freda's competitors would poach them.

The other problem with the Frederick Street shop was Autumn. Robin's mum, the ever-faithful and discreet Moira, had begged Robin to give his younger sister a job. Autumn had had more jobs in the eight years since she had left school than the Labour Exchange had had on offer. Yes, overindulged Autumn really believed that her employers should conduct their business around the hours that she was willing to work. She also required that her employers take her rather extensive social calendar into consideration...

Not wishing for his mother to be further upset by Autumn's failures, Robin had recently agreed to take her on in the business at Elm Row and train her up as a receptionist. He did, however, warn Autumn from the start that his employees – a group that would soon include her – had to put in a fair day's work.

To everyone's surprise, Autumn became a first-class employee. She really liked working in the salon and every day without fail she offered to model for the apprentice hairdressers and beauticians.

Anyone who looked at Robin and Autumn could not believe that a brother and sister could be so alike. It was not just that they both had dancing blue eyes, similar skin tones and blonde hair; they were also alike in the way that they walked, talked, charmed and smiled. However, there was one marked difference between them, and that was their appreciation of Freda. To Autumn's annoyance, Robin always consulted Freda about any shop business, because he knew that she would give him good, solid advice. However, from the very moment that Autumn arrived to work at A Cut Above, she believed that she should be number two in command and co-owner of the establishment. She even went as far as to hint to the staff that Freda was a gold-digger and had deliberately got herself pregnant by Robin. Needless to say, an atmosphere developed between Freda and Autumn, and it became clear that eventually one of them would have to go.

When Autumn became aware that Robin intended to open the more upmarket salon on Frederick Street, she was ecstatic – this was more than she had wished for. She started to work on Robin. Sweetly she simpered, 'Robin, I have been thinking. I wouldn't mind travelling a little further to and from work, so maybe I could transfer with you to Frederick Street? If I did, you would have the added advantage of someone with the right experience on reception when you first open up. It would also mean that Freda, who is so competent, could be left in charge here at Elm Row.'

Robin was not sure if Freda would agree to Autumn's offer, so he said, 'Leave it with me. After I have discussed it with Freda, I will get back to you.'

Autumn had to inhale deeply then, because she wished to shout at him, 'Look, she is just pinned on to you, whereas I am your sister! You should be seeing to it that I have the position that I am entitled to!'

However, whilst it was true that Autumn was not the Brain of Britain, she did have something that was more important: a good deal of animal cunning. Therefore, she said nothing in response to Robin, just meekly nodded her head.

The next day, when Robin and Freda were having their weekly business chat, Robin asked Freda if she had any objections to Autumn's proposal. Freda took her time to answer. It was true that she found Autumn overbearing and tiresome, and she could see difficulties arising if she was not reigned in. However, as Freda looked about their Elm Row shop, the thought of being the boss without having to put up with Autumn was just so appealing that she found herself smiling sweetly before saying, 'Yes. What a good idea. And now we have settled that, there is a delicate family matter that I wish to discuss with you.'

A week later, Thursday evening saw the grand opening of the new branch of A Cut Above. To Freda's surprise, Autumn laid on an excellent drinks and canapés reception for the invited guests. Naturally, it was also a family affair, and a smug smile came to Freda's face when she saw her sister, Susan, who was now a good-looking, willowy seventeen-years-old, circulating with the other guests. Susan had been urged by Freda to start her hairdressing career as an apprentice at one of their competitors' salons. Earlier that week, Freda had been advised by Robin that three of the hairdressers that had been trained up at Elm Row would be moving to Frederick Street because, according to Robin, they were the crème de la crème. Freda had raised no objections because it meant that there would be room for two promising new hairdressing apprentices at Elm Row, one of whom would be Susan.

Freda's delighted expression was a picture to behold as she watched her vivacious yet still-unspoiled sister mingle amongst the guests. However, when she noticed that Susan had stopped to engage in conversation with a handsome couple, a look of perplexity – or was it jealousy? – overtook Freda's features. So, she thought to herself, Ewan and Angela have come as a couple. She froze in anger and hurt, before starting to argue with herself. After all, was this not what she had urged him to do – to find himself a mate and get on with his life? It was, but now that she was faced with Ewan and the sophisticated, elegant Angela as a couple, she felt a lurch in the pit of her stomach and had to quell a desire to rush up to Ewan and say–

Freda's thoughts were interrupted by the sound of Robin tinkling a small bell, which brought a hush to the room. He summoned Freda to his side and she plastered onto her face a wide smile that did not reach her eyes.

'Ladies and gentlemen, family and friends, clients,' Robin began. He paused, hunching his shoulders and chuckling before adding, 'Especially those that I hope will become our regular clientele.' He stopped again to let the spontaneous laughter of the audience die down. 'We – that is my dear wife, Freda, and I – would like to thank you all for coming along tonight to assist us in the launch of our new venture. We are also grateful to everybody who helped make Elm Row the success that it is. Indeed, our customers and employees have become like our family – a strong, supportive system which gave us the courage to open up here, where the competition is exceptional.' He halted again and sought for Freda's hand. 'You won't believe this, but just before we opened up on Elm Row Freda whispered to me that she was pregnant with our twins, who are here tonight. At the time, we didn't know how we were going to juggle the new business and parenthood.' He stopped to tease the crowd before adding, 'Now, tonight, I have to tell you that a few days ago Freda whispered in my ear again. She told me that we will have to juggle the twins, two shops and the patter of tiny feet again when our third baby is born in July next year!'

The room echoed with loud clapping and cheering, especially from Stevie, who had confided to

Joey earlier that day that he didn't wish to attend such a 'ponsy affair'. Now he was so glad that he had. Freda, on the other hand, wished that the floor would open up and swallow her. When she glanced over at Ewan, the look of utter disbelief on his face told her that he was shocked and gutted that she had not confided in him about her condition.

Within the next few minutes Freda would discover that Ewan was not the only one feeling aggrieved by the announcement; her mother also felt more than miffed that she had not been told before other people. 'Freda,' Ellen hissed, still keeping a smile plastered on her face. 'I am your mother and soon to be the baby's grandmother, yet I have to find out along with everybody else at this shindig that you are pregnant.'

'Mum, I am sorry. Please try and believe that I was going to tell you tomorrow. Mum,' Freda whimpered, 'I am as angry as you are that Robin announced it tonight.'

Before Ellen could reply and ask her daughter the burning question of the expected child's parentage, Ewan had managed to manoeuvre himself over to Freda. As he bent forward to kiss her on the cheek and congratulate her, he whispered in her ear, 'Your news tonight alters everything. We have to meet and I won't be put off. No, Freda, this is not me trying to get you to speak to me on the phone and being told by one of your staff that you are too busy to take my call. You will talk to me or I will start shouting.'

After Ewan's warning, Freda could not think straight. She wished that the reception would come to a close, allowing her to go home and lie alone in her bed where she could think of what to do next.

Freda knew that Ewan would not wait any time before confronting her. So, when he arrived at A Cut Above on Elm Row just twenty-four hours after Robin had released the bomb, she was not surprised.

Once the door had closed on the last employee and he and Freda were alone in the shop, Ewan said, 'Now, don't try and deny that the child you are carrying is mine.'

'You are right about that,' Freda hissed, as she flung a wet towel in his face. 'And before you go on about how let down you feel that I didn't tell you, please consider how let down *I* feel – let down by you!'

'In what way?'

'You told me that I had nothing to worry about! You said that you had been careful, very careful, so how come I'm pregnant?'

'Are you now trying to say that I was the only one who got carried away? Let me remind you...'

Freda's face was now crimson and she cringed. No way did she wish to be reminded of the way she had so recklessly behaved. Tears brimmed in her eyes. All she had wished for was ten days, ten too-short days in a whole lifetime – was that too much to ask for? All she wanted was to love him and be loved by him, and now...

Seeing her distress, Ewan stepped forward and took her into his arms. 'Shhh, please don't cry. We have to think of what to do that would be best for all concerned.'

'Ewan,' Freda wailed, 'if you try to tell the world that this baby is yours then I will have to do the unforgivable. I'm not joking.'

He stepped back from her. 'Are you saying that you would abort our baby? Good grief, am I hearing right?'

'I would not wish to. In fact I desire with all my heart to keep this baby. Keep it so that I will always have some part of you in my life.' Freda tried to stay calm, but she was overwhelmed by an emotional outburst. 'Ewan, please don't make me think about an abortion. It is against my nature to do that. Can't you see? If I could not bring myself to abort my twins, who were conceived in such savage wickedness, do you think I would be able to live with myself if I had to abort our little one, who was conceived in such wonderful, genuine love?'

Holding her close to him again, Ewan murmured, 'Freda, I am assuming that you didn't tell Robin that I am the father of your baby?'

'No. I told him I got carried away in an on-board romance with Tommy Winters, and that we had parted and would not be meeting again.'

He sighed. 'All I am asking is that you tell Robin the truth, and ask him to let us marry.'

'Don't be ridiculous, Ewan!' Freda screamed, jumping back from him. 'That would mean my innocent children would grow up knowing that their true father was a monster! No! You already know, because I have repeatedly told you, that is a price too high and I will not have my children pay it. Now, you either agree to let things be and allow Robin to father the child, or I will abort it.'

Before shaking his head in utter defeat, Ewan opened his hands and gestured to Freda his resignation. All the while, his eyes implored her not to make him a stranger who his child would only see occasionally. He, like her, wished to be part of the child's life because he longed to have her – or at least part of her – with him always.

Guiltily aware of Ewan's distress and quandary, Freda wondered what she could do to lessen the impact of the nightmare he now found himself in – a nightmare from which he could not awaken. Crossing back to him, she placed her hands gently on his shoulders. 'Ewan, I am truly sorry that by loving you ... loving you so much that I ignored the danger and warning signs, I am ... I must ... please, Ewan, do not ask me to pay the very high price of sacrificing Jackie and Harry's happiness for our brief, intimate affair.'

He nodded to acknowledge that, as painful as it was, he would accede to her wishes. She wept, not only in relief but also for what might have been. Both of them were now awash with the memories of the utter joy of their romantic liaison.

'I don't suppose that before we part we could ... please, Freda, just once more?'

She was scared that if she did concede once more, it might be enough to send her resolve tumbling. The clock ticked by some agonising minutes as she deliberated. She shuddered. Why was it that she was torn between wishing she had never met Ewan, and yearning for more of him? She was also afraid of the deep sense of bleak loss that she knew she would feel when she finally removed him from her life. Then, to both of their surprise, she went over and switched off the front shop lights. Then, seeking his hand, she guided him into the back salon. As the door closed behind them, they were back on board the *Black Prince,* for the very last time.

Five months later, Freda was at her wits' end trying to control Autumn. The final straw came when one of Autumn's friends, Jeanie, came into the salon on Elm Row and asked if they could fit her in for a hairdo and makeover, as she hadn't the time to get to Frederick Street. Freda was tempted to say 'Definitely not!', but she knew that in doing so she would put further strain on her and Autumn's relationship.

Once the young lady had had all the most expensive and self-indulgent treats, she put on her coat and walked towards the door.

'Jeanie?' Freda called out to her.

'Oh, yes,' Jeanie replied, 'I am very pleased with the results of your staff.' She gave a little twirl so all could see just how good she looked.

'I know you are, but you still have to pay your bill.' Freda rang up the receipt and held it out to Jeanie.

'No, no,' replied Jeanie, 'I am one of Autumn's favourites. We do not pay for any hairdos, makeovers, manicures or massages. All that we have to do in payment is tell everyone that our wonderful appearance is down to us frequenting A Cut Above on Frederick Street.'

'That right? Well, let me tell you that my husband and I are running a business, not a charity! Here, take this bill and pay it, and from now on, even at the Frederick Street salon, you will be paying the going rate.'

Jeanie had the shop front door open now, but she did half turn to shout back to Freda, 'There is no way any of us could afford to have ourselves titivated up at A Cut Above prices! Besides, you can't ask me to pay.'

'I can't?'

'No. Autumn told me you are not a co-owner there so you have no authority. And what's more, she is going to make sure you jump before she gets her brother to ask you to leave.'

Before dumbfounded Freda could reply that Autumn was lying, the bell tinkled as the door slammed shut.

When Robin returned from London he was always in a jovial mood. However, when Freda informed him of Autumn's arrangement for her friends at Frederick Street, he was shocked. After mulling the problem over, he did as he always did and asked Freda what should be done.

'I have thought about it,' Freda said. 'I admit she is a very good receptionist, but we cannot afford to allow her to treat eight friends every week. Having said that, in no way do I think we should upset your mother by dismissing her, so we have to box clever.'

Robin smiled. 'And, dear Freda, how do you propose we do that?'

Freda hesitated, to give the impression that she was just thinking the matter through. In reality, she had already come up with the solution. 'Here, what do you think of this? You and I have trained up some exceptional hairdressers, and recently we have had some poached by our competitors. So, how about we select two of our up-and-coming stars, who are not only excelling in styling but also know how to count beans, and promote them to managers – one in Elm Row and one in Frederick Street.'

'But you and I do the managing.'

'Yes, and we are run ragged! And you – don't deny it – are already looking about for shops three and four.' She now looked him straight in the eye. 'You are also spending every second week in London now, so it makes sense to employ managers.'

He chortled, as he knew that what Freda had said made sense. However, what was she going to get out of the new arrangements? Gingerly, he asked, 'Does this mean that you will be able to take a back seat?'

Again Freda appeared to ponder, before answering, 'Robin, remember when I had the twins and I was so busy helping you with the new shop that I didn't get to spend precious time with them?' She ran her hands lovingly over her stomach. 'See, with this wee one, my last baby, I don't wish to repeat the mistakes I made with the twins. This time around I would like the time to enjoy the baby and appreciate every minute – time to find satisfaction in just being a mother.' Before Robin could respond, she quickly added, 'And before it is too late, I would like to have time – Mummy time – with Harry and Jackie.'

Her eyes were now pleading with Robin. He nodded, because he knew what she was saying. Yes, they had been so busy building up the business that they had lost track of what was really important in life – time with the children and with each other.

'So you will be leaving the business completely?' Robin asked.

'No, just drastically cutting back on the time I spend there. Don't worry, it will only be until the children have grown up and are making their own way in life.'

TWELVE

JUNE 1974

The sweltering sun was beating straight on to Freda's face, adding to her discomfort. All she wished to do was waddle her way out of the car park and into the Eastern General Hospital's maternity unit. Just then another agonising pain gripped her and she grabbed hold of Hannah's arm.

'Freda, please don't dig your nails into my arm like that!' Hannah gasped. 'My blouse is so thin that you are about to draw blood.'

'Look, I am in labour, not ecstasy! Surely you know how that feels.'

Hannah bit on her lip. 'No, I don't. And if anyone should know that I never will, it is you.'

Realising she had been crass and insensitive, Freda inhaled deeply. 'Sorry, Hannah. I know I should be screaming at Robin but he's on the

213

Edinburgh-bound train and I'll bet it doesn't get in until this is all over!'

'It's not his fault that he's not here, Freda. When he asked you yesterday if you thought that he should give London a miss this weekend you said that you thought you would be holding on for at least another two weeks.'

'Aye, I did think that, but how was I to know–' Freda stopped to audibly pant and moan – 'that the baby had ... other ... ideas.' Breathing heavily, she slumped against the wall for support. Not wishing to move from the wall, she said, 'Hannah, how selfish of me! I should have asked–' her voice was now at least three octaves louder and coming out in staccato – 'how is your new rooooooooomance going?'

'Like all the others he has moved on. Do you know, I think I would be judged as less of a freak by men if I had two heads!'

'Talking of heads, Hannah, I think the baby's head is near ... near ... nearly out!'

In desperation, Hannah looked down the long corridor and, to her relief, spotted a porter pushing a wheelchair with no one in it. 'Mister, mister, mister!' she cried, waving her hands and sprinting towards him, 'Please, my friend is about to give birth – can you help us?'

'Nae problem, lassie,' the jovial man replied. 'I wish I had a fiver for every baby that wanted to be born out here in the corridor.'

Leaving those words ringing in Hannah's ears, the porter quickly pushed the chair towards Freda. Soon, they were speeding towards the delivery room. Hannah held Freda's hand as the nursing sister examined Freda out in the corridor before saying, very quietly and calmly, 'Busy day today, so there is no room for you in the delivery room at the top of the corridor. I will just take you into this linen cupboard–'

'Take her into the linen cupboard?' Hannah interrupted. 'Look, whoever you are, my friend is of the opinion–'

The nurse pushed Freda into the cupboard and banged the door shut in Hannah's face, so the rest of her sentence was said to the door.

Ten minutes later, the sister emerged, pushing the wheelchair in which Freda was sitting. Hannah was gobsmacked, because Freda was openly crying as she looked down at the little bundle in her arms. The poor wee mite had come so quickly that the sister had just grabbed what was available to wrap her in, so she was swaddled in a National Health Service hand towel.

'Hannah, look at her. Isn't she just beautiful? Look at that cute little dimple in the middle of her chin!' Freda sobbed. 'Luckily the sister must have known that my baby was about to pop out when she pushed me into the cupboard.' The sister confirmed Freda's statement with a nod, and Freda continued, 'Know something, Hannah, that's what I'm going to call her – Poppy!'

Now it was Hannah's turn to weep. Yes, she did think that the tiny baby girl was beautiful, and she would have liked to take her into her arms. However, that possibility was put on hold when the sister said, addressing Freda's bundle, 'Right, my little friend, it's time to get you up to the labour suite for a wee wash!'

When Robin arrived at Freda's bedside two hours later, she was fast asleep. In order not to disturb her, he asked a nurse where his daughter was. 'In the nursery,' she replied, going to the door of the four-bed ward and pointing out the way.

Before going into the nursery, Robin looked through the room's glass window, noting that there were two other fathers and a couple of doting grannies already in the room admiring the rows of babies. He then decided to hang back, not because he thought that there were too many people there already, but because he did not wish to encounter one of the fathers.

By the time Robin got back to Freda's bedside, she was awake and sitting up, supported by pillows.

'You must have had a very easy time of it this time,' Robin teased, lifting her hand and kissing it.

'Easy time? Oh, no! If it had not been for a kind-hearted porter who got me into a wheelchair and a quick-thinking sister who bundled me into a linen cupboard, our baby daughter would have bounced off the floor and probably killed herself. But enough of that ... what do you think of her?'

'She is beautiful, just like her mum. Know something, her dad would not be able to deny her.'

Freda chuckled. 'Robin, don't be daft. Why would you wish to deny Poppy?'

'I will never deny her – I was thinking of her actual father.'

'But you have never met Tommy Winters, so how would you know what he looks like?'

'That's true, but I do know Ewan. And Freda, I also know you – I know you inside out.'

'What does that mean?'

'Just that when you told me that cock-and-bull story about how you threw all your propriety out of the cabin window and had a holiday romance with a complete stranger, I knew you were lying.' Freda squirmed, but Robin carried on. 'You see, I *know* you, and I realised that you must know the father of your baby very well, because you would not have done what you did unless you loved him, and loved him very much. I just couldn't figure out who it was, until I stood looking in at the nursery window and there, gazing lovingly down at Poppy, was Ewan.'

'What?' screeched Freda, sitting bolt upright and grabbing for Robin's hand. 'He promised me, he did!'

'Calm yourself Freda, people are looking at us. Now, all I wish to know is...' He hesitated and gulped, 'Are you and Ewan thinking of setting up home together, or will it be like Billy and I?'

'Neither. He and I parted on the journey home and he has agreed not to force any change in our relationship. Why he came today, I do not know. Nor do I know who alerted him.' She looked down at the counterpane bedspread as she was about to lie to Robin and she did not want him to see it in her eyes. 'Robin, I promise that since the cruise I have not been alone with him.'

'Oh Freda, I am so relieved that I won't be losing you or my children. Our twins mean so much to me. I am their father. I walked the floor with them when they were teething. I read a bedtime story to them every night I am at home. I am striving to build up our business so that they will never want for anything. And all that is not only for them, but for you too. Honestly, I am afraid to think of what life would be like for me without my family.'

'You never will be without us.' Freda looked him in the eyes again. 'The children are my first priority and therefore must be protected. For them, I will sacrifice anything – and for you too, Robin. Always you have been my best friend, the one person I could depend on when I was at my lowest ebb. Never will I leave you. Until death do us part. I promised you that and I meant it.'

Before Robin and Freda could say anything further, Hannah breezed in with a bouquet of flowers. 'Nice timing,' she said to Robin. 'Here, let me hand these flowers to Freda and then I will be able to hug the proud father.'

When Hannah released Robin from her bear hug, she babbled, 'Have you seen your pretty daughter? What do you think of the cute little dimple in the middle of her chin?'

Freda and Robin exchanged a worried glance. Of course, thought Freda, when Robin looked at Poppy he would also have noticed the tell-tale dimple and known for certain that Ewan was her father. Now, the problem was this: would any-body else make the connection?

Unaware of Robin and Freda's dilemma, Hannah blundered on, 'Here, see, when I was leaving today, I bumped into Ewan. He told me he was visiting his uncle in ENT, and I was just so full of the baby that I told him you were on the maternity ward and that you had just given birth to a daughter. He seemed to get a bit emotional ... I thought that was strange, him being a doctor, but I think he must have been upset about his uncle. Did he visit you on his way out?'

Freda shook her head. 'No,' was her emphatic response. 'Well, if he did, I was asleep.'

Freda and the baby had been home for two days when Ewan called in to see them. Luckily, it was Freda's mother's day off, and she had agreed to do some shopping for Freda. Of course, Ellen could only do that if she got to walk out with the baby in her new, top-of-the-range, coach-built, forest-green Marmet pram...

Before Ewan was seated, Freda decided that she had to grant him no quarter. 'What on earth did you think that you were doing, going into the nursery to look at Poppy?'

'Surely I would be less than human if I found out that my daughter had just been born but simply walked on by because I did not think enough of her to go and visit her?'

'Now, let's get this clear. From here on out, walk on by is exactly what you will do. You promised, and you knew the price that had to be paid when you made that promise. All I am asking is that you keep to it.'

He looked at her from the chair he had sat himself down on. Motherhood had, in his opinion, enhanced her attraction. All he wanted was to be with the woman he loved and who had carried his child, yet here she was slamming the door shut on his dreams again.

219

'Are you aware that Robin saw you in the hospital? Then, when he looked at Poppy and saw her little dimple, he immediately twigged that you were her father? Ewan, can't you see that now we won't even be able to meet up socially? That would be too cruel to Robin, who will always be wondering if I am about to run off with you.'

'Okay, I concede, but surely you will let me hold her today. Freda, please. Let me hold her just once.'

Surging emotion was weakening her determination. 'My mum has taken her out. I don't expect them back for at least an hour.'

'I could wait. I don't mind doing that.'

'But I mind.' Watching Ewan's face drop, Freda knew that not letting him hold his daughter was a step too far. Awash with guilt, she softened. 'She's going to be christened soon. I will invite you, along with Angela, to that occasion, and I will ensure then that you are able to hold her.'

She accepted that the arrangement that she had agreed to would be fraught with danger. For a moment, panic surged within her. Poppy looked so much like Ewan and she wondered just when others would see his features reflected in Poppy's. It was as if Poppy was defying Freda and had deliberately chosen to have the same light, soft, curly hair as her father. And why did she also have to have his dancing, bewitching eyes? Whenever those eyes looked at her, Freda was filled with so much love and emotion. However, the biggest giveaway of Poppy's true paternity, the one that Freda was sure people would notice, was the tantalising dimple in the centre of Poppy's chin.

THIRTEEN

JUNE 1975

From the day that Poppy arrived home from the maternity unit, Harry was besotted with her. Up until then, he had wanted to be a vet and to look after sick animals, but when he held Poppy in his arms for the first time, he announced that he was now going to be a baby doctor and hand out babies to all who wished for one. This being the case, Poppy's first birthday was a big event for him.

He asked everybody he knew personally to the party. Much to the disquiet of Robin, he even invited a smelly old tramp that seemed keen to start up a friendship with him. When Robin heard about this, he decided that he would go and speak to the man and, in the nicest possible way, withdraw the invitation.

Gathering up the children, Robin said, 'Right, kids – and you too, Jet – let's go and feed the ducks.'

When they got to the park, Harry allowed Jet off the lead and she bounded towards the seat where the old man was sitting. However, when the tramp saw that Harry was not on his own, as he usually was when he was walking Jet after school, he hurriedly got up from the bench and started to hobble away.

'Wait a minute, I want to talk to you!' Robin called out. The man looked furtively about and continued to attempt to put space between Robin and himself.

As luck would have it, the old man was not very steady on his feet and as he tried to speedily escape, he toppled over. Robin called out to Jackie to come and take charge of Poppy, who was strapped into her go car. He was then in a position to go over and assist the prostrate man. As he bent over to haul the vagrant to his feet, the man turned to face him. Robin reeled back and, without even thinking, rolled his right fist into a ball. Fortunately, before he could lash out at the man, he heard himself stutter, 'What in the name of heavens are you doing here? I thought you were long gone.'

The man, although tattered, still had some spirit. 'Aye, you hoped that when you dumped me bleeding and barely conscious on the Restalrig Circus allotment rubbish heap that would be the end of me. Aye, I bet that you thought that I had died there or, more likely, you hoped I had. But, sonny boy, I'm no' deid yet and I won't be for four months. Four months I hae to get even wi you aw.'

'Is this the reason you have made friends with my boy?'

'Aye, and after I met him and he told me how old he was I put two and two the gether – I reckon he's no' your boy but mine!'

'No, he's not,' Robin said sharply, 'Do you hear me? He is *not*.'

'That right? Well, tell you what, how about I put my hand up to smashing and battering your wife?' The man hesitated.

Robin's anger was growing out of control and he had the desire to finish off the job that Ellen had started when she stuck a knife in Drew's back. That awful night, when Ellen had arrived home and found Drew attacking Freda, she had lifted the knife and tried to stop him from harming her daughter. It was true that when Freda's grandfather had arrived at the house, he had decided that Drew deserved no compassion or treatment; instead, he should be dumped on the rubbish heap and left to sort himself out, or at least left for nature to decide what his fate should be. Robin remembered all too well how Grandad Jack, Stuart and himself had been outraged at what they found when they arrived at the house. They were all so sorry that they were too late ... too late to rescue Freda.

Robin was brought back to the present by Drew's voice, which was full of amusement. 'I think the kid is definitely mine. If you want to keep my mouth shut about that, you'll need to pay me, and pay me handsomely.'

'Pay you? Are you saying that after what you did to my wife, you want me to pay you? You know what, get lost.'

'Well, if you want me to do that, I could. You see, I only have four months left and I think I should have a wee bit of luxury. Now, if you cannae see your way to providing that luxury, then maybe I could start to be a storyteller.'

'Do you think you can blackmail me?'

'Naw. Just wanting what is my due. You unfeeling sods dumped me like a piece of shit and you thought – no, you bloody hoped – that I would die, but I didnae. And either my beloved wife or bloody stepdaughter stuck a knife in me.' Drew stopped to inhale some deep breaths. 'Bloody agony I suffered with that. Think they call it attempted murder. But, Mr Big Shot, the real reason that I've come is that I want to see my Susan again.' He sniffed before roughly wiping his nose with the back of his hand. 'My Susan is the one good thing that I did in my life... At least, that was what I believed until I saw Harry and his sister. So, I need dosh to get myself cleaned up so I can approach my lassie. I also need it because I want to die in a bed wi' clean sheets.'

Robin took time to answer Drew. He knew he must do what was best. Drew was saying that he only had four months to live, so it wouldn't take long to pay him off. But Drew had always been a liar. Robin shook his head then took a long, hard look at Drew. 'Okay,' he said, 'the money you will get. I will see to that. You can see Susan, but you will not say who you are. She thinks that you went to Amsterdam and got lost, so let her go on thinking that.' He paused to silently contemplate how he would pass the money over. His quick thinking came into play and he said, 'I will meet you on Thursday evening in the Golf Tavern on Duke Street.' He looked at Drew's ragged, filthy clothes before fishing for his wallet. He took out some notes, which he then pushed into Drew's hand. 'Get yourself tidied up or the barman at the Golf won't let you in. Now, after you have been paid off, you get yourself sorted out. Then, and only then, will I allow you to see Susan.' Wagging his finger and speaking through gritted teeth, Robin hissed, 'Finally, don't ever, ever come into this park again. If you dare to speak to Harry again, I will finish the job that Ellen managed to botch. Believe me, that is not a threat ... it's a promise.'

Poppy's birthday party was a joyous affair. Harry helped her blow out the big solitary candle on her cake. Jackie, who loved Poppy when she had her to herself but was a bit put out when everybody's attention was on Poppy and not her, hoped that Poppy would blow herself away too.

Once Angela had started to organise the children's games, Robin took the opportunity to get Ewan to himself. As soon as he felt that he had distanced himself and Ewan from earshot, he placed his arm on Ewan's arm. 'Ewan, I need to talk to you about something. Something I require your help with.'

Alarmed, Ewan quickly placed his hand on Robin's shoulder. 'For heaven's sake, don't tell me there's something wrong with Poppy or Freda?'

'No. Calm yourself and hear me out.' Robin then relayed in detail his meeting with Drew. At the end of the story, he looked at Ewan imploringly. 'Ewan, what I am wondering is this: how do I find out whether he is actually at death's door, or just pulling a fast one?'

Ewan pondered. 'Medical records are highly confidential, so no one is going to give you the information you require. But all is not lost. Here is what I propose: I will go into the Golf Tavern at the back of six, and try and engage...' He stopped to exhale a few short breaths before saying, 'I will try and engage the ... whatever-he-is in conversation, whilst I also attempt to assess him clinically. It won't be easy, as I can hardly ask him to show me his X-rays or let me sound his chest, but I should be able to judge if he is as bad as he claims.'

Relief seeped into Robin. He knew that Ewan was asking him to delay his arrival so that he would have time not only to appraise Drew, but also to gain his confidence. Then, when Drew became fretful and agitated by Robin's late arrival, Ewan hoped that he would be more likely to blurt out his anxieties and concerns.

It was always a mystery to Robin that when he wished to draw large sums of money out of the bank and it was not payday, the cashier always had the temerity to ask what he was going to do with the money. Normally, he would just smile and say, 'Got to keep my lovers in the style they have become accustomed to!' but today he felt anxious and annoyed so he quipped, 'No problem about this three thousand pounds; it is to pay a hit man to bump off a nosy bank teller.'

Whilst it was easy to retort to a cashier's question, Robin knew that it would be harder to convince Freda, who meticulously checked the bank accounts, that there was an acceptable reason for such a large withdrawal – he would have to come up with some kind of cock-and-bull story. After all, Freda knew that three thousand pounds per annum was the average wage that they paid their fully-qualified hairdressers. Additionally, it was more than enough for a deposit on a house. Yes, there was no way he would get it past

Freda, but he knew it was a risk he must take.

Later on in the day, on that important Thursday, Robin made his way to the Golf Tavern, acutely aware of the envelopes of cash he was carrying. The Golf Tavern was situated on busy Duke Street in Leith – nowhere near a golf course. It was, however, named the Golf Tavern in memory of 'gowff' being played on a five-hole course on Leith Links in the sixteenth century.

When Robin chose the Golf Tavern for his meeting with Drew he was aware of the history of golf in Leith but it was of no importance to him. No, Robin had decided on this particular hostelry for his meeting with Drew because it was comfortable and well managed.

When the meeting was finally over, Robin felt as tight as a drum. He had just watched Drew stuff two large envelopes containing three thousand pounds into his second-hand Burberry coat and slink out of the Golf Tavern. The door had just closed behind him when Ewan rose up from an adjoining table and plonked himself down opposite Robin.

'Right,' Robin began, rubbing his hands together in an effort to appear completely in control. 'What did you manage to find out?'

'Hmm,' Ewan replied, as he tried to work out just what he should impart to Robin. 'He is a very sick man. I would not expect him to live another two months, never mind–'

'Two months?' Robin expostulated. At the sound of this loud outburst, the pub's other customers fell silent and turned to stare at Robin and Ewan. Robin, undeterred by the unwanted attention, continued in a subdued tone, 'But you knew I was going to pay him off, so why didn't you signal to me to just hand over one envelope?'

'How much did you give him?'

Gulping, Robin played with a beer mat and whispered, 'Three thousand pounds!'

'Tell me you didn't?'

'Ewan, you are supposed to be cleverer than me – or so I thought! – but right now you are being a ninny. Firstly, you didn't give me a signal about Drew meeting his maker sooner than he had said, and now you are laughing at me! You can sneer, but in good faith I gave him what I thought he would need to get himself looked after for four months or so.'

'He's an alcoholic. You should have arranged to pay him a little each week.'

Looking up at the ceiling, Robin muttered, 'Dear Lord, give me patience.'

'What's done is done. Now, from what I understand, he has pancreatic cancer and needs palliative care.'

'What exactly does that mean?'

'I have told him that I will try to get him admitted to Corstorphine Hospital.' Ewan stopped to purse his lips.

'Unfortunately, that is the best I will be able to arrange for him. Pity he needs care now. If only he could have hung on until next year...'

'Why?' exclaimed Robin.

'I've heard that next year there are plans to build a hospice called St Columba's, similar to the ones down in London.

'Ewan, save me your compassion for him and

just get down to brass tacks.'

'As I've said, the man is dying. He will not have an easy death, which is why I am going to try to make things as comfortable for him as I possibly can.'

'Well, pardon me if I don't cry for him. You see, whatever he has to suffer will never be punishment enough for what he did to Freda.'

'Robin, please tell me that you do not mean that.'

'Oh but I bloody do. You see, you might have taken a Hippocratic oath to treat and feel sorrow for the likes of him, but you didn't see what he did to Freda so don't you dare try and make me feel guilty about how I feel about him.'

'Point taken. But Robin, don't forget that despite all that Freda suffered, she did give birth to the children. What would your life – and indeed Freda's – be like without them? I hated him at first too, but my time as a doctor has taught me that we must try to show compassion and forgiveness to our fellow men.'

Robin fell forward. As his head slumped onto the table he muttered, 'Dear God in heaven, I plead again for patience, because I don't know what planet he's from!'

Ignoring Robin's show of frustration, Ewan continued, 'Now, here is what I think should be done. I will look after Mr Black. By next week I should have him admitted to hospital. He wishes to see Susan, so I will approach her.'

'No, you won't.'

'Yes, I will. Then, when the end comes, I will make his funeral arrangements and try and retrieve as much of your money as I can. I will, of course, keep you up to date with what is happening.'

'Don't bother,' Robin huffed. He looked at Ewan's pint, which remained untouched because Ewan was not a beer drinker and had only ordered it so that he could socialise with Drew. 'Would you like a double dram? Because I sure could use one!'

Ewan nodded. 'Robin, try and understand how difficult it is for Drew Black to not be on good terms with Susan.'

Robin nodded, but said nothing. He knew that Ewan was reminding him how difficult it was for him not to hear Poppy say, 'Daddy, Daddy, my Daddy.'

Five weeks later, Ewan entered the Golf Tavern to find that Robin was already seated at a table, with a half pint of McEwan's Best and a double malt whisky in front of him.

As he sat down, Ewan lifted the whisky and sniffed. 'Celebrating, are we? I think we must be because unless I'm mistaken, this wee goldie is a Glenmorangie.'

'Aye, it is, and don't drink it over in the one gulp, because it's a double.'

'A double?'

'Yes. I thought that I should buy you a dram of Scotland's finest malt whisky as a thank you.'

Swirling the liquid around in the glass and inhaling again, Ewan said, 'I suppose you mean for yesterday?'

'Yes. I was tied up in Glasgow and I didn't know until I arrived home that Freda had gone to the funeral.'

Ewan nodded. 'Look, after I spoke to Susan – and, before you say anything, I only gave her the facts about Drew – I admit that I did suggest that she go and see him in hospital, and let him pass in peace. She decided that she wished to do that. I asked her not to tell her mother and, more importantly, Freda. How was I to know she would go and get them into a family circle? I didn't think that Ellen would want to go with Susan, even to support her. It was also reasonable to expect that Freda wouldn't go within a mile of Drew while he was still breathing. But, yesterday, Freda, Ellen and Susan huddled together in the cloister chapel and saw him off.'

Slurping from his half pint, Robin muttered, 'Into hell's fires, I hope.'

'Robin, don't scowl like that. He was Susan's father. No matter what he was guilty of, nothing could change that, nor the fact that she loved him.'

Time passed and they both sipped from the glasses. 'Tell you something though,' Ewan mused, 'I could not fathom why Freda seemed so *happy* when she found out that Drew had survived ... it was as if a weight had been lifted from her.'

A wicked little smile came to Robin's face. He was remembering a time when he and Freda had discussed Drew surfacing again. She had grabbed at her cheeks with both hands and muttered, 'Oh Robin, since that night I have been so worried that his body would turn up – I was convinced that my mum or I had killed him! Oh, isn't it just great that even though we wished him dead that night God let Drew live?'

'Robin, there's no hurry, but when you get down to earth again,' Ewan said, breaking into Robin's thoughts, 'I have something else to tell you.'

Robin stopped his daydreaming and focused on Ewan. 'It can't be that he didn't leave enough to pay for his funeral?'

'No. To be truthful, he didn't really get around to spending much of your money. Five hundred he gave to Susan–'

'Aye, I know that, and she is going to book a sunshine break on the Costa Brava for her and Ellen. Costa Brava ... and neither of them know that it's me that's bankrolling their jaunt!'

'Then there were the funeral costs, which he paid in advance. Now, before you say anything, he selected the coffin. He thought that as he never had the best in life, he should have the very best in death. Pity there was only five of us to see him go in such opulence.'

Looking happy and expectant, Robin chirped, 'So, you managed to salvage at least two thousand pounds of my money for me?'

'Not exactly.'

Robin stood up and made a grab for Ewan's tie. He screeched, 'Just what do you mean by "not exactly"?'

Pushing Robin back down, Ewan said quietly, 'You remember how I told you that we are hoping to have a St Columba's Hospice up and running next year? Down Trinity way, it is going to be–'

'So?'

'Robin, try and understand.'

'Understand what?'

'Drew was so pleased with the nursing care that

232

he received at Corstorphine. Every single member of staff was so good to him and they kept him free of pain. So when he was told that they were trying to raise funds to build and equip the new hospice–'

'Don't tell me. I am not hearing right, am I?'

'Yes, you are. You see, Robin, Drew's dying wish was to donate all that was left in the bags you gave him to St Columba's Hospice, to help them start up!'

FOURTEEN

OCTOBER 1976

October is one of the months in the year when there is still heat in the sun but you are aware, as the days grow shorter and the nights darker and longer, that the chill of winter is just around the corner.

However, not even the approaching winter could dampen the enthusiasm of Freda, Hannah and the children as they strolled along the beach at good old Portobello. The sun was high in the sky and the clear, buoyant surf seemed to fill them with energy.

As was usual now, Hannah spent every Saturday with Freda and the children. This arrangement was not planned; it just seemed to happen. Freda was well aware that because she had been there when Freda went into labour with Poppy, Han-

233

nah felt that she had the right to act as Poppy's surrogate mother – even when Freda was there. Furthermore, without her saying so, Freda knew that Hannah had given up on finding a suitable man who would wish to marry her. It is true that in life we sometimes have to stand back and watch family members or friends suffering. Freda had always felt Hannah's anguish. If she could have, she would have waved a wand and given Hannah the means to have a child and the opportunity to have a loving, meaningful relationship with a man. She had lost count of the number of times she had wished that she could purchase a uterus for Hannah. However, whilst this expenditure was within Freda's means now, medical science was not quite that advanced – yet.

Jet made a beeline for the crashing waves and Harry pursued her. Then, as she felt that she should be wherever Harry was, Poppy also started for the shoreline.

Hannah and Freda called out in unison, 'Harry, Poppy, come back! The sea is too rough for paddling in today.' Unfortunately, their words were hushed by the howling of the wind, which had grown energised. Grabbing each other's hands, Freda and Hannah started to run after the children.

Letting go of Hannah's hand, Freda stopped. She was staring at Poppy, who had turned and was now racing towards a silhouette that had called out to her. As the sun was blinding her, Freda was not sure who this person was – although she did think it was a man. Poppy, on the other hand, seemed to know the person; she was obviously eager to go towards them. Sheer panic gripped Freda. Someone was going to steal her child!

Poppy was just a few yards from the person when he leapt forward and scooped her up into his arms. 'You, you, you!' Freda thought she heard Poppy chant. Then, when she became aware who the person was, Freda drew up abruptly. Her panic turned to anger. Why was it, she thought, that Poppy was so attracted to Ewan? Whenever he was in their company she would scramble up onto his knees and scrunch up her little body in delight. His name was one of the first that she tried to say. It was her shortening of 'Ewan' to 'Ewe' that made Freda realise that, unconsciously, Poppy knew that Ewan was more than the 'uncle' she saw from time to time.

Ewan was now facing Freda. She spoke first, 'Now, please do not insult my intelligence and say that you thought you would go and have a wander on the beach and – lo and behold! – you bumped into us by accident!'

'No,' Ewan replied. 'My neighbour isn't well and, as Saturday is a day off for me, I offered to walk his dog.'

It was then that Freda noticed a huge, ugly, shaggy animal bounding towards her. Before the beast had even leapt at her, she had started to topple over. Rolling in the wet sand, Freda tried to distance herself from what she thought could be a lion. Gasping, she mumbled, 'Good grief, what kind of an animal is this? Is it a lion or something like that?'

'A lion! Don't be ridiculous. He's a Leonberger Mastiff, and the only danger you face is being

235

licked to death!'

Freda was not amused. Getting to her feet, she advanced towards Ewan. 'Is that right? Well, let me tell you that I am not amused and I do not buy your cock-and-bull story.' She huffed and puffed, starting to prod Ewan's shoulder with her right index finger. Then, as sheer, uncontrollable frustration bubbled, she spat, 'You promised that you would not seek Poppy out and–' Hannah, who was pulling Jackie and Harry along by the hand, was now within earshot, so Freda's final words had to be choked back.

Ignoring Freda's hostility, Ewan smiled at Jackie and Harry. 'No need to be afraid. He's a friendly dog. He doesn't know his own strength, so he likes throwing his weight about.' Ewan bent down to clap the beast on the back. 'Harry, his name is Napoleon.'

Looking askance at the dog, Hannah said, 'Well, to be truthful, Ewan, if *I* saw him bounding towards me I would just freeze, and I am not a child.'

'Come on now, Hannah, are you really saying that you would be scared of this pussycat?' Ewan teased, ruffling the dog's coat again.

Meanwhile, Freda's thoughts were in turmoil. To be truthful, it was not only Poppy who wished to hurl herself into Ewan's arms. It was Freda too. She knew that she had to keep him at a safe distance. Whenever she was close to him, she wished that she had never met him yet she was always unprepared for the sense of loss she experienced when she did not see him. Their affair had been brief – too brief – and yet the consequences would live with them forever, through Poppy.

'Right,' Freda heard herself say, after deciding that she required some distance between herself and Ewan, 'we have to get going. Daddy and I have to leave at six o'clock for Glasgow, and we won't be back until lunchtime tomorrow.' Feeling it was necessary to explain, she quickly added, 'It is the Scottish Hairdressers' Association annual dinner tonight. Robin will have a couple of social refreshments, so he may be over the drink-driving limit and I do not like driving in the dark.'

Ewan was now looking at Hannah. 'So Hannah, I take it you are childminding?'

'Yes!' Hannah squealed, hunching her shoulders in delight. 'And, as Freda just said, overnight, too!'

'Would you like a hand?' Ewan asked. 'I will be at a loose end once I have taken Napoleon back to his master.'

Hannah beamed and clapped her hands. 'That would be just super.'

'Hope you like macaroni cheese, because that's what Mum has made for our tea!' Harry piped up.

'Sure do, Harry,' Ewan replied. 'Know something, I can never say no to a plate of macaroni cheese.'

Ewan wished that the evening would go on forever. He loved being 'Dad'. He helped his two-year-old daughter feed herself before bath time, which was an hour of laughing and splashing that he hoped would never end. It was such a privilege to have Poppy all to himself that he was loath to take her out of the bath.

Hannah called out, 'For goodness sake, Ewan, take Poppy out of the bath! The twins have to get washed too and it is now eight o'clock. Wrap Poppy in a bath towel, then top up the bath with some hot water and throw Harry in.'

'What about Jackie? Shall I put her in too?'

'No. Three weeks ago, Jackie decided that she likes clean water. Now she washes herself – with the door shut and locked, of course!'

By nine o'clock, the children were in bed. Ewan had read a bedtime story to Poppy, who fell asleep before the end. Then it was Harry's turn, and he insisted that his story was an animal tale. Naturally Jackie decided that, as she was ever so grown up, she would read Enid Blyton's *Famous Five* books to herself.

Once Jet was positioned in the hallway, guarding the bedroom doors, Hannah felt it was time for a well-earned breather.

'Can I make you some tea and toast before you go?' Hannah asked Ewan.

'Pushing me out the door, are you?'

'No, but I do know that you only came to be with...' She nearly said Poppy, but caught herself at the last moment and instead added diplomatically, 'The children. Now that they are asleep, I am going to have a bath and curl up on the couch and watch–' she thought for a minute – *'The Bionic Woman*, because one day I hope to become one!'

Ewan laughed. 'Hannah, straight up, you are so good with Freda's children – have you never thought of marrying and having kids of your own?'

Hannah did not wish to answer this question,

so she sidestepped it. 'Well, Ewan, as you are so hooked on playing "Daddy", why don't you put an end to Angela's agony and get married and have your own wee ones?'

A long, uneasy silence fell between them. It was then that Ewan remembered what Freda had confided to him about Hannah not being able to have any children of her own. He cringed because in no way had he meant to hurt or embarrass Hannah. He was just about to apologise to her when the doorbell shrilled, startling both of them.

Rising, Hannah said, 'It can't be Ellen – she goes to the British Legion Club on a Saturday night and that goes on at least until midnight.' She went to the window and opened the curtains to look at the doorstep. 'Oh bother, it's the police. Bet you that one of the shops has been broken into!'

On hearing Hannah say 'police', Ewan stepped out of the room to open the outside door.

'Sorry to bother you, sir,' the male officer said, 'but is this the home of Robin and Freda Dalgleish?'

'Yes, but they are attending a function in Glasgow tonight... Am I able to assist you?'

'Could we come in?' the female officer asked.

'Certainly.' Ewan led the two officers into the lounge.

Without any prelims, the female officer said, 'I am WPC Shona Mackay of Lothian and Borders Police, and my colleague is Sergeant Green.'

Hannah was now wary. She knew that there were very few female officers in the force, and they were usually restricted to dealing with shoplifting, child abuse and the delivery of bad news.

'And you are?' WPC Mackay was looking questioningly at Hannah and Ewan.

'I am Hannah Lindsey and my friend here is Dr–' she thought that she should emphasise that Ewan was a doctor – 'Ewan Gibson. We are childminding this evening... Well, to be correct, *I* am childminding. Ewan is about to go home.'

The sergeant now took over. 'The children are in bed?'

'Yes... What is this all about?'

'How old are they?' the sergeant continued, ignoring Hannah's question.

'Harry and Jackie are nine years old. Poppy turned two in the summer.'

'Are you saying that Harry and Jackie are both nine years of age?' the female officer enquired.

'They are twins,' retorted Hannah.

The sergeant gave the WPC a warning glare. 'Look, Miss,' he said to Hannah. 'I have to be sure we are at the correct address, because we have very bad news to deliver.'

Before the sergeant could go on, Hannah rose from the couch. She heard herself scream, 'What do you mean?' She was now panicking. 'Ewan, ask this man to stop beating about the bush and tell us exactly why he is here!' she cried.

Ewan went over and sat Hannah down again. 'There, there, Hannah. Just breathe. Deep breaths.' He then looked imploringly at the sergeant.

'Sir,' the sergeant said quietly, 'I am very sorry, but there has been a major road accident on the Edinburgh to Glasgow road, just at the junction of Harthill.'

240

Hannah was now pulling at Ewan's shirtsleeve. 'Is he saying that Freda and Robin have been hurt and are now in hospital?'

Ewan looked directly at the sergeant, who was now just shaking his head. Taking hold of Hannah's two hands, Ewan squeezed her fingers tightly. 'I think what the sergeant is trying to say is that it is more serious than that.'

Hannah's tormented gaze was now on the WPC, silently imploring her to deny what Ewan was saying.

'Sorry, Miss,' the WPC began, 'the driver of a lorry carrying a skip lost control, and he veered into the other side of the road... No motor car, not even a brand new Cortina Mark IV, would have stood a chance.'

Gulping, Ewan asked, 'Were they both...?'

The sergeant nodded. 'It would have been instantaneous... I do not know if it is of any comfort to you, but they would not have felt a thing.'

Nothing except blind terror, Ewan thought, when they realised that they were leaving their children behind.

'Are their parents still alive?' the sergeant then asked. Nodding, Ewan gave him their details. The sergeant and the WPC then got up to leave, to go and inform Ellen, Moira and Stevie of the sad news.

In the hall, the sergeant turned to Ewan and Hannah and said, 'I don't know if this will mean anything to you, but when the emergency services got to the lady they noticed that at the moment of impact she must have raised her left hand to her right shoulder in a sort of salute.'

241

Hannah turned away from the officers. She knew that Freda must have thought of her precious dad in her final moments. Well, who was to say that he hadn't come to escort her to the world beyond?

When the officers closed the door behind them, Ewan fell against it. His whole body shook with sobs. Was ten days really all he was ever to have with the one woman he worshipped? Hannah didn't hear his anguish for she was too absorbed in her own pain, her body convulsing with grief. Freda had been her confidante. Without her, life had lost all its sweetness.

The rest of the night would always remain a mystery to Hannah. She knew that Freda's mother, Ellen, arrived, accompanied by her son, Stuart. Moira and Stevie followed a few minutes later. They were all in a state of shock, babbling incoherently. This was no wonder; Hannah couldn't even begin to imagine how they felt about the sudden loss of Robin and Freda. It was not until someone suggested that the children should be awakened and told of the accident that Hannah pulled herself together. She was adamant that the children should be left to sleep until the morning. Thankfully, Ewan agreed with her. Their next problem, as they saw it, was what would they tell Poppy? She was only two years old and would not understand. Shaking his head, Ewan declared that, should it be necessary, he would explain to her that Mummy and Daddy loved her very much but had to go away.

Before breakfast, Harry and Jackie were told about the accident. Sidling over to sit beside Hannah, Harry reached for her hand and mumbled through his tears, 'Please, Aunty Hannah, tell me that it wasn't too sore for them?'

Taking him up on her knees, Hannah replied, 'No. They didn't feel a thing.'

'And what is going to happen to us? Poppy is only two and too wee to go into a home.'

'Darling, the three of you will not be parted. Believe me, there is no way that any one of you will end up in care.' She then sat Harry further up on her knee, turning him around so that he could see his grandparents, uncles and aunts. 'Look at all these people. They will all be fighting to get custody of you. I promise that you will stay in your home here, go to the same school and have your same pals. We all love you and we will do our best for you.'

Poppy was sitting on Ewan's knee, unconcerned and enjoying seeing all the people in her home. However, it was as if she knew that Harry needed comfort. 'Harry,' she cooed, stretching out her arms to him, 'come here!'

Once Harry was settled beside Poppy on Ewan's knees, Hannah looked about for Jackie. She was surprised to find that Jackie had gone into the garden.

Jackie was sat on a bench, her shoulders hunched and her arms wrapped around her knees. Hannah approached quietly and sat down on the hard bench beside her.

'Jackie,' she began softly, 'how are you?'

'I want my mummy. And if I can't have her, I want to run and run and run away.'

Hannah was stunned; she just didn't know

what to say. Thankfully, Angela arrived. She had come out into the garden seeking Hannah, but she went over to Jackie and encircled her in her arms. 'It's all right to cry,' she said. 'You have a right to say that it is not fair. I know that you are worried, but we will all be here for you until things get sorted out.'

Jackie slumped against Angela. The sounds of the birds singing in the garden were drowned out by her heart-rending cries.

Angela had just got Jackie composed when Ewan came out of the house. He felt that the children needed a break from all the grief, so he suggested taking them over to the park.

Ewan and the children had just departed when Angela turned to Hannah. 'I can't imagine how you are feeling,' she said. 'You and Freda had such a special relationship. You will never know how much I envied that – how much I wished I could have been included.'

Hannah looked startled. 'But you could have been. You were the one who made us feel second class. You had everything–'

'Everything? How wrong you are! I spent my life pursuing an impossible dream. Do you know that it was only recently that I – fool that I am – accepted that I could never replace Freda? He will love her always.' Angela shrugged. 'Do you know what I would have given to have been able to talk to you or Freda about my hopes, my secrets, my disappointments...? But you were a duo. I was always kept at arm's length.'

'Oh Angela, we don't ... I mean, we didn't mean to shut you out. You always seemed to know where you were going and how you were going to get there... You made Freda and I feel like we were not in your league.'

'You were both also so lucky to have your mums.'

'But you seem to be so happy with Ewan's mother?'

'Yes, she likes me and I am her first choice for Ewan but that will never be.'

'I think you could be wrong, Angela. Freda being–' Hannah gulped – 'killed changes everything. It is true that he loved her, but it was always a non-starter. She would never have left Robin or–' Hannah stopped abruptly. She must never, ever tell anyone about the children's parentage; Freda had sworn her to secrecy. 'Look,' she continued, 'you are clever and attractive, and he will turn to you. Okay, you will have to accept that you are not his first choice or the love of his life, but would that not be a price worth paying?' She hesitated. Then, looking dreamy and faraway, she added, 'Angela, the cost is of no consequence when it means you achieve your dream.' Angela nodded. Hannah linked her arm through Angela's, before saying, 'And let me add, there is a vacancy in the friendship department and I would like to offer you the job.'

Ewan had just reached the top of Marionville Crescent when he heard Ellen call out, 'Ewan, wait for me! I need to get some fresh air too.'

Naturally, once they were inside the park gates, the children scampered off towards the duck pond.

'Ellen,' Ewan said, once he was sure that the children were out of earshot, 'I am so very sorry about what has happened.'

'Me too.'

'Last night I got to thinking about what would happen to the children and I just want to say ... I will be asking for custody of Poppy.'

'Just Poppy?'

'Well, I just thought that as the twins are older, you could probably care for them.'

'I could. And by the way, no one will need to support them financially – the family salons will more than provide for all their needs. At the present time, there are able people in place to manage the business side of things, but someday one or all of them may wish to be involved. They have been left well provided for.'

'I accept that, but I am thinking of Poppy's emotional needs...'

Ellen stopped. Before she answered, she looked towards her scampering grandchildren. 'Ewan,' she began, 'first things first. We must get through the funerals. They will be hard to cope with. Then, and only then, will we be able to access Freda and Robin's wills.'

'They made wills? Did they expect something to happen?'

'No. But Freda was very young when she lost her dad and I know that some things that happened after caused her much anguish and regret. She wanted to be prepared. So Ewan, there are wills, and the solicitors at the foot of Leith Walk are already–'

'Beveridge and Kellas?'

'Yes. Anyway, the wills will be watertight. Freda and Robin will have named a guardian for their children, and soon he or she will be appointed.'

'But if you get custody, you could–'

'No, Ewan, there is no way that Freda left the guardianship of her children to me. Sorry son, but like me you'll just have to hope that the guardian is someone you can get along with.'

'But I am Poppy's biological father!'

'Are you?' Ellen chuckled. 'That may be so but, until the new test comes into being, who else's word do we have for that?'

FIFTEEN

JULY 1979

The first Saturday in July signalled the start of the Edinburgh trades holidays, a favourite time for weddings. It was therefore no surprise that thirty-two-year-old Angela McDonald decided that Saturday, 7 July 1979 would be her long-anticipated wedding day.

Angela knew that most people would have expected her to purchase a bridal gown in the very latest fashion. However, instead she had climbed up into the attic of her father's home. From a chest, she had taken out the home-sewn dress her mother had worn when she married Angela's father in 1945. In wartime style, it was a sleek, satin creation that her mother had created from a shell-pink evening gown.

Just like her mother, Angela was good with a needle. She modernised the dress herself and when she walked into the church on her father's arm, her dream dress stunned all into silence.

Hannah, who had been given the honour of being the main attendant at the wedding, felt near to tears when she escorted Angela to her groom's side. Then, when Angela turned and smiled as she handed her over her wedding bouquet, Hannah thought about how it had been a long three years. During those three years, she and Angela had had to cope with losing Freda, and the subsequent startling events that no one could have foreseen.

As Hannah stepped back, she instinctively put out her free hand to take the charming five-year-old flower girl's hand in hers. Poppy, however, had a very different idea. She turned around to wave to her grannies in the congregation.

Before Hannah could chastise Poppy, the other bridesmaid, who just happened to be Jackie, loudly whispered, 'Poppy, you have been told that this is not your day. It is Aunt Angela's, so pay attention to what you are supposed to be doing!'

Not wishing to see his adored sister Poppy getting into trouble, the kilted pageboy dug into his sporran and pulled out a sweetie, which he handed to her.

'Thank you, Harry,' Poppy said. 'I'll do it all right now.'

For Angela, there was no reception in the Kintore Rooms in Queen Street. This was the most important day of her life, so there was to be no expense spared and the setting had to be opulent and glamorous. Her father had booked the prestigious and luxurious Prestonfield House Hotel. This was an old stately home built by the architect Sir William Bruce for the Dick family, who owned the vast estate. The added benefit of situating the house in the upmarket area of Duddingston was that it looked over to Edinburgh's extinct volcano, the majestic and historic Arthur's Seat. Since the 1960s, when it was opened up as a small five-star hotel and wedding venue, those and such as those had held their receptions there. Hannah had laughed when she heard that the function suites had once been the stables, but Angela had assured her that she would be amazed at how well the conversion had worked. Looking coquettish and sensuously licking her lips, Angela went on to confide to Hannah that she would also be spending her first night of wedded bliss at the hotel, possibly sleeping in the same bed that people such as Winston Churchill, Sean Connery, Margaret Thatcher and Elton John had once used.

Hannah didn't care who had slept in what bed at Prestonfield House, but she was bowled over by the sheer luxury and decadence of the hotel. It was like being transported to another world – a world far removed from Norton Park Secondary School, which she and her five old classmates had left in 1962. She gazed around her, her head full of memories. However, before she could get completely carried away, she met Ewan's mother in the ladies' powder room and was quickly bumped back down to earth.

'Oh Hannah, you must be green with envy,' gushed Mrs Gibson.

'Should I be?'

'Yes, you should. You see, my dear Angela is so sophisticated and ... oh! Just look at the opulence ... the finesse ... even here, in the powder room of the venue she selected! And did you note the detail in her dress, and the way she glided down the aisle? Do you know that from the moment she told me that she was going to marry Bruce Ogilvy...' Mrs Gibson leant in closer so that she could whisper to Hannah, 'You do know that he's a distant relative of the Buccleuchs? You know, the dukedom down in Bowhill, in the Borders.'

'Yes, I do know that Bruce is a very distant relative. So distant, he told me, that his dad is employed there to clean out the stables.'

'Rubbish. Anyway, I just knew that Angela wouldn't be letting that superior family down. No way would she be slinking into a registry office dressed in a knitted cardigan!'

'Mummy,' a little voice called out, and Hannah was glad to see Poppy being pushed in the door. 'Daddy says you are to hurry!' Poppy called, as she espied the soap and hand cream dispensers. 'Oh, nice creams! Can I have some on my hands?'

Without even saying goodbye to Mrs Gibson, Hannah smiled at Poppy and said, 'Of course you can. Then we must be going.'

When Hannah emerged from the toilet, clutching Poppy by the hand, she came face to face with Ewan.

'You look a bit...' Ewan began, but stopped at the sight of Hannah's face. 'Well, you *do!*'

'You would too if you had just spent ten minutes with your mother!'

'Oh, so we are back to my overlooking the gold again?'

'You've got it in one,' Hannah sighed. 'She never comes out and says it directly, but I know she means that you picked up the dross when you married me, because I have no class and turned up to marry you in a cardigan.'

Ewan's laughter reverberated around the room. 'But didn't I get a bargain? Along with you I got three kids, a dog and a budgie!'

'Ewan, your mother's attitude to me is no laughing matter. We have been married for two and a half years! Is she ever going to accept that we are a couple?'

'Calm yourself. Nobody in their right mind ever pays any attention to what my mother says. You should have told her that it was not a cardigan that you wore to get married; it was a Grazia knitted coat, a piece so popular with the upper crust that the Queen has one!'

Hannah was about to respond, but Ewan winked at her and they both started to laugh. 'Right, let's get our brood together and get ourselves home. See, if our next-door neighbour has not gone in and taken Jet for a walk, the poor soul will be standing at the back door with her legs crossed!' He didn't add anything more, but he thought that it was time he was truthful with her and tonight, after the children were tucked up in bed, was probably the right time to do it.

It took longer than usual to get the children settled. It had been a big day for them. Hannah allowed a warm smile to light up her face as she remembered how Angela had given the children pride of place in her big day. Angela had been such a good friend to the children and Hannah since they lost Freda and Robin.

Freda and Robin's wills were identical in every way: if one outlived the other, then everything was to go to the survivor, with no strings attached. Hannah would always remember that when the wills were read out, Angela was first to nod in agreement. Freda, being Freda, had also stated that if by some unusual circumstance neither of them survived, all of their worldly goods were to be divided equally between their three children, after Ellen, Moira and Stevie had each received one thousand pounds. However, if the children had not reached adulthood and still required a guardian, then custody was to go to Hannah Lindsey, and to her alone. She would be responsible for rearing them into adulthood and was to be given all the financial means that she required in order to do so.

The stunned reaction of all those who had gathered in the antiquated solicitor's office on Leith Walk would haunt Hannah always. From some of them, she could feel resentment. Susan and Autumn had thought that they would be given a senior management role in the business, but that decision was left to the solicitor and Hannah, who were the trustees, and would depend on whether the two young women measured up. Ewan had come along in the hope that Freda had left him Poppy, but there was no way that she would have allowed her children to be split up.

Freda had been right about her decision for the

children. They needed each other. Harry was protective of Poppy and it was important to him that he told her stories of what life was like when Mum and Dad were alive. Jackie withdrew into herself and would constantly put her left hand over her right shoulder, like she had seen her mummy do when she was worried. The first six months had been so difficult for the children that Hannah resigned from her job at the Council so that she could be a full time 'mum'. To be truthful, the children were so used to her that, before the accident, they had always called her plain 'Auntie'. Auntie tried her best, but she was not their mother; if Ewan had not spent all his free time assisting her, Hannah knew that she would not have been able to go on. She now tittered when she remembered the first time she had made macaroni cheese for the evening meal. Harry had sorrowfully announced that it was all right, but no one could make macaroni cheese like his mum. Angela had also been so very helpful. She became Hannah's confidante. When Hannah confided to her that there were times when she was sure she could not cope with the children's grief, anger and sense of injustice, Angela always held her hand and urged her to sleep on it, assuring her that whilst it might be raining today, the sun would shine again tomorrow.

No one was more surprised than Hannah when, after a long and yet somehow very short six months, Ewan made a proposal. They had just got the children to bed, and were relaxing in the living room. In a matter-of-fact way, whilst stirring his coffee, Ewan said, 'Look, don't you think it would make more sense if you and I got married?'

Hannah's response was to let her mouth gape.

'I mean, I have just bought the house on Argyle Crescent, so I have enough room for us all.'

'You mean, take the children away from their home?'

'Yes. But only if they agree, and I am sure that Poppy won't raise any objection–'

'At just coming up to three years old, I'm sure she wouldn't but–'

'And Harry will be pleased to move near Portobello beach because Jet loves it.'

Hannah started to wave her hands about. 'Just a minute, Ewan. I accept that you think us marrying would give more stability to the children but–' she swallowed hard and lowered her face – 'there is something you should know about me. Something that may – no, *will* – change your mind about becoming involved with me... Ewan,' she stammered, as her face fired, 'I am not all there.'

'Yes, I know that, or you would never have agreed to take on the children and the dog!'

'No, no, no. Not in my mind! You are a doctor so I will not have to draw you diagrams, but I was born with no uterus and an underdeveloped vagina.'

'Yes, I know. Freda confided that to me years ago and, like her, I didn't think you deserved that.'

'No, I don't. See, when any of my boyfriends decided they would like to make love to me, I would tell them of my problem and soon I wouldn't be able to see them for the dust!'

'Well, we could live a celibate life if you would

254

like. Or we could just ... try?'

So, to everybody's amazement, Ewan married Hannah.

However, before they had publicly announced their forthcoming nuptials, Hannah had asked Ewan to wait until she had told Angela personally.

'Why?' Ewan queried.

'Because, Ewan, when we were all at school together, Freda, Molly, Angela and I were all hopelessly in love with you. Molly was the first to get over you, Freda never did but she married Robin, and Angela, who I would not hurt for the world now, has always hoped that you would one day ask her to marry you... You see? I must tell her first, before someone offers her their smug condolences.'

Hannah's meeting with Angela brought another revelation that Hannah had to deal with. Before she actually faced Angela, Hannah had rehearsed and rehearsed what she was going to say. When Angela arrived at Marionville Crescent, Hannah invited her into the back room where they would not be disturbed. 'Angela,' she began, 'you will probably be a bit put out but ... well, there is no easy way to tell you. Oh Angela, please try and understand that I do not wish to hurt or humiliate you, but Ewan has asked me to marry him ... and I have accepted.'

An uneasy, stony silence invaded the room. After a few minutes had elapsed, Angela's facial expression relaxed. Taking Hannah's hand in hers, she said, 'Hannah, Ewan asking you to marry him has at last set me free. What a fool I have been! Know something, a lovely man, Bruce Ogilvy – you know him?'

Hannah nodded. 'Yes, he is a dishy senior solicitor in the Council.'

'He is all that. Now listen, I met him when I attended one of those Council Christmas parties you invited me to. He has been courting me ever since, but I have kept him at arm's length. Your news today has made me realise that I would be better off marrying a man who thinks that I will always be the love of his life, so that is what I am going to do. As to you, please, please, Hannah, think very carefully about marrying Ewan ... the love of his life was Freda. When she was killed, I hoped that he would turn to me to console him, but it was being involved with the children that brought him solace.' She pondered for a moment. 'Or, to be more specific, it was being involved with Poppy, who is so like him in every way that I think he may be her father?'

'He is.'

'Then you know that he is only marrying you so that he can have full access to the child – *his* child – borne by Freda, the one and only woman he has ever truly loved?'

Hannah's chest surged with mixed emotions. Time ticked by as she contemplated. Eventually, she wriggled her hand free from Angela's grasp and, looking her directly in the eye, she whispered, 'Angela, believe me when I say that I accept what you are saying is true, but Ewan is not all bad or selfish. After all, without being asked to, he has stood in for Robin and he is a good surrogate father to the three children. As I can never have children of my own–'

'You can't?'

'No, just a wee problem like not having a womb! Right now, though, it has its compensation in the fact that Freda's children will never be superseded by any offspring of mine.'

'That all may be so, but I still hope you won't go ahead with the marriage. Dear Hannah, you should be the love of someone's life. The love of Ewan's life was Freda, who is now a ghost. A phantom that he is willingly allowing to haunt him ... to consume his every thought.'

'I know all that but by marrying him, in time...'

Angela sighed. Exasperation was engulfing her. 'For goodness sake, Hannah,' she exclaimed, 'you cannot fight her and win!'

Hannah just shrugged.

Shaking her head, Angela accepted defeat. As much as she wished to, she knew that she would not be able to change Hannah's mind. So all she did was cackle, before adding, 'Talking of fighting, just you wait until his dear old mummy realises that he is going to marry you and not me.' She halted to savour the picture. 'Oh boy, Hannah, unless you are very careful, she could end up being your Achilles Heel!'

That was all in 1977. Now, it was 1979 and things had worked out better than Hannah had expected. However, she now knew Ewan very well and it was therefore only natural that she had guessed that he wished to discuss something with her – something very important to him. What could it be? Hannah acknowledged that she and Ewan were really good friends and recently she had thought that they might become more than that ... but perhaps that was wishful thinking on her part. She dared not raise her hopes that Ewan might wish to talk about their relationship.

The family had returned from Angela's wedding earlier that evening. The children were settled for the night and Jet had had her last wander around the garden; she had now taken up her position on the upstairs landing, where she thought she was guarding her three 'pups'. Hannah was seated on the couch in the downstairs lounge, reading the *Edinburgh Evening News*. She looked up when Ewan came into the lounge, carrying a tray with two glasses of wine on top. She folded the paper and laid it down, because she knew that crunch time had arrived.

Looking directly at Ewan, Hannah quietly but forcibly stated, 'No beating about the mulberry bushes, I know that you wish to get some things out into the open. To be truthful, I have felt for some time that there is something niggling you... Something that you wish to say to me... Something that requires some Dutch courage, in the form of a glass of wine.'

'It's Chianti from Valvona & Crolla,' he replied, handing one of the glasses to Hannah.

'That serious, is it?'

Ewan sat down on the couch beside her. Time seemed suspended; all that could be heard was the nocturnal singing of the birds in their garden and the rustle of the curtains as a welcoming, cool evening breeze blew in through the open French windows.

Eventually, Ewan began to rub his hands together. 'Hannah, I need to talk to you – ask you to forgive me.'

Hannah's pounding heart seemed to have taken up residence in her mouth. She swallowed hard in an attempt to allay her fears, but mounting anxiety had her thinking that he was about to confess to having an affair ... he was going to say he was leaving.

Unaware of the rising panic that was causing Hannah's imagination to run riot, Ewan sought for her hand. Her first instinct was to shy away from him, but she loved him and, to her shame, she knew she would put up with whatever he asked her to – just as long as he did not leave her.

Ewan took a deep breath and began, 'Forgive me, Hannah, for not being entirely honest with you from the start. It is true that I would have paid any price to be involved in Poppy's life, to be the main person for her. However, we do not choose whom we will fall in love with and, slowly but surely, Harry and Jackie also stole their way into my heart. I love them ... and I couldn't love them any more, even if I was their biological father.' He paused before adding, 'Life without them would be so lonely and meaningless. Last Friday, when I was finishing the evening surgery, I thought, "I must get home to my family". Then I remembered that Friday is the day that Moira and Stevie have the children over for tea. That is something else that I admire about you – the way that you have made sure that the children's grandparents are still welcome in our home and have an important part to play in the children's lives. Now, back to what I was about to confess to you... Hannah, even though I knew that the children would not be at home last Friday, I was still rushing to get home so that you and I could spend a little time together. That got me thinking ... I now realise that I have grown to love you so very much. The children are growing up. Poppy starts at Towerbank School in August, and the twins are off to Portobello High School then – and that is just the start of the children preparing to grow up and leave us. However, I know that is the right way for them to go and I don't feel sorry, because when they have all flown the nest I hope that you and I are given time to just enjoy each other – to grow old together. Hannah, what I am trying to say is that yes, I loved Freda and I will always be grateful for the ten days we had together, but I adore you just as much. Now, whatever time I get to spend in this world, I wish to spend with you.'

Tears of joy were running down Hannah's cheeks. 'Oh Ewan, we found ourselves over the last three years, and then we found each other. You have only just discovered what I have known for over a year now. You see, my dear, when we first married you carried out the duties of a husband because you were obliged to.' She pursed her lips and swallowed hard; the next words she wished to say to him were so very difficult for her, but it was important that they were said. Placing her hand on his cheek, she softly murmured, 'Now, you are so considerate, tender and passionate when we make love that I have started to wonder if, at last, you see me as desirable, in spite of–'

Tenderly, Ewan put his hand over her mouth.

'Hannah, please. From now on, never ever again say—'

'No, I won't ever say that I am not all there. I have found it hard to accept myself over the years, but I am learning to love myself, despite my insecurities. Thanks to dear Freda entrusting me with her children, I am now the loving and contented mother of three. And now thanks to you, my darling, I know that I am desirable, too. Oh Ewan, I finally feel fulfilled.'

The publishers hope that this book has given you enjoyable reading. Large Print Books are especially designed to be as easy to see and hold as possible. If you wish a complete list of our books please ask at your local library or write directly to:

Magna Large Print Books
Magna House, Long Preston,
Skipton, North Yorkshire.
BD23 4ND

This Large Print Book for the partially sighted, who cannot read normal print, is published under the auspices of

THE ULVERSCROFT FOUNDATION